The Mountain Man's Dog

Gary Corbin

This book is a work of fiction. Names, characters, businesses, incidents, and dialogue are either drawn from the author's imagination or are used fictitiously, and are not to be construed as real. Any resemblance to actual events or persons, living or dead, is entirely coincidental.

To Sandy, Beauty, Oliver, and Georgia

CONTENTS

PART 1

Stuck With a Dog

CHAPTER 1

Lehigh slowed down around the S-curves on Brady Mountain Road even before the speed limit sign told him to. The fog rolled in thicker here due to the nearby lakes, intensifying the dark and making the night seem much later than it was. A guy never knew what the night fog might throw out of the woods in Oregon's Cascade Mountains, especially in late September. He didn't want adventure on a Thursday night. He just needed some groceries, stuff that old man Patterson's market didn't carry, and anyways, he closed at five o'clock. So, as much as he hated doing it, Lehigh had to drive down the mountain into town.

Just go to WinCo, get some groceries, and leave. No distractions.

He braked just in time not to kill a coyote darting across the highway. It startled him and sweat rolled down his back in spite of the chill. He shook his head and took a heavy breath. Focus on driving, dumb-ass. Don't get all riled up.

He kept his speed down below forty. Good thing, as it enabled him to brake in time once again, this time to avoid hitting a yellow hound dog limping across the road. Well, normally he'd call it a good thing. In coming years, Lehigh often argued it was anything but. He wasn't much of a dog person, ever since Uncle Ted's German Shepherd near tore his hand off as a kid. Or so he remembered. The injury grew with every retelling.

Lehigh didn't so much fear dogs as loathe them. Dogs were nothing but a nuisance: noisy, smelly, always needing attention and cleaning up after. Kind of like a kid that never grows up. Still a committed bachelor at thirty-seven, his position on kids was pretty clear.

He came to a full stop for the yellow hound. It limped so badly, it hardly moved, really. Its brown eyes reflected the glare of the truck's headlights, making them shine red like the indicator lights on his dashboard. The dog froze in his tracks as Lehigh waited. Then it lay right down across the center stripe, its bleeding belly exposed and vulnerable.

Dumb-assed dog. He could get killed like that. Of course, that might well have been the dog's intention. Dogs, his uncle used to say, can smell their own death, and will go take care of it when the time comes. Maybe the dog wanted him to run it over.

Hmm. Tempting.

He shook his head. Nope. Can't do it. Dogs may be mean, stupid little bastards, but he couldn't just up and kill one of 'em. Maybe Uncle Ted's nasty old shepherd, but not one that hadn't done anything to him first.

He left the old Ford running, tucked his shaggy brown hair into the Dodgers hat he kept on the seat and stepped out into the fog. The dog looked up at him, stared a second, then lay his head back down on the pavement. Lehigh approached him, taking small steps, still wary, twenty-nine years after feeling that shepherd dog's teeth on his fingers. He could just move the pup aside a bit. Move him and be on his way.

He fetched the wide aluminum shovel out of the back of his truck, just in case he had to prod the old hound to move. The dog looked friendly, but one never knows what a dog's going to do. What if he's rabid, like Uncle Ted's dog? You just never know. Those shots hurt like hell for days and days. He had no desire to go through that again.

The lazy flap of the dog's snakelike tail against the damp black pavement told him rabies were probably not an issue. Its pink tongue flickered between furry lips, anticipating rescue. The dog's brown irises and black pupils filled the top hemisphere of its eye sockets in a steady, whimpering stare. Its bleeding belly and forlorn face melted Lehigh's apprehension. Dogs may be a nuisance, he reckoned, but this one was just hurting.

He set the shovel down and held his hand out, palm down, in front of the dog's nose, the way Uncle Ted had taught him. Wet, gentle lapping on his knuckles confirmed the dog's friendliness—or at least, its trust. "Let me take a look at you, boy," he said in as soothing a voice as he could muster. He used the handle of the shovel to lift the dog's hind leg, exposing more of its belly and crotch.

"Huh. I guess I shouldn't call you boy no more," he said, a little embarrassed. She licked his hand again. He looked closer at the cut. She'd somehow sliced herself across the belly, maybe jumping over a freshly-pruned hedge, or a barbed-wire fence, or maybe a cat or raccoon had clawed her. The ragged cut caused her skin to gape an inch or so apart. It would need stitches, probably several.

"Well, you ain't gonna walk into a vet's office all on your own," he said. "But the sheriff's office is on the way to town. Maybe he'll get you there. Which means, I've got to get you to him. C'mere, girl."

The dog found his eyes with her own, and laid her head back down on the pavement. He nudged her backside with his foot. "C'mon girl, get up." She stayed put and glanced at him sideways, panting just a little. Moisture from the dog's breath danced in the beam of his truck's headlights.

"You gonna make me pick you up and carry you?" She didn't look heavy. But to pick her up, he'd have to risk putting at least one hand near her head. Near her open mouth.

Pain. Fingers. Bleeding...

He shook his head. This dog knew more about pain and bleeding than he ever would. Come on, Lehigh, do what you gotta do here.

He crossed around the dog and slid the edge of his shovel under her furry back. At first she remained dead weight, a passenger in the next step of her journey. He pried her body up from the pavement, using the shovel as a lever and his foot as a fulcrum. He grunted under the awkward exertion. Six-one, one-ninety-five, he ought to be able to lift this skinny mutt with ease, but not from this position.

Just before he let go to start over, the dog responded. With a herky-jerky motion she stumbled to her feet and sauntered to the open door of his pickup's cab, panting, a hopeful and grateful dog-smile painted on her weary face.

"Wait," Lehigh said. To his surprise, the dog obeyed. He scratched the stubble on his chin. "You been around people." That changed his strategy a bit. He had intended to put her in the bed of the pickup, but he discarded that thought like an empty carcass. Instead he spread a small tarp onto the passenger's side of the seat. The dog put her front paws on the truck's sidestep and convulsed in a pathetic attempt to climb further. Fresh blood trickled down her hind leg. Lehigh winced. Careful not to touch the wound, he pressed the flat blade of the shovel against the dog's hindquarters and pushed her onto the floor of the truck, then guided her onto the tarp.

"I don't reckon you've done anything wrong," he said after climbing in next to her, "but I think it's time you and Sheriff Summers got acquainted."

The dog responded with a quick lick of her lips, heavy panting, and a low, prolonged whine.

***

Mt. Hood County Sheriff Dallas "Buck" Summers hated being interrupted. Especially this close to completing the daily paper's WordFind puzzle—a rare accomplishment on Thursdays. For some reason Thursday's puzzles seemed harder than the other days. But Buck had only three more words to find. Then he could unscramble the leftover, uncircled letters to answer the Indiana Jones trivia question on the comics page. He was scanning the grid for the word "snakepit" when a jangle of bells from the doorway in the foyer announced his visitor.

"Please just be someone needing directions, or a phone, or something," he muttered. He pressed his pencil on the start of row seven to mark his place, just in case. Directions, a map, even a jump of a dead battery—easy things like that, Deputy Dwayne Latner could handle. Not much else, but surely that.

No such luck.

"Someone here to see you, Sheriff," Dwayne said a moment later. Summers, having progressed only one more row of letters, penciled an "8" in the white space next to the grid. He craned his neck to see over his feet, propped comfortably on his desk. Dwayne's lanky frame leaned against the open door, one hand scratching the salt-and-pepper stubble on his leathery face. Summers wondered how a man's beard could grow so fast and thick while the hair on his head grew only thinner, if at all.

"What's he want?" He took his feet off the desk, set the newspaper in his bottom drawer and slid it shut. He stood, tucked his shirt into his slacks and loosened the belt straining over his bulging belly, then checked his watch. Almost dinnertime.

"It's Lee Carter. Says he found a hurt dog in the road, up a mile or so his way."

"So? What's he want me to do about it?"

"I dunno. I guess he wants to jaw a bit with you about it."

Summers regarded his hapless deputy a moment, hoping yet to find a way to pawn this problem off and get back to his puzzle, but he knew he would just be delaying the inevitable. "Fine, then. Show him in."

"Will do, Sheriff."

Lehigh strode through the doorway a few seconds later. "Thanks for seeing me, Buck. Did Dwayne tell you why I'm here?"

"Sure did. But why the hell'd you come here? You know we don't got no facilities here to take care of a dog."

Lehigh corkscrewed his face into a deep frown. "I know, Sheriff. But I figured you folks would know what to do and where to bring her, and you could get her there faster in a squad car than I could in my pickup. Flash a few lights, sound a siren. Know what I'm saying?"

Summers hissed in irritation and shook his head. "Nothing doing, Carter. We ain't running no animal am-boo-lance service.

He's all yours. How bad off is the dumb mutt, anyhoo?"

"She's bleeding. Her gut's cut somehow. Probably needs stitches and a few shots. C'mon, Buck. Help me out here."

"Sorry. We're short-staffed, just me and Dwayne tonight. I send him off on this little joyride and then I got nobody to send out if a call comes in. All I can do is tell you where to take him. You familiar with Clarkesville Animal Hospital?"

Lehigh's eyes narrowed. "Course I am. Isn't there anyplace else?"

"No place open now. Why? What's wrong with them? Anyway, they'd be operating on the dog, not on you."

"You know damn well what's wrong."

"Do I?" He snuck a peek at his bottom drawer. Just three more words to go on that puzzle.

Lehigh crossed his arms. "I'd just as soon drop this damned dog back on the highway as set foot in that place. And I'm sure the feeling is mutual."

"Aw, come on, Lehigh. She's not still mad at you."

"She hasn't exactly kept me on her Christmas card list."

"That was a long time ago. What, ten, twelve years? Nobody could stay mad that long."

"Stacy could. And does. So, unless you want a dead dog on your conscience—"

"Whoa, whoa. Stop right there. This dog ain't gonna become my problem. In fact, you'd better get going if you're gonna make it before they close." He stole another peek at the bottom drawer, then wagged a hand toward the door.

"I tell you, I ain't going there."

Summers's face darkened. "Look here, son. You better get that dog down to Clarkesville, pronto, or I will march you into that jail cell just the other side of that wall on a charge of cruelty to animals. Are we clear?" He punctuated each word with a jabbing finger, each jab closer to Lehigh's nose than the last.

Lehigh glowered back at him a moment, then shrugged. "All right, Buck. If you put it that way." He tipped his baseball hat in a mock salute. "Thanks for your…help."

"Say hi to Ms. McBride and her daddy for me," Summers

called after him. He smirked and listened for the telltale jangle of bells to confirm Lehigh's departure from the station. "Now, where was I? Oh, yes. Snakepit."

***

The hound stayed quiet on the ride into town, whimpering only when Lehigh hit the deeper potholes. She lay with her belly facing forward and her tail by the door, so that her moist exhalations dampened the right leg of Lehigh's jeans. The thick gray tarp absorbed the blood seeping from her wound. "No doubt my upholstery's stained," he said. The dog apologized with a doleful stare. "Aw, it don't matter. It's all full of coffee and Dr. Pepper anyhow." She lifted her head and craned her neck to look at him. Then, like a wounded soldier certain of his death, she laid her head on his thigh for comfort. The touch of the dog's head startled him and he jerked his leg upwards, thumping her snout into his rib cage, and she retreated into a curl on the tarp, tail tucked between her legs as if to absorb her lost blood.

"I'm sorry, girl," Lehigh said. "This is as fast as I can go. Stupid Sheriff." He held his hand in midair over the dog's head, unsure of whether to pet her, scratch her ear, or leave her alone. She broke his indecision by lifting her head up until her brow grazed his fingertips, then dipped and rose again, coaxing his hand into contact: touch me, comfort me. He rested his hand on her head and stroked her scalp. With each stroke, she lowered her head a smidge until, minutes later, it rested on his lap.

"I feel like I'm giving aid and comfort to the enemy," he said. The dog opened her eyes and gazed upward, delivering an unspoken message: We are not enemies. I trust you. "You shouldn't," Lehigh said. The vet would probably put her to sleep, he reckoned. A stray dog with no collar, bleeding for who knows how long, with nowhere to go and no one to pay for its care, might have been better off left alone. At least then it could die its own way.

It. So much easier to say "it" than "she." "She" implied some knowledge of the beast. "It" made the dog seem like more of a stranger. That's best. Stay strangers. Or enemies. Like dogs always have been.

Clarkesville Animal Hospital, a mostly-volunteer clinic, was clear on the northeast side of town, exactly opposite the part of town he'd intended to go. That meant an extra twenty minutes of driving. Luckily, there was a Safeway nearby. That'd do for groceries, even though it cost more. Damned Sheriff.

He checked the dog's cut when he stopped for a red light in mid-town. The dog's bleeding had slowed. That's either good in that the wound was clotting up, or bad in that she'd already lost too much blood.

It. It had lost too much blood.

He took his hand off the dog's head and put it back on the steering wheel. She rewarded him with a dull, brown-eyed stare, unaccusing, unsuspicious, accepting. Okay, she seemed to be saying, I know you need both hands to drive.

It. It seemed to be saying.

After about five minutes, he rested his hand on the dog's side, and left it there until he pulled into the clinic's tiny lot.

Shutting off the motor, he kicked open the driver's side door, stopping its rebound with an extended toe, and leaned over to scoop the dog, tarp and all, into his arms. The dog had yet to indicate a tendency to bite—she hadn't emitted so much as a growl during the bumpy forty-five minute ride—but no point in taking chances now. She weighed less than he expected—forty pounds or so, about ten too few—but he struggled to pull her out of the truck at that angle without jostling her and aggravating the wound.

The clinic, a one-story converted ranch house, sat on a double lot just off the four-lane main drag in Clarkesville. Built in the 1960's or so, its decorative shutters and thin horizontal siding needed painting, and moss filled the open tabs of the composite shingle roof. But they'd paved and striped the parking lot sometime in the past fifteen years, and not a speck of trash littered the grounds. The heavy front door sported a sign boasting of new late Thursday hours.

"Just my luck," Lehigh said. He managed the lever-style

handle, pushed the door open, and carried his burden inside. Soft-focus pictures of beautiful pets needing homes adorned the white walls of the waiting room. The gray linoleum tile smelled of fresh disinfectant. He set the stoic animal on the broad Formica counter, pinged the service bell and waited.

"I'll just be a moment," a woman's voice called from down the hall. Lehigh nodded to nobody and bent over, his face level with the dog's.

"Now don't you worry," he said to the dog's sad brown eyes. "The folks here'll know just what to do. They'll fix ya up and find someone to take care of you."

"Lee?" the woman's voice called. "Lehigh Carter, is that you?"

Moments later, Stacy Lynn McBride, daughter of State Senator George Lindsay McBride, appeared behind the counter. She'd aged twelve years since he'd last seen her, but she showed almost no sign of it. Long black hair pulled back into a pony tail framed the smooth skin of her face, tanned a deeper shade of copper by the summer sun. Ten pounds heavier (five of which she'd needed anyway) and a couple of laugh lines later, her clear blue eyes still sparked fire in his gut. She remained the only woman ever to tell him those three magic words, and to hear them from him: "I love you." She'd stolen his virginity, taught him which liquors could mix, and even, one time, convinced him to try smoking pot. In countless ways, she'd changed his life.

Then, in one big way, she changed it all again. Suddenly she wouldn't take his calls for a week. Then she hand-delivered a letter to his mailbox that began: "Dear Lee, I hope you will someday understand…"

That same woman now stood, mouth agape, not six feet from him, as unnaturally still as the statue of Captain William Clark in the center of town—and as still as his own heart for the beat's length it took to absorb the fact that she actually seemed happy to see him.

"Hey, Stacy," he whispered.

She blinked once, noticed the dog, and the surprise on her face doubled. She walked through the Dutch door next to the counter into the waiting area. Their hug lasted maybe a second and a half. "I can't believe you're here."

"I found this dog," he said. "I tried bringing her to the sheriff's, but–"

"Let me look at her." She examined the dog's belly, made a face. "It doesn't look infected. She'll need stitches and a rabies shot. Probably some fluids, too. Poor thing must be starved." She met Lee's eyes again. "You did the right thing, bringing her here."

"Thanks. Buck suggested it. Anyway, it seemed right. But I didn't know–"

"I'll need you to fill out some forms." She returned to the business side of the counter and pushed a clipboard at him, her eyes focused on a spot somewhere on the counter between them.

Pet's name, the first line read.

"Hell, I don't know anything about this dog. I just picked her up off the street so she wouldn't die on the highway. Can't ya'll just–"

"We can't treat her without some information. Just tell us what you can." She scooped the dog off the tarp and disappeared down the hallway.

He struggled with the forms. They asked more about him than the dog. "That don't make no sense," he muttered. "All's I'm doing is dropping the dog off. She ain't mine." But he filled it in anyway. At least this way, they could call and let him know what happens to it.

"We'll have to keep her overnight," Stacy said, re-entering a few minutes later. She managed to look him in the eyes now. "You can pick her up in the morning. Since it's a rescue, we can pay the majority of the bill from the charity account. You can pay the rest by check or cash."

"Whoa! Wait a minute. She's not my dog. I just–"

"Lehigh Carter. Don't you pretend for one minute that you are abandoning this dog here tonight." Stacy's pale blue eyes narrowed and her face reflected foreboding anger for a moment before softening into a gentle smile. "Besides, there's a great place for breakfast around the corner. My treat for the hero who rescued this lucky little dog."

Standing outside, hat in hand, Lehigh felt a churning in his gut that he hadn't felt in a long time.

Twelve years, to be exact.

***

"The trouble is, I can't pick that dog up tomorrow morning." He practiced his speech to Stacy as he searched Safeway's aisles for the groceries on his list. He needed to go back to the clinic and tell her that, and tell her that he couldn't meet her for breakfast, either, even if she was buying. Which a woman shouldn't do, anyway, even as a reward for something. Which he shouldn't get, besides, because he wasn't rescuing the dog, not in the sense of taking it home and adopting it.

So, that was one reason. He couldn't adopt a dog right now. Not now, or any time. He didn't like dogs. Worse, they didn't like him. She would be disappointed, sure, but she'd understand. She'd have to. This must happen all the time. She'd have a dozen names in a file somewhere, and she'd call one or two, and the dog would be adopted by dinner time tomorrow, making a houseful of kids happy.

So long as they don't get their fingers bit. But he wouldn't say anything about that. That, she probably wouldn't understand. Or, maybe she'd understand, but she'd give him that dismissive scoff of hers and change the subject.

Come to think of it, she probably wouldn't understand much of any of it. Understanding was not among her finer traits, at least not twelve years ago.

Which raised the second point. He couldn't meet her for breakfast. First off, he had to work. Second, he wouldn't be picking up the dog—he would have already explained all this. And third…he just couldn't meet her there anyway. Just forget it.

"Excuse me?" A gray-haired woman in a print knee-length dress stared at him with a strained look on her face, the kind that makes you think the person has just tasted something awful.

"Ma'am?"

"Were you talking to me?" Her knuckles shone white against the red bar on the shopping cart. Her eyes narrowed, accusing.

"No, ma'am. I didn't even mean to be talking out loud." He grabbed a box of corn meal off the shelf, dropped it into his cart, and moved past her, just catching sight of her head wagging in impatient disapproval.

Damn. He didn't even need corn meal.

So, third, or fifth, or whatever the heck number he was on, it wasn't a good idea to be meeting up with Stacy again. It smacked of a date, and hadn't she gotten married some time back? No longer Stacy McBride, she was now Stacy—what? He couldn't remember. But no matter. He couldn't be meeting a married woman for breakfast, nor lunch, dinner, anything. Not tomorrow, not any day.

And no dog.

He rubbed his fingers as he looked over the various offerings of coffee. Everything's different here at Safeway compared to WinCo.

He shivered. Everything's different.

CHAPTER 2

Even under the best circumstances, Lehigh hated shopping. It didn't help matters that the damned dog had him so distracted. The dog, and...her.

As a result, it took over an hour to find everything. Even working from a list—and he always worked from a list—he kept missing things and had to repeat some aisles several times. He liked to buy store brands. They were cheap, and usually the same damned product as the name brand, in a different box. But Safeway's store brands were different than WinCo's. It took him a while to sort out which was which.

Why did that dog have to lie down in front of his truck? And why did Stacy McBride have to be working at the animal hospital tonight, of all nights? Didn't the boss get to work day shift anymore?

Standing in the long checkout line behind a young mother and her eight-year-old son, whose principal talent seemed to be snagging candy bars off shelves perched kids-eye-height, he made his decision. He'd drive back to the clinic tonight and tell Stacy he wasn't coming back for the dog, nor for breakfast in the morning.

Of course, he'd call first. It was the only decent thing to do.

Whether from guilt or a sudden surge of generosity—if there's even a difference between the two—Lehigh answered the cashier's friendly greeting with, "Uh, actually, there is one more thing I need. Where's the dog food at?"

He hurried to the indicated aisle. He grabbed two cans of

Alpo Extra Meaty, a package of rawhide dog chews, and a box of peanut butter flavored biscuits—too much for one dog, but maybe the clinic could use the extra.

"Your dog is going to feel extra special." The checkout girl's braces reflected the neon flashing in the store's front window. "What kind of dog do you have?"

"I don't have a dog," he said. Her furrowed brow demanded an explanation. "It's—for a friend's dog. She got hurt."

"The friend, or the dog?" Beep, beep, beep. "That'll be $79.65."

"The dog. Will you take a check?"

"With picture ID. What happened to the dog?"

"I don't know."

More puzzlement and this time a shrug of her shoulders.

He scribbled on the check. "I mean, she got a cut on her belly, but I don't know how. I found her like that on the highway."

She rolled her eyes. "O-kay…" She copied his license number onto the check and returned his license to him. "You have a nice night. I hope your friend's dog gets better."

"I know it don't make sense," Lehigh muttered as he pushed his cart through the automatic door. "None of this makes any damn sense."

***

"I'm sorry, sir. Ms. McBride left half an hour ago. I believe she said something about getting some Chinese food."

Lehigh sighed into the receiver, adding even more static-like sounds to the scratchy line. A stiff wind rattled the folding door of the glass phone booth. He propped the back of his foot against it, which helped some, and plugged his free ear with one finger. Still it was hard to hear.

Tonight, of all nights, he forgot to bring his cell phone. "Did she say when she'd be back?"

"No, Mr. Carter. I'm not sure she will be back tonight. Would you like to leave a number where she can call you in the morning?"

"No, ma'am. Thank you." The wind blew the door open as soon as he released his foot, and something—dust, a leaf particle, or a bit of trash maybe—flew into his eye. He squeezed it shut until he could get back to the truck, where he flushed it with some water from jugs he kept in the back. A good forester is always prepared.

He drove along Route 229, the main drag in Clarkesville, looking for the Chinese place. Last he could recall, there was only one, somewhere among the various local shops gradually being replaced by chain stores. The Color Tile store used to be Peterson's Lights and Linoleum. Ace Hardware replaced Clarke's Tool and Lumber. Burger King, McDonald's, KFC and Taco Bell crowded the corners where the good drive-ins used to be. He stopped for gas at what had always been a Shell—but a moment later he wasn't sure.

"Where's the Chinese place?" he asked the cashier, a skinny kid with glasses and braces.

"Fong's? Or the new Szechuan place? Fong's is up the road another mile or two. The other one, you gotta go right on Lost Lake Drive, then into the new food court. They may be closed, though. Hey, you want a Powerball ticket? It's up over ninety million."

He declined the lottery ticket, thanked the clerk, and counted out enough cash to pay for the gas. $49.40. When did gas hit three bucks a gallon again?

He found Fong's a few minutes later. Once inside, the smell wrinkled his nose. He never much cared for Cantonese. He declined the host's offer of a nice table by the window. A quick scan of the room told him Stacy must have gone for the spicier Szechuan place. Back in the car, his stomach growled, reminding him he'd skipped dinner. He cruised the strip for a burger place, anything but a chain—a frustrating and unsuccessful search. What happened to Sheryl's Shake Shop? They used to have the best burgers and terrific shakes in the metal cup that you poured into the tall curved glass yourself. Pizza Hut stood there now. The old Italian place had become an Office Depot. They sold paper made from his wood, so he reckoned that not all change is bad.

He opted for drive-through at the KFC. "Regular or new Cajun spicy?" the young girl asked over the static.

"Regular." He shook his head. More damned change. When would it stop?

***

"Stacy, that man called back for you."

Stacy paused in her review of the forms that Anne-Marie had processed that day. The old gal had a heart of gold, but she wasn't the sharpest knife in the drawer, and it showed on her paperwork most of all. If she weren't a volunteer, she'd have been fired ages ago.

"What man?" It had been a busy night. Please God, not Paul again. That man had to learn some boundaries.

"Mr. Carter. The man that brought in the yellow lab with a cut on its belly." Anne-Marie's face wore a suspicious look, like she'd just tasted something horrible and wanted to spit.

"Oh. What did he say?" Stacy gripped the pages in her fingers, wrinkling them, then set them down to smooth the edges.

"He asked where you went to dinner."

Alarm bells rang in Stacy's brain. God, no. Not another stalker. The first guy she'd dated after her divorce had made her life intolerable, eventually prompting her return to Clarkesville.

But, wait. This was the same Anne-Marie who had once told her then-jealous-boyfriend, now ex-husband: "Leave her alone. She's already got a man." That one took hours to explain.

"He called to ask where I went to dinner?" Stacy asked. "How did he know I had gone to dinner?" She couldn't even pretend to read the forms now. She turned to face Anne-Marie, folding linens on the examining table. While horrible at paperwork, she excelled at laundry. The stack of towels towered up to Anne-Marie's ample chin and hid most of her pudgy torso.

"Well…he called and asked for you. I told him you'd gone out. He asked where. He seemed desperate to talk to you."

Desperate? Stacy discounted this by half. Anne-Marie loved

to dramatize. "Did he leave a number where I could reach him?"

"No. He said he'd call back in the morning." But Anne-Marie's face and tone of voice seemed troubled.

Damned Anne-Marie. Mind like a steel sieve. God knows what really happened. "Thank you, Anne-Marie. I appreciate you telling me."

Anne-Marie's face brightened and she picked up one stack of linens. Her pink skin flushed red, highlighting the salt-and-pepper fringes of her dark brown hair. "I'll put these away. Anything else you need me for? I want to get home in time to watch Survivor tonight. That awful boy from Texas needs to get kicked off so the Oregon girl can win. That's what I'm rooting for. How about you?"

"I'm sure you're right, Anne-Marie." Stacy smiled and waved a hand at her. "Go on home. I can handle the little bit we've got left."

"Oh, no, Ms. McBride. I'll stay–"

"No, really. You go. Say hi to Jimmy for me."

"Poor Jimmy. He had TV dinner tonight. It's the one bad thing about me working here. I can't properly take care of my man." But Anne-Marie hummed as she put on her coat and hat. She paused by the door. "Should I come back tomorrow? It's really no trouble."

"Sure. I'll see you then." Stacy waited for the door to click shut, then dug through the stack for Lee Carter's intake form.

He didn't answer by the tenth ring, and no machine picked up. "Well, Lucky," she said to the yellow hound, "he'll just have to tell me whatever he had to say in the morning."

She'd named the dog "Lucky" earlier this evening when she read what Lehigh entered on the intake form. "Stray" is all he'd written, and that was no kind of name for a dog.

The man refused to attach himself to this animal. Would it make a difference if it were a human female instead of a canine? She shook her head. No. Some things never change. He'd had it so good once, but he'd let it all slip away, and for much the same reason.

***

Donna, Stacy's best friend since high school and maid of honor eleven years before, waited for her at Chi-Chi's on the strip with frozen margaritas already sweating onto the cocktail napkins. As always, she dressed to impress men: low-rider designer jeans one size too small, 3-inch spike heels, and a V-neck blouse that exposed the lacy trimmings of her push-up bra. If she added any more support, Stacy often told her, she'd get her own toll-free number.

"What took you so long?" Donna asked when Stacy approached the table. She had to shout over the piped-in sounds of trumpets and tambourines. "You didn't call that no-good used car salesman again, did you?"

"Someday you're going to have to learn what 'supportive friend' means," Stacy replied with a grin. "Paul's an okay guy. I don't know why you think he's so sleazy." She slung her jacket over the back of her chair and took a taste of her drink. "Perfect."

"They do make great margaritas here," Donna said. "Cheers." They clinked. "I can't put my finger on it, but all I know is, he can't be trusted. I'm sorry, that's just how I see it. I'm your friend. I have to tell you the truth."

"You have nothing to base that on."

Donna checked her hair in a make-up mirror. Perfect, of course. "Paul's a skirt-chaser. He leers at every good-looking woman he sees."

"He leers at you?"

"No. I ain't good-looking enough."

They laughed. Two men at the next table stopped gawking at her, as if they'd feared the remark had been directed at them. Which, in part, it was.

Stacy clinked Donna's glass again. "Still looking good, sister. I wish I had those legs. And those boobs."

"It's the blonde hair they like, and you can get the same bottle of it at Safeway."

"But not those boobs."

"Nope. Those you gotta see Dr. Gorman for. So what did sleaze-bag have to say?"

Stacy shook her head and sipped her drink, already half-gone. She set it down. "I didn't talk to Paul tonight. Anne-Marie left early again and I had—a busy night."

"Wait! What were you going to say just then?" Donna leaned forward to whisper to her. "Did you meet a new guy? Somebody new who came into the clinic?" A moment later she leaned back in her seat, a smug smile on her face. "I knew it! Good for you. What's his name?"

"I didn't say—"

"Come on, you can't hide anything from me. Not after twenty-five years. Remember I caught you lying that time in Truth or Dare about Bobby McCafferty putting his hand down your pants?"

"Donna, for heaven's sake. I was thirteen."

"And you've never been able to lie to me since. Now come on. Spill."

Stacy sighed. "Well. It's not a new man, exactly. It's sort of a blast from the past."

"Not Steven?"

Stacy shuddered. "No. That would be more like an atom bomb from the past."

Donna finished her drink and signaled for two more. "Who, then?"

Stacy cleared her throat and stared into her glass. "Do you remember Lee Carter?"

"Lehigh Carter? Mr. Don't-Know-if-I'm-Ready, Can't-Decide-Whether-to-Crap-or-Get-Off-the-Pot Carter? Mr.–"

"Okay, I get your point." Stacy laughed a little. "Yes, that handsome bugger. He rescued a dog off the highway. Could've knocked me over with a feather."

"Stacy. Don't you dare go there."

"What? I'm not going anywhere."

"You're lying again. I can see it in your eyes. You squint whenever you fib."

"I'm not, I swear! I just…was surprised, that's all."

Donna stared at her for several seconds and thanked the waitress for their fresh drinks. "Stacy. Listen to me. I'd rather you stick with Mr. Sleazo than go through that heartache again. Please."

"Maybe he's changed."

"Men don't change."

"He did rescue a dog. He used to hate dogs."

"One of your many incompatibilities."

"But no more." Stacy took a long pull on her margarita.

Donna rolled her eyes. "Did he say he loved dogs? It's not his dog. It's a stray. Okay, so he has some compassion. But he hasn't changed his stripes."

"Interesting point. About the dog."

"He's no different. He—"

"No. We don't know that." Stacy gave Donna a conspiratorial smile. "Yet." She sipped her drink. "Let's see how the animal clinic's new stray-pet adoption policy works on Lehigh Carter."

"What new policy?"

Another wicked grin. "The one you're going to help me make up right now."

Donna's hoots of laughter startled the stares off the two men's faces at the next table, but the two women pretended not to notice.

CHAPTER 3

Lehigh finished his morning tasks early. The saplings on the family-owned property required no attention and the recent rain made the ground too soggy to do any thinning. He needed to drive out to the other landholdings, the ones he managed under contract for extra cash, but not until late in the afternoon.

He returned to his office—a converted garage with an old wooden desk, a gunmetal gray filing cabinet, and a space heater—to catch up on desk work, his least favorite activity. His calls to potential buyers met his latest pet peeve, voicemail. That left only one option—the bottom of the to-do list. Paperwork. He opened a dusty manila folder and read the figures on the page. Out of date, of course. He scanned the pages, updating the numbers by hand with measurements he'd taken earlier that morning. His accountant always badgered him to get a computer for this sort of work, but he preferred the feel of pencil on paper. Paper made, perhaps, from his own trees.

His mind returned too many times to the yellow dog he'd found on the road, and to Stacy. She'd just have to understand about him not meeting her for breakfast. After all, she hadn't really asked him—she'd told him. The more he thought about that, the more it bugged him. She'd always been that way, expecting people to do things her way, because she said so. Damn him if he didn't usually just go along.

Except twelve years ago. She'd expected him to propose to her, which he'd intended to do, but his own way, not hers. At his own pace, not on her timetable. Sometimes life just doesn't go according to schedule.

His mechanical pencil dug deeper into the page. She'd have to find someone else to take care of that dog. It wasn't his. He'd felt sorry for the poor critter, lying there bleeding like that. Doing a good deed shouldn't shoulder a man with additional responsibility. He had plenty enough of that already. Over 800 acres of woodlands in family holdings to manage, another 1,500 for other customers, a house to maintain—and Pappy's ranch to keep up, if Maw would let him. More than enough. He didn't need a dog to add to that list. Nor a demanding woman, by God. Above all, not that.

Besides, he hated dogs. Really.

The jangling of the phone interrupted him carving a "7" into the page—the circumference, in inches, of one of the saplings at the base. The lead of his pencil snapped and he drove the metal tip clean through to the sheet underneath.

"Damn!" He jammed the pencil into the "I Heart Trees" cup on his desk and reached for the receiver. Enough paperwork. Anyway, client calls took priority.

"Lee? It's Stacy. Where have you been? I've been waiting for you all morning."

If she heard his heavy sigh, she didn't let on.

"I tried calling last night to let you know that I couldn't make it this morning," he said. "Didn't Ann-Marie tell you I called?"

"She said you were looking for me. I have to tell you, I was very disappointed that you didn't show up this morning. So was Lucky."

"Well, I—wait a minute. Who's Lucky?"

"Your dog, silly. That cute yellow lab-hound mix you brought in last night. She's all ready to go home."

He rubbed his aching brow. "Well, I hope you find her a home. She's not coming to live here."

"Lehigh Carter, I'm surprised at you. Condemning a dog to death like that."

He rolled his chair away from the desk—too hard. The chair slammed into the paneling behind him and the curls of the phone cord tangled in a knot suspended over his lap. "Wait a minute. What the heck's that about? I saved that dog's life. What's this about it dying?"

Her turn to sigh. "We have a policy at the clinic. If you bring an animal in, you take it out. If you can't care for it...well, we can't keep it here, so we have to euthanize them."

He stood, waving his free arm in the air in protest. "I didn't know that. If I'd-a known, I wouldn't-a brought her in."

"Are you saying you'd have let that poor dog bleed to death on the street?"

"No, of course not." He rubbed his temples. "But Stacy, I can't take care of a dog. I have too much on my plate already."

She snorted. Words flew from her mouth in a torrent. "What? Babysitting trees? Just how demanding is that? You can't spend five minutes a day putting out a bowl of food and water for a poor, homeless mutt? With all that land, you wouldn't even have to walk it—just let it run. She could go with you into the field, keep you company. Why, I bet–"

"Okay! Okay! I hear you." Lehigh massaged the back of his neck and shook his head. A minute ago it all seemed so clear. Now...damn her, how did she always manage to do this?

"Good. When can you come pick her up? We'll have a starter pack of food, treats, and a collar all waiting for you. Her tags show which shots we gave her and when. You'll need to bring a check for $47.50."

"What? Wait–"

"That's over a hundred dollars off, since it's a rescue. How about we meet for lunch? The staff can have Lucky all ready for you by the time we're done eating."

"I don't know, Stacy. I–"

"Should I just put her down, then?" Her whisper-quiet voice nearly broke. Damn that voice. It made him feel guilty. Which, of course, was her damned intention.

"Stacy, for Pete's sakes." Another deep sigh. Maybe Pappy could take him. It was a long shot, but...

He couldn't even listen to the words that left his mouth next. "Shirley's Diner at noon okay?"

Damn that mouth. Must, must, must reconnect it to the brain

again real soon.

***

Lehigh strained to hear Stacy's question over the din from the restaurant's kitchen. The hostess had seated them right next to the swinging doors, and it sounded like a civil war battle in there, with plates and metal pans as the chief weapons.

"I'm sorry, I couldn't hear you," he said when her lips stopped moving. "Maybe Shirley's wasn't the best choice. I'm sorry."

"That's okay," she shouted. "I thought it was romantic." The doors closed, muffling the din from the kitchen as she said "romantic," and her voice carried across the dining room, turning heads.

"Romantic? What do you mean?"

She snorted, stared, and waved a loose hand at him. "Are you telling me you don't remember? We had our first meal together here, outside of the high school cafeteria. Remember? Cheerleaders treating the football team's seniors for homecoming. I had such a crush on you then, and you never noticed me."

Lehigh did a spit-take with his Dr. Pepper. "What the heck are you talking about? You were Miss Popular. I couldn't get within 20 feet of you until you got home from college."

The kitchen doors swung open again and World War Shirley's resumed. At least this time they benefitted from it, as their waitress, a gravelly-voiced matron named Connie, delivered their food. "Chicken Caesar for the lady, burger and fries for the gentleman. Can I get you some more coffee, miss?"

"Decaf, please." They dug into their meals while the noise ebbed and flowed from the kitchen. When it quieted, Stacy said, "So what I asked earlier was, what do you think of the name 'Lucky'?"

Lehigh shrugged. "I dunno. S'fine I guess. Seems fitting." He took a big bite of burger.

"I thought so. She seems to have gotten very lucky to have found you last night. I–I sort of know how she feels." Her face flushed and she stuffed a wad of lettuce into her mouth.

Lehigh chomped into his burger. Never talk with your mouth full, Maw always said. Chew slowly, she always added. That suited him fine just now. Except the dry burger made that difficult. He set it back on the plate and sipped his Dr. Pepper. After several silent seconds he swallowed and reached for the ketchup bottle. "So whatever happened to that guy you married? That doctor fellow, Daniel something-or-other?"

"Dentist. Steven Daniels. J. Steven Daniels the Third, to be precise." Her affected British accent and fluttering eyelids made Lehigh laugh. Another swing of the double-doors and Connie returned with a pot of coffee.

"How's your meals, kids?" Connie asked without making eye contact. She poured coffee with one hand and used the other to shove the frame of her black horn-rimmed glasses back into her tight gray beehive.

"Fine," Lehigh said.

"Actually," Stacy said, "my chicken's a little underdone. Could you have them–"

"I'll take care of it tootie-sweetie." Connie snapped her gum and disappeared with Stacy's plate.

"Easy come, easy go," Stacy said. "Just like my ex-husband."

"You were about to tell me about him." The cap of the ketchup bottle slipped out of his hands and skidded across the table, splattering the stack of imitation sugar packets with red goo.

"Was I? Oh, please, don't wait—your food will get cold."

"S'awright. So, you got married, moved away for awhile, right?"

Stacy sighed and stole a French fry from Lehigh's plate. "And divorced, five years ago. No kids." Another heavy sigh. "We lived in Hood River. I came back and opened the clinic a year later."

He nodded, remembering some hoopla around all that, and shook the open ketchup bottle over his plate without success. "So I take it you finished veterinary school, then?"

She shook her head, a glum expression on her face. "My

credits had expired, and I would have had to start over. But I figured, you don't have to be a vet to open a clinic or care for animals. Just money, and…I scrounged some together."

He considered asking how, and thought better of it. "And you still ain't got remarried yet? Have more fries."

"I shouldn't," she said, and grabbed one."These go straight to my hips."

"Lucky fries." Lehigh reddened as soon as he said it, but Stacy laughed.

"Lee. Are you flirting with me?"

He reddened further, unable to think of a graceful reply. He *was* flirting, but he couldn't figure out why. Ketchup flowed in a sudden torrent onto his open-faced burger.

She dipped a second fry into the ocean of ketchup on his sandwich. "I guess I just haven't met the right man. I always wondered about you—what happened to you. Whether I'd ever see you again."

"Well, now you have." He spread the ketchup around with a French fry and closed the two halves of burger bun together. Stacy opened her mouth to reply, but the cacophony from the kitchen resumed and Connie reappeared with her salad.

"Here we go, Sweetie," Connie said in too loud of a voice. "Anything else I can get you two?"

"Is there a quieter table?" Stacy asked. "It's hard to talk here."

Connie glared at her a moment, then shook her head. "Sorry, honey. We've got a line out the door and a jam-packed dining room. I'll ask the boys to keep it down in there." She nodded her head once toward the kitchen doors.

"S'awright," Lehigh said. "We'll make do."

Stacy made a face, then shoved her fork into her salad. "Thanks anyway, Connie." She waited until the waitress disappeared, then said, "Okay, Mr. Make-do. Talk to me about what you've been up to the last twelve years."

He chewed a huge mouthful of burger, took another big bite, then set it on his plate. It took him a few moments to swallow— time to think.

"Well, you know. Working a lot. I visit Pappy every other Sunday after church."

"You're going to church?"

He shook his head and stuffed two more fries into his mouth. Chewed. Swallowed. "Not me. Maw. Pappy retired, and I took over the business. It keeps me occupied." Sort of. In busy months.

"Well," she said around a mouthful of Romaine and chicken, "now you'll have a dog to keep you a little busier."

Lehigh suspected he'd have more than the dog on his hands. Hell's bells. He shouldn't be here. He and Stacy were through. They blew their chance twelve years ago. He was happier alone.

"I'll need your help with the dog," he said to his own amazement. "If I keep it. I don't know nothing about 'em."

"Dogs are simple." Stacy forked a huge chunk of Romaine. "Feed them, water them, scoop their poop and let 'em run. Especially a Lab-hound mix like Lucky. She'll need lots of room to stretch her legs."

"I guess we're a good match, then." He stuffed the burger into his mouth to shut himself up.

"You like living alone, up there in the woods?" She kept her tone light, but her eyes burned into his with determination. He replied with a nod and a shrug.

"Yes...sort of?" she asked. "As in, yes, you like the woods, but not so much the alone part?"

He swallowed and took a sip of his drink. "It's not so bad, living alone. Sometimes I kind of like it. Most times, in fact."

"Most times? What about the other times?"

He held his burger inches from his face. "If you're asking if I miss people, the answer is no."

She smiled wryly. "I guess it's good that you'll be having a dog."

"As long as she doesn't bite, I guess."

It. It doesn't bite.

He shoved too much burger into his mouth. That'd keep it shut a while.

***

Half an hour later, Lehigh parked his truck next to Stacy's car in the animal clinic lot. He pulled the key from the ignition and leaned back in the seat, expelling heavy air from his lungs. A dog. Of all things, he was adopting a dog. How stupid. Flat-out crazy. He'd have to talk to Pappy. Maybe he'd take her.

Three taps on the driver's side window snapped him out of his reverie. "Are you coming inside?" Stacy grinned. "Don't chicken out now."

"I'm not chicken." He opened the door. She chuckled. Damn her, pushing his buttons. She played him like a damned pinball wizard sometimes.

Lucky wagged her tail and cowered in submission when Anne-Marie brought her out to the lobby for him. "Hey, Lucky," he said. "Reckon that's a pretty good name for you. Seeing as I haven't thought of anything better."

The dog's tongue slipped in and out of her lips, as if practicing her kisses. He extended the back of his hand to her snout. She licked him once, then rolled onto her back, exposing her newly-stitched belly.

"Take it easy with her for the next few weeks," Stacy said. "You shouldn't have to do anything to the stitches, but keep an eye on them. If they ooze or pus, let me know. Lucky will probably lick it off—oh, don't make a face. Dogs do a lot worse than that."

"Don't I know it." He shuddered.

Okay. He definitely needed a new plan. This one wasn't going to work.

CHAPTER 4

"You're trying to trap that man." Donna tossed chopped carrots into the wooden salad bowl and set the knife to work on a pile of radishes, still attached to their long green stalks. "I know what you're up to, Stacy, and it's a very bad idea."

"You mind your own business." Stacy turned the gas burner down to let the marinara simmer. Basic supermarket sauce, but she'd added some spices to liven it up. The smell of garlic filled her sinuses. She might have added too much. She shook her head. "I know what I'm doing."

"So do I," Donna said. "The question is, does he?"

Stacy huffed her hair away from her face and stirred a pot of half-cooked penne pasta. Ah, to have a six-burner gas stove like this one at home. She'd learned to cook in this spacious, well-equipped room and no other kitchen would ever measure up. "Lehigh's a grown man now," she said. "He can make up his own mind about things."

"Only if he knows what you're up to. How many radishes in the salad?"

"One per person is my rule of thumb. Unless you don't like them."

"Nobody likes them. I'll do four. You need to talk to him, tell him you're interested." Donna sliced through the thick red roots with ease.

Oh, to have good Henckel knives at home. But not on Stacy's salary. "I'm not so sure I am interested. Besides, it's up to him. He's the man."

"Ha!" Donna slapped the chef's knife onto the cutting board and knotted her arms across her chest. "When has that ever made a difference to you? Stacy McBride, you are your father's daughter. You see something you want, you take it."

"Keep your voice down." Stacy checked the pasta. "These walls are thin. Reverend Scott and his wife don't need to hear this. Not to mention my parents." At that moment, Senator McBride's booming laugh erupted in the next room, joined by the polite laughter of three others. "I'll have to remember that one, Reverend!" McBride said.

Donna adjusted the shoulder straps of her black knee-length dress to cover her lacy undergarments and resumed chopping. "No, but Lee Carter does need to hear it, and he's all the way across town. How's he doing with that dog, anyway?"

"Really well." Stacy grinned. "Thanks for helping me on that. That was an ingenious plan, if I do say so myself."

"You're not being honest with him."

Stacy shook the wooden stirring spoon at her. "He's a man, Donna. When has a man ever been honest with you?"

Donna smirked, shrugged, and tossed her hair to one side. "Okay. Point taken. But if you trick him into it, he won't last. He'll be gone, just like last time."

"I did not trick him, last time or ever!" Stacy splashed the spoon into the sauce, spraying red dots all over her flower-print apron, hand, and arm. It stung, but didn't hit anywhere it could stain. She wiped the sauce off her skin. Thank God for sleeveless dresses. "He was the one who couldn't talk about his feelings. He's the one who kept it all bottled up inside him. What am I supposed to do? Wait around all my life, wondering—"

"Is everything okay, dear?"

Stacy turned to the short, matronly figure leaning one hand against the kitchen doorway. "It's all right, Mom. Can I get you some more cranberry juice?"

"You can," Catherine McBride said, her hazel eyes twinkling, "and you can throw in a splash of Ketel One while you're at it. Hello, Donna, dear."

"Hello, Catherine." Donna gave her a polite hug. Her approving wink disappeared into the older woman's large silvery-brown curls. "I'll get the cocktail, Stacy. You keep dinner on track. Your mom and I have some catching up to do." She ignored Stacy's icy glare and prepared Catherine's drink, chatting with her about neighbors and old friends.

"I'm so glad you didn't talk about you-know-who," Stacy said when Catherine rejoined the other guests in the living room.

"I would never do that to you," Donna said. "I may be a sly and cunning bitch, but I never rat out my friends to their moms. Just because we're grown-ups doesn't change that. Now, come on girl. Spill. There's lots you haven't said."

Stacy chuckled, adjusting the stove's flame to prevent the pasta from boiling over. "There's lots I don't yet know. But you'll know as soon as I do."

The land line rang as Stacy pulled the pasta pot off the stove. "Would you like me to get that for you, dear?" her mom asked from the living room.

"Bah! It's probably just a telemarketer," Senator McBride's voice boomed. "Why, I have half a mind to introduce legislation to ban dinnertime sales calls."

"I'll get it, Mom," Stacy called back. "I'm expecting a call."

"Who?" Donna asked.

"Nobody," she said in a low voice. "I just don't want Daddy to start one of his rants."

"Amen to that." Donna hefted the giant bread plate in her arms. "I'll get things started. Hurry up—I don't want to be left alone in there."

"Mom?" Stacy shouted over the ringing phone. "Would you mind helping Donna get dinner out?" She ignored Donna's evil eye and picked up the receiver.

"Stacy? That you? This is Lehigh."

"Oh, hi, Lee," she said. Donna's evil eye turned into a knowing smirk. Stacy brought the phone onto the back porch and closed the sliding door behind her.

"Did I catch you at a bad time?" he asked.

"Kind of. I'm just putting dinner on the table. Daddy's hoping the good Reverend Scott can sway some of his flock to back his campaign. How's Lucky doing?"

"That's why I called. She's...well, she plumb ain't eating. I never heard of a dog who wouldn't eat."

"Does she seem sick?"

"I don't know. She's just kind of laying there. She's not perky or nothing."

"What are you feeding her?"

"The canned stuff you sent me home with. She seemed to like it okay earlier today."

"How much have you given her?"

"One can at breakfast, one at lunch. I figured, dinner, she'd need a little more."

Stacy suppressed a chuckle. "She's probably just not hungry. You've already given her twice what a dog that size needs in a day."

"Oh." A long pause.

Stacy shook her head, glad that he couldn't see her ear-to-ear grin. "Good for you for being so attentive to Lucky," she said. "She's very lucky indeed to have you looking after her."

"She's gonna have to change her name to Fatty if she stays with me, I guess," he said. "I've got a lot to learn."

"Don't we all? I tell you what. How about I come by tomorrow and check in on her? If you have any questions, I can answer them for you. Maybe we could take her on a little walk."

She winced. Here she goes again, taking all the initiative. Dammit.

"Well, that'd be mighty nice of you. But, well, I'm visiting Pappy in the morning, and then I gotta work and all, and..."

"On a Sunday?" Stacy asked. "Look, it's up to you. It's just an offer of help, that's all." She didn't mean it to come out as sharply as it did. Or did she?

"Well, okay, I guess," he said. "I don't have much in the way of fixin's to eat or anything."

"I'm not inviting myself over for dinner. Just a quick look-in on Lucky. How about two o'clock?"

"Much appreciate it, Stace."

She hung up smiling, and imagined him smiling, too.

***

Her mom clasped her hands together in delight when Stacy stepped back into the kitchen. "Did I hear you say that was Lee Carter who called?" she asked in a near-whisper.

"I don't recall saying that at all." Stacy glared at Donna, who pretended that she needed to continue tossing the salad. "Haven't you brought that salad out there yet?"

"Have you been seeing him lately?" Catherine asked. "You know, I always thought he was such a nice boy."

"Yes, Mother, I know you did." Stacy sighed. "And no, we haven't been seeing each other—"

"Mm-hmmm!" Donna's throat-clearing sounded painful.

"But he did come in to the clinic the other day with a dog he's adopting, and I'm helping him out a little with her," Stacy said.

"Mm-hmmm!" Donna choked. Stacy shoved a chunk of cucumber into Donna's mouth.

"I thought he didn't really like dogs," Catherine said. "Didn't you once tell me—"

"Catherine?" the senator's voice echoed from the living room. "Stacy? Are we dining any time soon? The Reverend and Mrs. Scott are starving!"

"Yes, dear," Mom called back in her soft voice. "Why don't you all take a seat at the table, and we'll bring—"

"What? I can't hear you, Catherine. Why don't you come in here and talk to me, where I can hear you?" In a lower voice he said, "You know I love that dear woman, but sometimes she does so drive me crazy!"

"Go on in, Mom," Stacy said. "Donna and I can finish up in here."

"Are you sure? Here, I'll bring in the pasta." Catherine picked up the bowl and headed toward the dining room. Stacy whirled to face Donna.

"How many times do I need to remind you not to discuss men with my mother?" She stomped her foot. "You know what will happen now. Endless questions over dinner, none of which I'll have answers for. Oh, I could strangle you sometimes."

Donna rolled her eyes and handed Stacy the salad bowl. "I

didn't tell her—she overheard you. But so what? It beats talking religion and politics with the Reverend and the Senator. Oh, how did I let you talk me into this dinner?"

"Free food and good wine," Stacy said. "Speaking of which, let's get this stuff out there. If I know my dad, he's chewing on the good plates by now."

"Tell me something first." Donna armed herself with food-laden serving dishes. "Why did you invite me rather than sleaze-bag? Sorry, I mean Paul. Doesn't he work for your father's campaign? And this seems like sort of a couples thing. You two should—"

"Exactly why I didn't invite him. That, and the fact that we haven't talked in four days."

Donna shrugged. "Let's get in there before Senator McBride passes a law banning same-sex dinner partners."

"Oh, he would never do that." Stacy laughed. "After all, most campaign dinners are with men."

***

Driving the pickup. Sunny day, but getting darker, fast. Fog rises from the tree-lined murk as the road curves. Lehigh slows down, mindful of deer or other critters that could leap out onto the highway at any time. The cab feels more crowded than usual—cramped. He thought he was alone, but someone is riding with him now, someone heavy who presses against him and paws at him and touches his skin with a cold wet nose—

"Off the bed, Lucky." He woke and pushed the dog away from him, but carefully so as not to disturb her stitches. Lucky stretched to all fours and sent him a doleful look before she slid off the side of the bed, two legs at a time, with another sad glance between each step.

"One thing's for sure—you weren't feral." Someone, somewhere, was missing their furry sleeping companion tonight. He checked the alarm by the bed. 5:35. Correction: someone was missing their dog this morning.

Well, almost time to get up anyway. Lucky followed him to the kitchen. He let her outside and started a pot of coffee. The newspaper wouldn't be here yet—whoever delivered on Sundays couldn't seem to get it there before six most times. He still had yesterday's crossword to finish. Seems he had a little less alone time lately.

But less time lonely, too.

He ran water into the sink and washed the few dishes he gathered from around the place: an Oregon State University coffee cup on his desk, a plate and soup bowl he'd left on the end table in the living room last night, a cutting board on which he'd sliced some Tillamook Cheddar for his Ritz crackers on the side. Getting sloppy in his old age. That won't do. Not with a woman coming around today–

Dammit. Gotta stop that type of thinking right now. She's just coming to check on the dog. Nothing more.

Speaking of the dog…

He stepped outside, first cup of coffee in his hand in a mug from International Paper, one he'd picked up at a trade show many years before. He listened in the darkness for the heavy rustling that a walking dog makes in dried leaves and underbrush, much louder and clumsier than a squirrel or deer.

Nothing.

He walked around his house, keeping an eye and ear open to the woods. Pink skywash crept over the eastern horizon. No sign of the dog. He gulped some coffee and considered his options. Should he go look for her, or wait? She was a stray. Which means, she could stray again. Injured, too, so she'd be easy prey for coyotes and the occasional wolf that roamed these forests. He sighed–

Then jumped half out of his skin as his 6:00 a.m. alarm sounded just inside the bedroom window to his immediate left.

Lehigh returned indoors, shut off his alarm and refilled his coffee mug. He pondered what to do about Lucky. If he just waited, would she return on her own? Probably not. A dog smart enough to do that would have made it back to her previous owner's home, wouldn't she?

Well, maybe that's what she was doing now.

He expected to feel relieved by that thought, but an

unwanted sadness weighed on him instead. In the few days since he found her, he'd actually gotten attached to the old gal. Her gentle, even disposition grew on him, and she followed him everywhere, with her big brown eyes showing appreciation at every turn.

Nothing like Uncle Ted's dogs.

He set packages of eggs and bacon on the counter and pulled an iron skillet from the rack. Stacy would come by this afternoon to check on Lucky. That's it—no more. Just to check on the dog, give him some advice, and thank you very much, kind ma'am.

The skillet slipped from his hands and clattered onto the stove. Dammit.

Would she really make an hour's drive, round trip, just for a dog?

Maybe. Those animal lovers, you never know. But he did know this: no dog, no visit. Except to help find her. Maybe.

He pulled on a light jacket and baseball hat, checked his flashlight, and grabbed the leash from its new hook by the door. He headed straight into the woods east of his house, where Lucky had followed him yesterday. Lehigh called her name a few times and retraced yesterday's path. She knew her new name already—surprisingly fast. Dogs had always seemed dumb before. Dumb and mean. But not this one. Lucky was challenging, and changing, his belief about dogs.

Damned dog. Likely to mess everything up. Everything's just fine right now. Nothing broken. Nothing needed fixing.

Except now some things needed changing back. Like, right now, he couldn't get Stacy off his mind. Damned woman. Last thing he needed right now was a woman in his life.

"Lucky!" he called. "Lu–ucky! Come here, girl!"

The dark woods absorbed his words like water into a dry sponge. Mosses, lichens, and leafy underbrush carpeted the ground, and a thick canopy blanketed its roof. No rain at the moment, but the ground remained mushy from the on-and-off drizzle of the previous few weeks. Faint calls of birds seemed distant, but Lehigh knew they were closer than one would guess from the volume. Sound did not carry well in these woods.

"Lucky!" he called again, louder. A rustling noise to his right caught his attention. The underbrush rattled in a zig-zag line toward him until the yellow hound's head popped into the clearing where Lehigh stood.

"There you are!" Lehigh tried to say, but the words stuck in his throat. He knelt to greet her. She bounded into his arms, knocking him back to the ground. He laughed and stroked her head and back, not minding at all when her sloppy pink tongue lapped away the hot salty flow under his eyes.

***

While Lucky had been an occasional, silent companion for the first few days, now she stuck to Lehigh like flypaper. If he moved, she moved. If he so much as coughed, Lucky responded with an alert stare. Twice that morning he tripped over her—the first time as he got into the shower, and she'd braked hard, an inch shy of the flow of steamy water. The second time, Lehigh stopped his fall on the hot kitchen stove, and he snapped at her. After that, she retreated into a spot a foot or so behind him, and stayed there.

He went outside to stack some firewood he'd collected the day before, placing it under the back shed's wide overhang out of the rain. Lucky followed him, then sat to watch his curious labors. She appeared stronger, healthier, more energetic—happy. Lucky's enthusiasm resembled a child's. Everything became a game. If he tossed a stick onto a pile or dropped a sock while folding laundry, she retrieved it, but refused to surrender it to his outstretched hand. Instead she danced just out of reach, her head hinting away from him as if she wanted to be chased into the woods. She ate her food with eager dispatch, filling her mouth and staring at him with gratitude between bites. Or so it seemed. In reality he had almost no knowledge of or experience with dogs. Just the nasty one at Uncle Ted's, really.

He knew almost nothing about Lucky in particular, either. Nothing about her breed, her history, even her age. He could tell she'd been a house pet before, very comfortable around people—him, anyway, and the staff at the vet clinic. Yet she had run away, and he'd found her wearing no collar or ID tags. Perhaps her former owners would come claim her somehow.

Lehigh paused in his work and swallowed a lump in his throat. Of course they would. Who wouldn't want this dog? A dog person would, anyhow. Hell, he would never call himself a dog person, and even he had gone looking for this one.

If someone did show up to claim her, he'd have to give her up, and let them have her back. Even though they were careless enough to let her run away.

Those jerks. How could they?

Of course, he'd just done the same thing. Must be an easy thing to do. Look away for a minute, and bam! She's off and running, where to God only knows, and who can keep up with her? So maybe they're not such jerks.

Still. Maybe they were. And if so…well, then they'd chat about who owned the dog now.

He glanced toward the dog—or, rather, the empty spot where she had been lying. "Lucky?" he called. "Where you at, girl?"

A noise at the back door of his house drew his attention. Lucky bounded toward him…from the house.

Carrying a now-empty carton of bacon in her mouth.

Damn it. If the former owners came, they could have her.

PART 2

Political Affairs

CHAPTER 5

Pappy sat alone in the kitchen, as always, chain-smoking hand-rolled cigarettes and watching Sunday talk shows with the sound turned down. Probably had turned off his hearing aid, too, hidden under the silver tousled mop that passed for hair. Stooped forward onto his hand-made wooden cane, he nevertheless looked as strong as ever, his wiry frame and leathery skin befitting a lifetime of hard work in the outdoors.

"Maw's off to church again, I take it?" Lehigh asked in a loud voice. The heavy smell of tobacco and stale coffee filled his nose, and his eyes watered.

Pappy nodded, eyes locked on the TV screen. "Then grocery shopping. Same as always."

"Nothing ever changes, I guess."

A shrug. "Just get older and fatter."

Lehigh smirked at the familiar joke. Pappy carried not an ounce of fat on his body. "I see you got the wood chopped. I'd have done it for you."

Pappy waved him off. "Gives me something to do. How's business?"

"Oh, fine. Same as always." He helped himself to some weak coffee and refreshed his father's cup.

"Better get me more syrup," Pappy said.

Lehigh found a bottle of Log Cabin in the fridge and squeezed a glop into the mug. Pappy took a noisy sip, swirled the cup in his hand, and emptied his mouthful back into it before starting the process over again.

"I could get you a spoon," Lehigh said.

"I'm fine mixing it this way."

Lehigh sat next to him at the table and waited for a commercial break. The louder, fast-paced pitch of a local tire dealer broke the monotony of the talk show's droning guests after a few minutes. He raised his voice. "Ever felt like breaking up your routine, Pap?"

Pappy squinted at him sideways. "Nope." A pause. "Why?"

"Well, I was wondering. T'other day, I rescued a hound dog, bleeding on the highway."

Pappy's eyebrows raised. "You?" He lit another cigarette, then stubbed out the first in an overflowing ashtray. Lehigh reached for it, but Pappy batted his hand away. "I'll get it. I'm not lame." The old man stretched his arm opposite Lehigh and emptied the ashtray over an open trash can in the corner. About three quarters made it into the rectangular opening. The rest snow-flurried onto the floor.

"I'll get the broom," Lehigh said.

"You will not." Pappy's hand interrupted Lehigh's rise, thumping him mid-chest and popping him back into his chair. "I'll get it later." He flicked his cigarette into the empty tray and blew smoke from his nose onto his flannel shirt.

"Okay. Well, as I was saying, there's this dog."

"How did you end up with a dog?" Pappy's bushy eyebrows somersaulted across his brow. He sipped his coffee, this time swallowing.

"I found her on the highway."

"Surprised you didn't run him over."

"Me too, kind of. But anyways, I didn't. I brought him to a vet and somehow got talked into keeping him. Ah, her. It."

Pappy flashed a wicked grin. "I can guess how. Blonde, brunette, or redhead?"

Lehigh sighed. "Stacy Mc–"

"Aw, damn, son. Tell me no." A deep scowl replaced the grin.

"I wish I could."

"You get caught up with her again, you're a fool."

Lehigh fidgeted. "Well, that's where you can help me."

Again the suspicious glare. Pappy turned back to the TV.

"See," Lehigh said, "I was hoping maybe you and Maw could–"

"Absolutely not." A long drag on the cigarette, several flecks into the ashtray, emphatic shakes of the head. "No dog. No."

"I thought you liked dogs. You always said, if not for me–"

"I like 'em fine, from a distance."

"You sound like me now."

Pappy snorted, then coughed. Smoke poured out of his mouth and nostrils.

"You okay?" Lehigh asked.

"I'll be fine," Pappy said in a strained voice, "so long as your Maw don't find no stray dog on our property when she gets back. You know your Maw's not keen on dogs."

"Maw's not keen on much of anything. Particularly me. But–"

"Don't talk like that about your Maw. As for the dog, forget about it. Besides, it might do you some good. Teach you a lesson about taking on someone else's problems."

"Pappy, I–"

"Hush. My program's coming back on." The Washington, DC pundits resumed their low-volume shouting match on Pappy's TV.

Lehigh sipped his coffee. This damned dog. There had to be another way. There just had to be.

***

Stacy parked her two-year-old Volvo Wagon behind Lehigh's truck at the end of the long gravel drive leading to his house. She considered parking to one side, but weeds and mud had swallowed up the gravel. Park there, and her tires might not find purchase when it came time to leave in an hour. A few hours, tops.

Maybe she should ask him to fix up that spot for her—or anyone, really—to use.

She shook her head. She was getting way ahead of herself here.

She considered changing into the nicer shoes she'd brought—she kept two or three pair in the car, since a politician's daughter never knows when the occasion may call for a quick-change—but opted to stick with her tennies. The grass looked wet and muddy, and she'd need the more comfortable shoes for walking the dog.

A walk. She sighed. "What a nice idea, Lehigh…"

She shook her head again and got out of the car. She grabbed a small brown sack of dog goodies from the back seat and left the larger bag of kibble for the moment. Lee would gracefully offer to carry the thirty-pound sack in for her while she rested her feet by the fire.

"Stace? That you?" Lehigh's voice interrupted her reverie, followed by the pounding thump-a-thump of a galloping hound.

"Hey! Off, Lucky! Off!" The dog's paws smeared mud on her black slacks and unzipped fleece jacket. Lucky obeyed her command and danced in circles in front of her, emitting tiny barks and whines of excitement.

"So it's 'off', is it?" Lehigh held the front door open. Stacy made her way closer to the house, dodging Lucky's mad succession of figure-eights. "I hadn't been able to figure that one out. I tried 'down' and 'stop' and…well, anyway. She's sure glad to see you."

"I'm glad to see you, Lehigh." Stacy held the bag of dog goodies out toward him.

He missed his cue with the bag, still catching up to her verbal one. "Oh, uh, I'm glad to see you, too." He pushed the door open wider for her. She held the bag closer to him and cleared her throat. He scooted his body against the door frame to let her pass.

"These are for you. I mean, Lucky." She thrust the bag against his chest. He let go of the storm door to take the bag. The door closed rapidly on her butt, bumping her forward. Surprised, she lost her balance, and tripped over the step into his living room. He reached to catch her, but her fall propelled her forward, and his hand slid from her shoulders to her breast. He snapped his hand away, but it got tangled in her unzipped jacket. Her body crashed toward the floor, dragging him and the day's groceries on top of them in a tangled heap.

"Ouch!" Stacy yelled. "Get off my leg!"

"I'm sorry!" Lehigh scrambled onto all fours and tried to tug his hand free, still trapped beneath her. She raised her upper body, bumping his other elbow, and he tumbled forward again. He jerked his hand the other direction, intending to plant it on the floor, but his finger hooked the V-neck of her blouse, yanking the fabric to one side and torquing her breast.

"Hey, watch that," she said. "I'm still attached to those."

"Sorry, sorry." Lehigh stood, red-faced, and offered her a hand to get up. "That was an accident, I promise."

"Oh, I'm sure it was. Wait a sec, I have to put everything back in place." She sat up and adjusted her clothing. No real damage done. Her blouse gaped open, but he'd seen her bra before, and then some. Once upon a time, that was not accidental. She reached for his outstretched hand–

"Lucky!" she shouted. The dog had made quick work of digging through the bag of goodies, now scattered across Lehigh's linoleum. "Lee, get the dog! She's having a feast."

"Lucky! Stop!" He stepped closer and slapped the dog's hindquarters. Lucky yelped and her tail end skidded counter-clockwise. Unfazed, she buried her face into a new pile of rawhide treats.

"Lehigh Carter!" Stacy jumped to her feet, her face red-hot. She grabbed him by the shoulders and whirled him around toward her. "Don't you ever—ever!—strike that poor animal again, or you're gonna get it where you can least afford it."

Lehigh stood, pale and frozen like a mountain lake. "Lucky! Down!" Stacy yelled. She grabbed the dog's collar and shook it. Lucky snapped at the air by her wrist. "No!" Stacy said. "Down!" She planted her free hand behind the dog's ears and pushed her into the living area, several feet from the enticing treats. "Down!" Following Stacy's downward-arcing hand, the dog lay on the floor, head up, her eyes large under Stacy's commanding stare.

"Stay," Stacy said in a firm voice. She wagged her finger

inches from the dog's snout and patted her backside. The dog whimpered, but flattened onto the floor.

"She listens to you good." Lehigh swept biscuit crumbs into a dustpan.

"That makes one of you," Stacy said. "What the hell were you thinking, smacking her like that? That's no way to treat a dog."

"I didn't know what to do!" Lehigh's voice rose. His neck and face flushed. "I don't know how to raise a dog. I told you that the very first day you pushed her onto me. So if you don't like it, you can take her back right now." He tossed the debris into the trash can and slapped the broom upright into the corner.

"I—? Pushed?" Stacy glared at him, her hand frozen mid-pat on the dog's now placid head. "Lehigh Carter," she said between her teeth. "I never knew you to be a quitter."

"I ain't a quitter," he said. "Cookies?" Without waiting for a response, he emptied a package of Oreos onto a dinner plate and poured whole milk into two small glasses. "I'm just not so sure I want to even get started."

"Well, some things never change." Stacy sat on the sofa and petted Lucky, who lay panting by her feet. She shook her head. Damned man. He'd never change.

Lehigh set the plate on the coffee table in front of Stacy and sat next to her. "Look, this whole dog thing. I—"

"Down!" Stacy grabbed for the lunging dog, but missed. Lucky buried her head into the plate of cookies, lapping up two at a time with her long tongue and spraying crumbs as she chomped. "No!" Stacy said. "Lucky! Drop it! Now!" She shook the dog's collar hard enough to jerk its head back. Soggy cookie bits flew onto Lehigh's lap. She turned to Lehigh. "Get those cookies out of here. Chocolate is toxic to dogs. Go on, get it away from her!"

Lehigh stood with the plate. Soggy cookies fell from his lap to the floor. Lucky, ever attentive, dove for them. Stacy jerked her back just in time.

"Scoop that up too," she said.

"What? It's all full of dog spit."

"Get used to it. Go on, get it."

Lehigh made a face like he'd just smelled something awful, but he bent to scoop up the soggy chocolate. As he did, more cookies fell from the plate in his hand and broke into pieces on the floor. Lucky lunged again.

"Oh for heaven's sake!" Stacy yelled. "Get those damned cookies out of here!"

Lehigh stared at her a moment, then tossed the plate and its few remaining treats into the kitchen and kicked cookie crumbs across the floor. "The hell with it!" he yelled. "Screw the cookies. Screw the dog. And screw you!"

Lucky cowered to the floor, head between her paws. Stacy's jaw hung open like a rusty gate.

"Did you just say 'screw me'?" she asked in a whisper.

Staring hard at the floor, then cringing, Lehigh answered in a hoarse voice. "Yes. I'm sorry."

Stacy shook her head. "Lee Carter, that's the most emotion I think I've ever seen you display. Ever." Her hands shook on her lap, fingers twisting into a knot.

Lehigh took a deep breath. A moment passed. The dog snorted. Stacy's fingers twitched. He shrugged. "Yeah, well, I…" His eyes met hers, then fell to the floor. He gripped the back of a chair as if to hold on for dear life.

And then he closed the gap between them in a swift step, and their mouths joined, sucking, tasting, breathing in each others' exhaled air. His body pressed hard against her, his arms wrapped around her like a vise. His weight and momentum tumbled her backward to the floor. Hands touched, groped, squeezed their bodies together. They fumbled with belts, snaps, buttons, straps. Moments later the cool autumn air chilled hot naked skin joining blissfully on the sofa's soft fabric, the sound of spilled milk being lapped into a large canine mouth ignored amidst their own gasps and moans.

***

Binoculars lowered on the driver's side of a silver Dodge

Charger parked behind a tangle of untended hedges overgrown with blackberries a few hundred feet down Lehigh's long gravel driveway. The heavy-set brown-haired man holding the binoculars jotted a few notes onto a small notepad attached to his dashboard with double-stick tape. The man had seen what he'd come for: the woman he'd been following had entered the house of the long-haired guy over an hour before and hadn't come back out. He couldn't see everything going on inside, but he saw them in a passionate embrace, sucking each other's face and grabbing at each other like teenagers. Then the guy had picked her up and carried her off, and he could pretty well imagine what happened next.

He adjusted the earbud attached via a thin white wire to his phone and pressed the entry at the bottom of his speed dial list. His current employer answered on the second ring.

"You with her?" His employer was not one for pleasantries.

"She's with a guy."

"What guy?"

He squinted at his notes. He needed glasses. "No positive ID. Some logger dude with long hair."

"What's she doing with him?"

"She ain't playing cribbage."

"Don't be obtuse. Answer my question."

The man frowned, not entirely sure what "obtuse" meant. "They're in the bedroom, and they ain't catching up on their sleep."

"Dammit! I want pictures, I want names–"

"You want me poking my nose into their damned bedroom?"

A long pause. "No. Run the address and let me know who it is. And when she leaves."

The man cut the connection. He had a lot of work to do, and he needed to do it without being noticed, and before the woman returned to her car.

But he smiled. He loved the work. And his employer paid well.

***

Paul van Paten cursed out loud, despite being alone in his black BMW. Alone, that is, with several hundred strangers, each in their own vehicles on westbound Interstate 84 in Portland. Sunday afternoon traffic had gotten as bad as rush hour lately.

The phone call he'd just received put him in a foul mood, and he needed to get over it for the next call on his agenda. Nasty just wouldn't cut it with people like this. He took deep, calming breaths, willing his heartbeat to slow and his blood pressure to drop. He thought of the success he'd enjoyed recently in his law practice, and with the Senator's campaign, and the bright prospects ahead of him after the election. Normally, he'd also bring to mind the beautiful, dark-haired woman he hoped would become his wife. But at the moment, she engendered the opposite reaction in him.

The traffic eased, helping to relax his spirits, and he dialed a number into his phone. A man answered with a sibilant, raspy voice. "Well, well. If it isn't my favorite fund raiser."

"I'm honored."

The man laughed. "Don't be. How goes the campaign?"

"Spendidly. We picked up two new editorial endorsements this week."

"I know. I paid for both of them."

Paul smiled. "And we appreciate your efforts."

"I'm working on more. As you know."

"Which is why I'm calling." Paul cleared his throat. "We may need to, ah, accelerate it just a bit. Say…within the week? Would that be possible?"

Another laugh, this one humorless. "Anything is possible, for a price. And do you know what our price is?"

Paul held his breath a moment, then exhaled. "We can't move legislation until the session opens in January."

"Now you offer me excuses?"

The drawn-out S's in "excuses" stung Paul's ear. He sighed. "I'll see what I can do."

"As will I," said the man. "As will I."

CHAPTER 6

Lehigh tugged at his baseball cap, trying to force a better fit on his head, but the damp cloth stuck to his wet mop of brown hair. Rivulets of rain water splashed off the bill onto his face. He blinked a few drops out of his eyes and peered through the gray drizzle at the stand of Douglas firs before him.

For the life of him, he could not remember what he'd been looking for ten seconds before.

He shook his head and gave in to the distractions bubbling in the back of his brain: Stacy, the dog, and the sudden, strange new turn his life had just taken.

Now he'd gone and done it.

They'd attacked each other's bodies with ferocious, pent-up lust. They'd torn at each others' clothes, kissing, biting, and touching every inch of skin and hair and private part God gave them. He'd picked her up and carried her into the bedroom, kissing her neck as she squirmed and groaned and heaved in his muscular arms. He tossed her onto the rumpled covers like an armload of kindling on a roaring campfire. She'd rolled, spread her legs, and then the fire really started.

A heavy raindrop splashed his right eye, shocking him back to the present. Lucky sniffed at his knee, then grinned up at him, panting, impatient. A red bandana drooped around the dog's neck. Stacy had put that on her when she left this morning.

This morning!

Twelve years had passed since they'd been intimate—physically and emotionally. For twelve years, he'd managed to convince himself that all that emotional stuff didn't justify the time and energy it demanded of a man. It just makes a guy all soft and torn up inside. Weak. Childlike. Pitiful.

Yeah, pitiful. Like right now.

Okay. Task at hand: check for blight on these trees. Parasites, growth issues, diseases. Determine if this stand needs thinning yet. He checked the canopy and ground cover. Time to clear out some underbrush, for sure. He'd get that good migrant labor crew back in here once they finished picking the fruit harvest in Hood River.

He picked up a branch that had fallen, and the dog's ears perked up. "You want this?" he asked the dog. Lucky's tail shot up and her front legs tensed. Lehigh broke off a piece and tossed it. Lucky raced after the stick and bounded back with it moments later. Lehigh grinned and tossed it again. For the better part of the next hour, they played fetch while Lehigh checked the trees on the perimeter of the stand. It should have only taken half that time, but the fresh air and verdant colors of the ferns and evergreens made the time fly.

He completed his loop and checked the time. He picked up the pace and called to the dog, who returned to his side, stick in mouth. "Come on, Lucky." He trudged back toward the truck, parked just up the hill about 200 yards, barely visible through the trees and mist. His breath fogged the air and his heartbeat accelerated with each step. His body had aged and fallen out of shape. That wouldn't do, now that he was—

What? In love? No. No, no, no! *Involved*. That's the word they'd used, chatting at 2 a.m. before the next bout of lustful insanity began.

When he reached the truck, he pulled a notepad and a pen out of his pocket. He wrote the date on top of the page, then—

Nothing.

Something about Doug firs…canopy…What the hell? Lucky sniffed at the ground cover a few feet away, waiting.

"Screw it." He spat. "Lucky, let's go." He opened the truck door, and the dog bounded in.

***

Lucky sniffed at his heels all morning while he made his rounds. He tripped over the dog more than a few times.

"What's up with you today?" he snapped around 11 a.m."What are you smelling? Is something–"

Different? Hell, yeah.

"Smart dog," he said with a rueful grin. "Come on, let's go get some lunch." Living up to the compliment, Lucky's ears perked up at the word "go" (or maybe "lunch") and raced back to the truck.

Back home twenty minutes later, he made himself a sandwich and gave Lucky a sliver of beef jerky, then checked messages. Two. He deleted the first, a sales call from a local sprayer. The second one doubled his heart rate from word one.

"Lee." Stacy's voice. "I think I may have left my earrings behind. Could you look for them and let me know? Bye!" She punctuated her sign-off with the tiniest little giggle.

"Stacy," he said to the air, "I'm supposed to be working…"

Hell. Not on Sunday.

No, wait. That was yesterday. Today was…ah…yeah. Monday. Right.

He carried his sandwich with him and searched the bedroom. That brought a smile to his face. "Well, if they're in the sheets, I'll never find them." He chuckled at the rumpled mess they'd left behind. No earrings on the night stand or dresser—just a tissue she'd used to wipe away extra makeup. Next he checked the bathroom. No dice. Just a few long black hairs in the sink. Moving to the living room, a sense of unease grew within him. He searched the sofa cushions, the coffee table, the stereo cabinet…oh, yeah. A button had popped off her shirt. Somehow she'd forgotten to take it with her. Her morning coffee cup, smeared with red lipstick, rested next to his on the end table. Under it, a note in her handwriting and a purple-ink pen, her trademark.

More unease.

She was doing it again. Marking her territory.

"She's got no right," he said. Lucky jumped at the loudness of his voice. "No right a-tall." He stood in the center of the kitchen, hands on hips, glaring at the countertop, stacked with breakfast dishes, cleaned and dried in the rack instead of soaking in the sink, where they could have waited until dinner. Folded dish towels hung from the oven handle, no longer where he usually left them, crumpled into a ball on the counter.

"She's gonna come in and change everything!" He threw his hands into the air. Lucky lay down on the floor and tucked her head into her paws. "Next thing you know, her things will be everywhere. There won't be any room for me and my stuff! In my own house!"

He stomped out of the kitchen, into the living room, intending to flip himself onto the couch and call her, right now, to tell her no, this has got to stop right now, RIGHT NOW dammit–

He stepped on something hard, felt it smush into the rug. He leaned over and picked it up.

An earring. Now with a slightly bent pin.

He spotted a matching gold sparkly object over by the fireplace, next to one of his socks. He didn't even remember taking off his socks.

Oh, yeah. She took off his socks.

He fought it. Didn't want to feel it. Dammit, don't don't don't don't–

Grin. Heh. Yeah.

***

A half hour later, the phone jangled Lehigh's focus out of his balance sheets, something he hated working on even without the distraction of more pleasant thoughts. He picked up on the second ring. The throaty bark of a Rottweiler roared in the background before Stacy's breathy hello.

"Work going well?" she asked him after an embarrassed silence.

"Well, honestly, I'm having trouble keeping my mind on it."

"Mmm. I wonder why."

"You know why." His voice took on a smoothness he hadn't intended. The sound of her lusty sigh somehow overcame the background noise. He let it linger.

She broke the silence again. "Did you find my earrings?"

"Oh! Yeah. Ah, in the carpet. I meant to call you."

"Good!" Her voice dropped a register. "I'd like to get them back from you...soon."

Tightness gripped his chest. Decision time.

He waited a beat, took a deep breath, exhaled. "I could bring them to you..."

She waited. He searched for words. He needed to speak, tell her when he could come by. Tomorrow, next week, maybe later–

"...tonight."

"That would be lovely," she said in a whisper. But then her tone changed. "Oh, shoot. I'm having dinner at my parents' house tonight. The Senator's wooing another contributor."

"Oh. Well, another time then." Staccato bursts of air escaped from his lips. His shoulders sagged, releasing dammed-up tension he hadn't noticed until just now.

"Perhaps you could join us?"

The tightness returned tenfold and his breath caught in his throat. "Dinner with your parents? Stacy, your dad–"

"My mother always loved you. Come on, please? I can't do these dreadful things alone anymore."

"I could never do them in the first place."

"I remember." The silence hung again, this time heavy and anxious. "Please, Lee? It's not a big event. Just a small dinner party."

"What will they think, me showing up all of a sudden after all these years? They'll think we're–"

"Involved, Lee?"

He fought for another word, but lost the battle. "Yeah. Involved."

"Well, what do you think? Are we involved, or aren't we? Did last night mean anything, or was it just a casual roll in the hay?"

"I don't do casual. You know that."

"Nor do I."

"I know." He stood, then paced behind his chair. "Stacy. You're still…the only one I've ever…you know. Had."

"Had? Don't make it sound so romantic."

"Sorry. Made…love to."

She paused. "I'm sorry too. That's…sweet, Lehigh."

"Not so much. It's just what it is." He stopped pacing, leaned on the back of his chair.

"So. Where does that leave us?"

He toyed with the earrings on his desk. Another deep breath, then: "What time is dinner?"

***

Oregon Senate President Pro Tempore George Lindsay McBride cradled the large black receiver to his ear, careful to prevent the tangled cord from tipping over the framed family photo perched precisely in the spot on his desk that his very expensive political consultants prescribed. He preferred cordless, but he put up with the black cord for appearance's sake. Demonstrating strict adherence to quirky traditions, even outdated ones like ancient phones, helped maintain his carefully crafted image. Or, as the consultants called it, his persona. With a persona comes a price.

"Did it come through?" he asked the familiar voice at the end of the line.

"It's in the pipeline," said the voice through static.

Damned cell phones. He tried to keep the grumpiness out of his voice, but failed. "In the pipeline, meaning, what? The check is in the mail?"

"These people don't write checks," the voice replied.

"Hush!" McBride wiped his brow. "Don't be foolish. You're on a damned cell phone." A few years back, the Feds trapped some Congressmen by intercepting their wireless phone conversations. Congress acted soon after to limit the FBI's power to eavesdrop—on Congressmen. State senators and gubernatorial candidates remained fair game. "Did they give you a number?"

"Five digits, beginning with a five."

McBride smiled. Nice. That'd fund a lot of state fair appearances and TV attack ads. His opponents – ruthless, anti-logger, anti-rural, anti-business, hell, anti-American liberals from Portland – needed to be kept on the defensive. "Good work, my boy. You'll make all the arrangements, then?"

"As we discussed."

McBride nodded. "There is a place for you on my winning team, my friend. A very important place."

"I've been thinking about that," the voice said.

"Something specific?"

"Very." The voice paused. "But it requires the cooperation of someone else very close to both of us."

McBride's bushy eyebrows spread wide across his forehead. "Ah. I see. That sort of position. Well, as I've told you many times, I can't offer you that…position. You must earn that one directly."

A heavy sigh broke through the static. "One word from you, and–"

"It would all go south." The Senator rubbed his temple. "It's delicate. You know that. There are other people involved."

"Which is why I need your help."

"And you shall have it. But we need to do this another way. Think, man. Think about your standing in this world. Trusted aide to the governor? Top executive, managing millions of public dollars and thousands of employees? All we need to do is decide which department. There are so many to choose from for a man of your…talents."

"First, you must win, Senator."

McBride nodded. "We'll win. Of that, I have no doubt."

"If you put that money I just found you to good use."

"Hush, man! Don't be so crass. People may be listening."

Laughter. "Count on it, Senator. They're listening. Your job is to make sure you're saying something they want to hear."

Color seeped up McBride's neck and face. "Don't you think that I–"

"What this man wants to hear," the voice said with a sneer, "is the offer of that position. Win or lose, Senator, I want that *position.*"

Two beeps, and the line went dead.

CHAPTER 7

"Stacy? Your mom is here." Anne-Marie fidgeted in the doorway of the small examining room, her crisp uniform even whiter than the drab clinic walls. Stacy long ago gave up trying to convince Anne-Marie that volunteers didn't need to dress like nurses. If not for the uniform, the old gal might quit.

"Thank you, Anne-Marie. Please tell her I'll be out as soon as I'm finished with this client." A ten-pound brown-spotted Chihuahua stared up at her with bulging eyes. Its lazy tongue drooped to one side, wagging in time with its nervous panting. A young Hispanic woman in a print dress and two-inch heels fretted in silence next to the stainless steel examination table.

Anne-Marie shuffled backwards out of the room, not quite closing the door behind her. Stacy checked her watch: 11:48. Mom had arrived early, as usual.

"We're going to have to watch Lili's diet, probably put her on some low-fat food for a bit," Stacy advised the woman. "And no more French fries!"

Stacy's stomach rumbled. French fries sounded great right now. But not if she intended to fit into that black dress for dinner. Which she most certainly did.

Minutes later, she hurried to her mother's car. "We'll have to eat quickly," Mom said. "McDonald's okay?"

"I prefer Wendy's," Stacy said. "All I really want is a salad." Liar. She wanted a double cheeseburger with bacon.

"A salad? Are you dieting again?" Mom rolled her eyes. "You don't need to at all, you know. Not at all. You're too skinny already, if you ask me."

"I'm not in the mood for an argument, Mother. Besides, we'll be eating a heavy meal tonight." The Olds 98 smelled of cigar smoke and stale air freshener. "You let Dad smoke in here again?"

"*Let* him? Hardly. George McBride does what–"

"George McBride wants. Yes, I know." Stacy rolled her eyes in tandem with her mother. "Every so often he ought to do something that Catherine McBride wants."

"He does, dear. Every so often." Mom started the car. Stacy stared out the window. Dusty, one-story buildings slid past on the side of the road, framed by fluffy white clouds. A few sported tinges of dark gray.

"You're awfully quiet, dear. Is something wrong?"

"No! I mean, uh, no. I'm just thinking."

"Well, think about dinner, please," Mom said. "We have a lot of shopping to do in forty-five minutes."

"It's not the shopping part that concerns me. Are you sure about the chocolate mousse for dessert? That seems so involved and you don't have a lot of time."

"It doesn't take long, and it's Speaker Ramsey's favorite," Mom said. "He's a very important person and George very much needs his endorsement. Are you concerned about your weight again, dear? Or is Paul pestering you about it again? He should talk. He seems to like chocolate rather well."

"No...no, actually, Mom, Paul won't be joining us tonight. We sort of broke up. I'll be bringing a different guest."

"Sort of? How does one 'sort of' break up with a boy?"

"He's hardly a boy. He's thirty-eight."

Catherine pulled into the Wendy's lot and waited for a car pulling out of a spot by the front door. "Stop avoiding my questions. You have until we leave this restaurant to tell me what's up with Paul—and who's coming to dinner with you. You know how your father hates surprises."

"Can't we use the drive-up window, just this once?"

Catherine's glare answered for her. Stacy got out of the car in silence.

***

Sitting at a tiny table in uncomfortable chairs, Catherine asked Stacy again about Paul.

"He just stopped calling a few weeks ago," Stacy said. "And, well, I stopped answering when he did call. I guess we both lost interest."

"I thought you saw him last Tuesday?"

"He stopped by the clinic briefly. We didn't really talk."

"And he hasn't called you since? Tsk, tsk."

Stacy cleared her throat. "He's left a few voicemails." Twice a day.

"Sounds like Paul hasn't been told about his lack of interest."

Stacy reddened and stabbed at her salad with a plastic fork.

Catherine picked at her chicken sandwich. "So, who's the new boy you're bringing to dinner tonight?"

Stacy choked, but pretended she had salad sticking in her throat. She drew out the more-than-requisite amount of chest-beating, coughing, and deep breaths, but Catherine could not be deterred.

"You were going to tell me about this new boy of yours."

She coughed again. "It's not exactly a new boy. It's sort of an old friend."

"Friend?"

"Yes, friend." Another stab at a hunk of iceberg lettuce swimming in Italian Lite.

"Does this old friend have a name?"

"Of course he does."

"Don't be coy with me, dear. You're proposing to bring a man into my house–"

"How do you know it's a man?" Stacy asked around a mouthful of lettuce.

"Don't interrupt. You're bringing a man into my house for dinner with some very powerful people who are very important to your father. The decision of whether he crosses my threshold is not entirely yours."

Stacy swallowed her overly-masticated salad and cleared her throat. "It's Lee Carter, Mom."

Catherine's face softened into a smile. "Lehigh. I hoped it

was him. I always liked that boy."

Stacy nodded. "But Daddy didn't."

Catherine patted Stacy's hand. "Don't you worry. I'll take care of George McBride."

Stacy hid her grimace behind a leathery wedge of orange tomato. No one "takes care" of George McBride. Not without regrets later, anyway.

***

Anne-Marie greeted Stacy at the door when she returned to work. "Stacy, that man called again."

Stacy hung her coat in the closet and let out a silent sigh. Anne-Marie's deliberate vagueness could frustrate Saint Peter.

"That man being...?"

"He says he's your boyfriend." The older woman scowled.

"Did he say what his name was?" Stacy strode behind the counter and checked for a pink phone message slip. None. Why, if somebody had called, hadn't she–?

"He said not to leave you a message," Anne-Marie said. "But I thought you'd like to know."

"Anne-Marie, if someone calls for me, please—please— always take a message. No exceptions. Okay?"

"Yes'm. But he insisted."

Stacy sighed again, this time not hiding her exasperation. "And who was it that was so insistent?"

"He said he was your boyfriend, and needed to talk to you. That's all."

Stacy frowned. That sounded like Paul. "Very well. Thank you. Now, don't we have a one p.m. appointment with a schnauzer?"

"No, Ma'am. Dr. Zwick cancelled, said he needed to reschedule. Your next appointment is at one-fifteen with Betsy Kellerman and her toy poodle. I wouldn't expect her before one-twenty though. You know how she's always late."

"Thank you, Anne-Marie. Would you bring me her file? I'll be back in the office. I have a few calls to make."

"Yes'm."

Stacy closed the office door behind her and dialed Paul's number. He answered on the second ring. "Did you call me?"

"I told her not to bother you. I was just saying hi, but then I thought, no problem, I'll just see you tonight."

"Tonight? What do you mean?"

"Your father invited me to join his little dinner party. He wants the Speaker to meet his campaign treasurer. Hey, I'm surprised you didn't tell me about it yourself."

"Paul, we need to talk."

"You aren't kidding. I miss you. Why haven't you called me back? I've been trying to reach you for a week."

"Stacy?" Anne-Marie called from outside. "Betsy Kellerman showed up early. Can you see her right away? I think something's terribly wrong with Extra. She's bleeding, and–"

"I'll be right out." She uncovered the phone's mouthpiece. "Paul, I'm sorry—I have an emergency here. Can I call you back?"

"Actually I'll be unreachable the rest of the day. But I'll see you tonight, and we'll talk then. Bye, hon!"

Stacy guided the receiver back into its cradle, then buried her head in her hands. "Now," she said, "I have a problem."

***

Lehigh's office answering machine took three messages from her that afternoon, each one more vague and frantic than the one before. "Lee, call me!" constituted the last one, squeezed in while ducking out of an examination of a cockatoo that'd lost its appetite.

Stacy didn't have much of one, either. Not with the knots stress had tied in her stomach.

She could still prevent disaster. Paul planned to meet her at her parents' house, while Lehigh would pick her up at home. She could explain the situation to Lehigh and hope he'd understand. She could make it up to him with what he preferred anyway— alone time. It could all work out. Maybe.

Her phone rang as she walked in the door from work. Her hopes rose. She picked up the receiver. "Lehigh?"

"What do you think you're doing, inviting two boyfriends—if that's what you'd call them—to dinner at my house and embarrassing your father like this?" her mother screamed. "Do you know who Arthur Ramsey is? And how important he is to your father's campaign and career? Stacy Lynn McBride, I am so ashamed of you. What are you think–"

"Stop!" Stacy shouted. "Mother, please. Take a breath and let me explain. I–"

"Do not interrupt me," Catherine said. "I raised you to be a polite, intelligent woman. What you're doing here is anything but. It is unconscionable. You need to fix this and I don't mean later. If both of those men show up tonight there will be trouble with your name written all over it. Do you understand me?"

Stacy waited for the pause, then let out a long, slow breath. "Mother. I didn't invite Paul—Daddy apparently did. I just found out about it this afternoon—apparently, same as you. He and Daddy must have played golf this weekend or something."

"Well, how was your father to know you'd run off with Lehigh Carter again? The last anyone knew, you and Paul were still an item. God knows why you'd want anything to do with a Portland lawyer. Well, I don't second-guess your choices, dear. But this—oh!"

Another heavy sigh. "I know. It's a great big mess. I'll just have to break it to Lehigh when—oh, wait. My call-waiting is beeping. It's probably him now. Can you hold on or should I call you back?"

"Normally I'd insist that you let it go to voicemail," Catherine said. "But this one time, I'll make an exception. Call me back when you've worked it out."

"Okay, Mom. Bye." She pushed the "flash" button on her phone.

Silence.

Then a beep, and a message: voice mail waiting. She dialed in her access code and password. Lehigh's voice greeted her. "Stacy, I'm stuck in a client meeting," he said, "and it's going long. I'll just have to meet you at your folks' house. I'm really sorry."

She hung up and speed-dialed Lehigh's cell phone, but it went straight to voicemail. "Lee. Stacy. Please call me. It's important." Pound, two, one. "Call marked as urgent," said the robotic female voice.

She waited. Five minutes. Ten.

She needed to shower, but she couldn't afford to miss his call. She called him again. Once more, voicemail. "Lee, Stacy again. It's really, really urgent."

Ten more minutes. She undressed, ran the water, kept her cell phone nearby.

Maybe he'd called, and she'd missed it? She checked the phone again. No.

Her mother had asked her to come early and help, but she'd begged off. Now she would compound that sin by being late.

She stepped into the shower, began a quick soap-down–

The phone!

Not her cell, though. The house phone. The one all the way downstairs, in the kitchen. She cursed her decision to remove the extension from the bedroom two months ago, at Paul's request—he hated being "interrupted."

She pulled on a robe, dried her legs from the knees down and pounded down the stairs. Three rings, four. It would go to voicemail on five. She dove for the phone and knocked it to the floor. She tumbled after it, banging her knee on the telephone table. "Ouch!" she yelled. "Wait, I'll be right with you."

"Stacy, what is going on here?" Catherine's voice shouted from a few feet away. "Paul is here already, you're not, and Lehigh Carter just called to ask what wine he could bring. As if I don't provide wine for my guests!"

She picked up the receiver. "Mom, I–"

"I mean it's very sweet of him, but goodness gracious, hasn't he been to a formal dinner before? And why haven't you told him what's going on? You–"

"Mom!" Stacy yelled. "I will! I've been trying to call him, but—Oh, damn. There goes my cell phone now!" She set the phone down and ran up the stairs, her mom's squawks fading behind her. The phone stopped ringing before she reached the top of the stairs.

"Missed call: Lehigh," the display read. The phone beeped, indicating a new voicemail message. She carried it back downstairs to finish up with Mom, but her land-line greeted her with a dial tone. She sat on the sofa and called her cell's voicemail.

"Stacy, it's Lehigh. Sorry we keep missing each other. I was in a dead zone for a bit. Oh, damn, it's beeping at me—the battery's low, so once I hang up, I'll be turning it off to recharge it. Anyway, I'm on my way to your mom's. See you there."

Stacy hung up the phone and cried.

***

Calls back to his phone confirmed that she'd missed her window of opportunity. Her last message, a sobbing, incomprehensible mess, bore only the vaguest resemblance to English.

She pulled herself together and reshowered. Her hair got wet in spots, forcing her to spend even more precious minutes under the dryer. She eschewed her original dress plan—a silky, above-the-knee black strapless—for a blue calf-length with a shawl. No need to add fuel to the fire by looking even the slightest bit sexy.

She left home already twenty minutes late, and she could only imagine the scene at her parents' house. With luck, she could sort things out before Speaker Ramsey arrived, at least with respect to the dinner. As for the rest of her life…maybe she could join a convent somewhere. Like, Peru.

She pulled into the drive. Her heart sank. A silver Cadillac with vanity plates—"RAMSEY"—took up two spots in the drive. Next to it sat Paul's black BMW. Behind it, Lehigh's pickup. She cursed. Twice.

The inside of Lehigh's truck provided the only good news of the day: the pink-tongued grin of a golden canine.

"Lucky!" she squealed. The dog bounded to her feet, thumped her tail on the dash and pressed dog snot onto the driver's side window. "Oh, pretty girl, I didn't know you'd be here! But why are you stuck in that silly old truck?"

Lucky sat, licked at her lips and sniffed at the window, cracked open just a few inches. Stacy tested the door handle. Sure enough, good old trusting Lehigh had left it unlocked. A sneaky, evil, thrilling idea came to her. "You need to come out and play," she said. Lucky stood and pawed at the window, as if she sensed adventure.

Stacy yanked open the door. With a clatter of paws and claws, Lucky bounded out of the truck and into the sprawling yard of Senator and Mrs. George McBride. She sped diagonally to the far corner of the estate, then zig-zagged back along the perimeter at breakneck speed, finishing with a set of figure-eights around the pickup and a well-trimmed star magnolia.

A roaring, gravelly voice inside the house interrupted Stacy's laughter. "What is that dog doing on my property?"

Pompous George, right on cue.

Lehigh's shout followed. "Lucky!"

"Carter!" Senator George McBride yelled, still not visible to his grinning daughter. "Is that your animal?"

Stacy stepped around the vehicle in the circular drive, giving her a view through the picture window to the gathered dinner guests sipping drinks and munching hors d'oeuvres from trays held by black-tie-clad caterers. Her father pointed and puffed in the doorway.

"It's okay, Daddy," she said. "I'm the one who let Lucky out. I wanted to play with her."

"Play with her in your own yard!" McBride yelled. Lehigh tumbled out the door. McBride shouted at him. "It's not appropriate to bring pets to a dinner party—especially when some of our guests are allergic to dogs!" Lehigh ran to the cowering dog, grabbed her collar and dragged her to her feet. After a moment's resistance, Lucky ambled along toward the truck. Stacy intercepted their path.

"Be gentle with her," she said. "It's not her fault."

Lehigh spat. "I'm aware of the fact that she can't open car doors on her own. Last I checked, dogs ain't got fingers or thumbs."

"I'm sorry, Lehigh. I needed to get you outside, where we

could talk."

"You mean, out of earshot of your boyfriend?" He opened the driver's side door, ignoring her cringe. Lucky hopped onto the seat and spread out, panting onto the beach towel covering the passenger's side.

"I'm sorry about that, too. Paul and I–"

"You don't need to explain anything to me." He slammed the door shut and leaned his back against it, crossing his arms over his chest. He locked his eyes on Stacy's. "Except for one thing. Why you invited me to dinner with him, without any warning—and then don't show up for the first half hour—I gotta say, that's one fantastically uncomfortable situation."

"I didn't know he'd be here until after I invited you. Then I tried calling you, over and over–"

"Bad day for me to be in the field." He looked away, then shrugged. "It's okay. I needed to see this, I guess. You, your family, your fiancé–"

"My what?"

"Paul. You know him." He turned away.

"Don't be snide. Why did you call him that?" She stepped in front of him again.

"He called *himself* your fiancé." Lehigh locked eyes with her. "Your dad shook his hand and welcomed him to the family. I felt two inches tall at that moment."

"I'm so sorry. He–"

"What am I, your final fling?"

"No!" Tears welled in her eyes.

"And tonight, what's this, a ceremonial sacrifice? I'd have said sacrificial virgin but clearly we don't have any of those present."

She gripped his arms above the elbow. "Stop it, and listen to me."

"Fine. I'm done. Oh, wait, one more thing. Congratulations on your engagement."

"We are not engaged!" Her voice echoed off the stone walls of her parents' massive house, and heads turned to stare at them from the far side of the picture window.

Including her father's. And Paul's. And Speaker Ramsey's.

At that moment, she noticed the open windows in the living room.

"You'd better work that out between the two of you," Lehigh said. "I'll leave you to it."

"Lee, don't go just yet. Please. I need to talk to you."

He climbed into the truck, closed the door, and lowered the window. "We do need to talk, Stace. But you have other things to take care of first." He raised the window halfway, then stopped. "Enjoy your dinner."

He managed to avoid churning gravel until his truck left the driveway.

Stacy stared after him with a mix of grief and relief. While angry, Lehigh hadn't dumped her, and the minor confrontation prevented the major embarrassment that would have greeted her had she gone inside. But he could be a very stubborn, recalcitrant man, as twelve years of silence had proven.

She turned from the view of his disappearing taillights to find the stares of her father's dinner guests still upon her. In particular, two stood out: the pale blues of her father, ornamented with furrowed white eyebrows, and the steely grays of Paul, blazing above the firm line of his mouth.

Stacy felt very, very small.

Of all things, at that moment her cell phone rang. She answered it. "Hello?"

"Come in through the kitchen, dear," her mother said through the receiver. "I need your help in here."

"Thank you." Tears collected in the corners of her eyes. "I feel like such an idiot."

"I have just the thing for that," Catherine said.

She did: a bright red Cosmopolitan and a long, tender hug.

"Oh, Mom," Stacy said. "I screwed up pretty badly here, didn't I?"

"It's not so bad, dear." Catherine patted her back. "But you do need to have a little chat with Paul. After dinner, please."

"I don't know if I can go in there and sit across from him right now. Did Daddy tell you—"

"He did. As you know, I'm less enthusiastic about him than your father is. But if it's what you want…"

"It's not, Mom. Not at all. And knowing this, I can't—"

"Stacy? Honey, is that you?" Paul's voice drifted into the kitchen. Stacy downed the rest of her drink, about three-fourths of the glass, in one gulp.

Paul entered the spacious room. "There you are." He sidled up to her, wrapped an arm around her and leaned in for a warm kiss. Stacy leaned away, and Catherine assisted with a loud clearing of her throat.

"Shall we join the others, then?" Catherine tugged at Paul's starched white sleeve and nodded toward the living room.

"In a moment." Stacy turned to Paul. "I need another minute to talk to Mom while she refills my drink. Save me a stuffed mushroom cap, would you, please?"

"Sure." Paul's 6'2" athletic frame seemed to shrink with Stacy's dismissal. "But it's almost time to sit down to dinner. Don't be long, okay?" His second attempt at a kiss found only Stacy's flushed cheek. He left with doubt and confusion clouding his boyish face.

"Another Cosmopolitan?" Catherine asked.

Stacy nodded. "Better make it a double."

CHAPTER 8

Lehigh gripped the steering wheel with a ferocity he hadn't felt in years. Had it been the neck of a living, breathing animal—and a particular few human animals sprang right to mind—they'd not have lasted a New York minute before choking to death. Or being beheaded, which better fit his black mood.

Lucky edged close to him once, but dodged an annoyed swipe of his hand just in time and spent the next several minutes tucking herself into the crack between the passenger door and the seat. Her second whimper elicited an angry human growl. After that, she remained silent.

Another growl—this one from his stomach—reminded Lehigh that he hadn't eaten since mid-morning. His light early lunch had seemed like such a good idea when he'd expected to be dining on fresh salmon or a juicy prime rib from the McBride's caterers. On impulse he pulled into a KFC drive-through and ordered a three-piece meal. "All white meat," he shouted into the static of the ordering kiosk. If he couldn't have prime cuts of fancy meat, at least he could eat the best of the greasy worst. He ate it while driving and flicked occasional bits of chicken to the grateful dog.

Once home, he turned his cell phone off and unplugged the land line. He popped open a can of Old Milwaukie and plugged a DVD into the player—"The 39 Steps"—but paid scant attention to the black-and-white images flickering across the screen, or the gritty dialog that so often absorbed him in previous viewings. He had his own dark mysteries to solve, starting with why the hell he believed anything a woman ever told him. Neither the beer nor the movie provided any clues.

Around 10:30, Lucky interrupted his brooding with a quick scratch at the back door. The poor girl hadn't had her usual evening constitutional. He pulled on a light jacket and baseball hat and opened the door.

Lucky shot outside like a meteor seeking the horizon, a burst of energy in a blurry arc of motion racing toward oblivion. In moments she'd disappeared into the woods, out of sight. "Lucky!" he called after her. The rustle of leaves and branches faded into silence.

He sighed, following her trajectory some thirty yards into the forest. He'd never find her in the trees at night, and she left neither a visible nor audible sign of her whereabouts. He returned to the house, flicked on the porch light and settled into his easy chair to wait.

***

"As of tonight, Senator," Paul said, "we're well ahead of our October first target of five million dollars in contributions." He pushed a thin stack of stapled pages, thick with numbers, across the expansive desk. "By the time you formally announce your candidacy in January, you should have twice that, if present trends continue. According to what my friends in Salem tell me, that ought to keep any serious challenger out of the race for the party nomination."

"Excellent." Senator McBride let the pages lie untouched. He slid open his bottom desk drawer and removed a small wooden box. He lifted its mahogany lid and offered the selection of Cubans to his campaign treasurer.

"Still trying to quit." Paul patted an imaginary pack of Marlboros in his shirt pocket. "But you go ahead."

"Tell me," the Senator said after his first puff of blue smoke filled the dim light between them, "what's in the official report?"

"That's not due until December thirty-first, so technically, nothing yet," Paul said. "But clearly we'll need to, ah, repackage a few of these donations so they, um, more neatly align with regula–"

"Don't bore me with details." McBride sent a stream of blue

into the center of the smoke ring he'd just unleashed. "What's the bottom line? How much of that five million is reportable?"

Paul hesitated. "Well, sir, as we've discussed—"

"Don't call me 'sir.' We're partners in this effort and, hell, you're practically my son-in-law. Call me George." He took another satisfied puff and blew another perfect smoke ring.

Paul nodded. "Very well…George. In order to preserve your deniability, it's essential that you don't know certain details, so that if it ever came out—"

"Which it won't," McBride said. "Stop dilly-dallying. Anyway I don't want details. Just one number. If my next contributor asks me what my official total is, what do I tell him?"

Paul picked up the report and licked his lips. "Almost two million. Most of which came from your Super PACs. The Campaign for Cascadian Freedom, and the Responsible Forestry Fund. The other three million, well…that's the unofficial part."

The Senator leaned forward, pointing his cigar's smoky cinders at his most trusted aide. "Are you telling me that over half of my campaign funds exceeded or otherwise violated reporting guidelines?" He stared hard at his treasurer's nodding head, then smiled.

"Nice," he said. "Keep up the good work."

Paul waved blue smoke away from his face. "One more thing…George. About that son-in-law thing. I'm afraid your daughter may be getting cold feet. Or worse." His eyebrows fused in a concerned grimace.

"Worse? What do you mean?"

"She may be double-timing me with another man. Specifically, that idiot hayseed Lehigh Carter, the one whose dog nearly ruined tonight's dinner party. I guess he's an old flame of hers?"

The Man Who Would Be Governor scowled. A bitter taste formed in his mouth. "That's not acceptable," he said. "Not acceptable at all. We'll need a plan…and some of that, how do you call it? Unofficial funding."

Paul smiled. "I was hoping you'd say that."

***

Lehigh's eyes shot open. A pleasant dream evaporated from his consciousness, just out of memory's reach. Odd sights and sounds surrounded him. The colors, the space, the noise disoriented him. No alarm, no comfortable bed, no soft white curtains glowing through the darkness from his bedroom window. Instead he sat in an easy chair, with bright lights glaring into his face. Some golden oldie competed with static on low volume behind him. Darkness clung to unadorned picture windows. A chill hung in the air.

He sat up, recognized at length the simple rustic décor of his own living room. The darkness outside meant that the porch light had burnt out. He stretched himself out of the chair, rubbed the crick that had settled into his back, and craned his neck to check the clock on the kitchen wall. 12:17. Way past his bedtime, and Lucky's feeding time. Surprised she didn't come begging for it.

The memory of her dashing off into the woods returned with a painful stab to the gut. Damn! What if she'd returned while he slept, scratched at the door, and gave up, only to wander off somewhere…back to the highway maybe? To be picked up by someone else, a true dog-lover perhaps, one who would know how to take proper care of her…

A rattling of his storm door interrupted his worry. The pale yellow tail end of a slumping mutt appeared through the screen. He strode to it and threw open the door.

"Lucky!" He knelt to greet the happy mutt. She barreled into him head-first. Her tongue lapped his face and neck and her paws climbed his chest. Her skinny tail wagged and her back feet clacked a random percussive beat on the kitchen linoleum. "Good girl." Lehigh rubbed his palms along her back and atop her bobbing head. Her tongue tickled his skin as she lapped his face, now wet with dog spit.

"Okay, okay, girl." He laughed and pushed her face away from his lips. "These lips are spoken for."

Or were. Until the catastrophe of this evening, the humiliation of being the fifth wheel, the Other Man…His lips were fair game again. Probably for another twelve years.

But not for a damned dog.

"Let's get you some food." Lehigh straightened and strode to the cupboard where he stored her kibble. She followed with a limp in her stride. "What's up?" he asked. "Did you hurt yourself?" Drops of blood trailed behind her on the floor, and paw-smeared red streaks blotted the area by the door where they'd lingered upon greeting. A dark trickle eked a path down her hind leg. "Let me see your belly." She stood still, her expression blank. Obviously he'd used words well outside of her known list of commands. "Sit." She obeyed.

He knelt and lifted her front paws. Torn stitches exposed her open wound to the elements once again, bloody, and from the looks of things, painful.

"Looks like we'd better take a ride downtown, Lucky." Not what he wanted to do after midnight. At least this time he wouldn't be greeted by that meddlesome, lying Stacy McBride.

But the clinic's phone went unanswered. "Looks like it'll have to wait until morning," he said. Lucky lay on the kitchen floor and whimpered. Blood dripped from her belly. "Damn," he said. "Okay, let me see what I can do." He found clean dry towels and pressed them against her wound. The bleeding slowed after a bit. He got fresh towels and did it again. Around 3 a.m. the bleeding slowed to a trickle. He pressed his last clean towel against the cut, tied an old shirt around her body to secure the makeshift bandage, and flopped into bed.

The 6 a.m. alarm rang moments later. Lucky struggled to her feet next to Lehigh's bed, leaving a fresh red streak atop the dried brown crust on her pillow. Lehigh coaxed on a pair of jeans, a flannel shirt and a pair of boots and led the dog onto her towel on the passenger's seat of the truck.

Fog enveloped the dark, wooded highway, limiting visibility to less than a hundred feet. Somewhere out there the sunrise brightened someone's morning, but not his. Lucky whimpered and glanced at him, faith and hope in her sad brown eyes. He pressed the accelerator, pushing his speed fifteen over the speed limit. Screw it. He knew the road well, and if a deputy stopped him, well, it's an emergency. Bleeding dog. Every second counts. He had to get there before...

Before her.

Don't be there, he said to the Stacy in his head. He didn't know when she started work. No sooner than seven. He hoped for eight. A little extra time would help.

He rounded a bend a little too fast, and Lucky slid head-first into the hard vinyl armrest on the door. She whined a little and scooted back toward him.

"Sorry, girl." He petted her side. She somehow reached him with her languid tongue and showed appreciation to his salty fingers. He pushed his arm closer, making it easier for her mouth to reach him. His finger brushed against her teeth–

He jerked his arm back, a reflex, unthinking action, startling the dog. The truck lurched left—his whole body had reacted, including his left arm, which yanked the wheel counterclockwise. He jerked it back to straight, and now Lucky slid closer to him. Her tail poked his thigh, and her hind legs clawed at the open air.

"All right, girl, I'll slow down." He wiped his hand on his pants. The imprints of her teeth still tingled on his fingertips, and the quickening effect on his pulse lingered. She whimpered again. "Sorry, girl," he said. She was not his uncle's fierce sheep dog, the aggressive attack dog that had scarred his psyche, and his skin. Her soulful brown eyes spoke of loyalty and trust, of submission to his stubborn will, of faith in his alleged generosity.

Alleged, at best. Sure, he'd rescued her from a lonely death along the highway, bought her some food, given her a warm place to sleep. But anyone else would have done the same—maybe more. Stacy would do more. Stacy would–

Stacy's Volvo was parked in the clinic's lot.

"Damn it all to hell." He sat in the truck and took several deep breaths. "I should go," he said. "There's another veterinarian across town. We could be there in twenty minutes."

Lucky moaned and pawed at the door.

"Shoot," he said. "All right. We'll stay here." He eased Lucky out of the truck on the driver's side, cradling her and the blood-stained towel in his arms. He kicked the truck door shut with his heel and carried her into the clinic. She licked his face once when he paused before the swinging glass door, as if to say, "Thank you. I trust you."

He didn't trust his own feelings at that moment. He pushed open the door.

Anne-Marie looked up from her People magazine. Her eyes grew large. "Oh, dear. Is something the matter with Lucky?"

"Her stitches came undone," Lehigh said. "She'll need 'em retied, I guess."

"I'll go get Ms. McBride." Anne-Marie rose from her seat.

"No!"

Anne-Marie froze in mid-rise. Lucky wiggled in his arms and he nearly dropped her. "Is there anyone else here who can help her?"

"The doctors don't come in until seven," Anne-Marie said. "For the next fifteen minutes, it's just me and Stacy."

"What kind of animal clinic doesn't have a vet on staff during business hours?" Lehigh asked.

"The kind that takes far too many charity cases and can't afford it." Stacy's face appeared behind Anne-Marie, clouded with anger. "If you'd like the address of a private veterinary surgeon's office in Hood River, I'd be happy to provide one. You should be able to get there by eight-thirty, Mr. Carter."

"Charity case?" He hefted Lucky six inches higher, almost to his chin. "I've spent over a hundred bucks on this dog in the last week, and she wasn't even mine when I brought her in. You people tricked me into keeping her."

Anne-Marie gave Stacy a knowing glance, then slunk out of sight.

Stacy folded her arms across her chest. "Did you want the dog euthanized? That's what we would have had to do."

"The hell if I know. Maybe. Last week I wouldn't have cared. Now…no. Damn you!"

Stacy stared at him for a hard beat, then shrugged. "Bring her in." She opened the door next to the reception counter and held it while Lehigh stepped through. Stacy pointed down the hall.

"First door on the left. Set her on the table. I'll be right in. I'm going to call Dr. Lewis, see if she can't come in a little early. But she may be on her way already."

Lehigh nodded and did as instructed. Lucky sprawled on the examination table, stainless steel covered with white terry-cloth, and gazed sadly at him.

"It's okay, girl," he said. "The doctor will be here soon to fix you up. Then we can go home and get some rest."

The door closed with a thud behind him. He turned, expecting to greet a scrub-clad doctor or aide...

Rather than the passionate kiss that engulfed him.

The kiss lasted ten, twenty seconds. Maybe an hour. Lehigh lost track of time, place, everything, except the soft caresses of Stacy's lips and her tongue's hungry search of his mouth. He tasted her teeth, her breath, her excitement and passion, smelled her hair and skin and perfume, felt her arms on his neck and the small of her back in his rough hands.

She broke the embrace as she began it—with startling abruptness. She pushed him away and combed her fingers through her hair. He opened his mouth to protest, and to ask her why—so many questions, why—and stopped when the heavy metal door swung open. A tiny, round, bespectacled woman in a white lab coat over blue scrubs shuffled into the room.

"Mr. Carter, I'm Dr. Lewis." She extended her hand for a shake. "I heard our poor girl Lucky tried some at-home suture removal?"

"I'm not sure exactly what happened." Lehigh wiped lipstick off his mouth. "She ran off into the woods last night and came back bleeding." He tried to catch Stacy's eye, but she aimed her flushed face at some undefined spot between Lehigh and Lucky about waist-high.

"Let me take a look." Dr. Lewis stepped between Lehigh and the table and examined the dog's exposed, bleeding belly. Lehigh took a half-step back to give her more room to work, and to allow him a better view of the unpredictable woman who had attacked him with such impetuous passion a few moments before.

Stacy steepled her fingers in front of her heaving chest. She still did not look at him, nor at the dog. She seemed entranced. He wanted to pull her aside, out of the room, ask her what the hell was going on. But right then, his injured dog needed his attention.

Oh, yeah. The dog.

"It looks like she snagged herself on some underbrush." Dr. Lewis cleaned the wound with a damp cloth. Lucky stared doe-eyed at Lehigh. A faint whimper escaped from her open mouth. "Then, probably, she pulled the rest out herself. Easy enough to fix, but we'll want to put a cone on her this time. Once they start chewing on something like this, they tend to keep doing it."

"Okay," Lehigh said. "I can come back later to pick her up." He edged toward the door.

"It won't take but a few minutes," Dr. Lewis said. "Half-hour, tops. You might want to wait."

"Yes, why don't you wait here? I mean, in my office." The sound of Stacy's voice surprised him. "I want to go over something with you." Her misty eyes spoke of wanting and remorse. Or so he wanted to believe.

"I could use a cup of coffee," he said to Stacy's perfect lips. Perfect and off-limits. Taken. Engaged. Yet, moments before, planted on his.

Stacy opened the door and held it open. "My treat, Mr. Carter."

He floated out of the room, forgetting all about his injured dog, and followed her to the clinic's lobby.

Stacy pulled on her coat. "I'll be back in a half-hour," she said over her shoulder to Anne-Marie. The older woman wore a troubled expression but did not respond, other than to scowl at Lehigh. He did not return her stare. Glassy-eyed, he walked Stacy to her car.

"I'll drive," she said. "I have a place in mind."

"Ain't we just going across the street?"

She shook her head. "Too many people there. I want privacy."

He held the door for her, then got in on the passenger's side. Before he could close the door, Stacy's mouth covered his and her hands held his head in an impassioned embrace.

"What happened to privacy?" Lehigh asked when she pulled back to take a breath. He took the opportunity to buckle his seat belt.

"Sorry," she said, red-faced. "I just didn't expect to see you this morning. I wondered if I'd ever see you again. I'm just so happy." She started the car and backed out of the parking space.

Lehigh pointed to the curtains falling back in a tiny window at the front of the clinic. "Is she going to be trouble?"

Stacy sighed. "Anne-Marie doesn't approve of my interest in you. She's pretty traditional. She sees Paul, a guy from an old-money Portland family, so established, so smooth, and wonders why I don't marry him. Come to think of it, my father wonders the same thing."

"Last night I thought that was the plan."

Stacy reddened again. "That's why I want to go somewhere private. I want to explain all of that, without anyone I know eavesdropping."

"Good idea, but where in Clarkesville do you not know anybody?"

A few minutes later she pulled into a nearly-empty parking lot for a place called "Mr. Downey's."

"A 'gentleman's club'?" Lehigh asked. "Are you serious?"

"I know the owner—an old friend of the family," she said. "There's a private room in back. I have a key—"

"You have a key to a private room at a strip club?" Lehigh shook his head in wonder. "What next? You show me your burlesque act?"

"It's not like that." She pulled into a spot behind the squat adobe building. "I mean...not anymore." Her face turned from red to scarlet. "Haven't you ever wondered how places like this stay open in towns like Clarkesville?"

"I'm lost."

Stacy smirked. "It's all about who you know...and whose political campaigns you donate to."

"And who you have dirt on."

"It's not what you think." She dangled a key in front of him on a long leather shoelace. "Let's just say, Mr. Downey owes me."

***

Lehigh paused a moment at the entrance to the tiny apartment, his mouth agape. Stacy entered ahead of him and didn't seem to notice his shock. She closed the heavy drapes and flicked on various lamps scattered about the room.

"I guess stripping pays pretty darn well." He ran his hand along the back of the soft leather sofa pressed against the oversized picture window and facing a 65-inch high-definition TV. An expensive looking stereo system with five free-standing speakers surrounded the white leather sofa, matching love seat, and glass-top coffee table. The plush carpet absorbed nearly an inch of his footprint, and a fully-stocked bar appeared ready to serve a party of fifty.

"Mr. Downey likes to entertain," Stacy said. "And it's not the dancers per se that earn him the money—it's the booze. And whatever, um, side business he can generate. That's what this suite is for."

"What sort of side business?"

"I'd rather not talk about that yet. I want to talk about us."

Lehigh sat with an exasperated sigh on the sofa and folded his arms across his chest. "Half of 'us' is you. There are things about you that I think I ought to know about. Things I should have known twelve years ago. Such as why you worked at a strip club—"

"I was never a dancer." She filled the coffee-maker with water and scooped grounds into a filter.

He nodded. "I'm relieved. Actually, no. I was having a hard time imagining you taking your clothes off for pay. Not only is it completely out of character for you, but the Senator would flat-out kill you."

"Kill, filet, and roast over a high flame." She poured water into the coffee-maker's reservoir and sat next to him. The rich aroma filled the room.

Lehigh uncrossed his arms and turned toward her. "So why do you have a key to the luxury suite backing a strip club? What exactly is your relationship with this Mr. Downey?"

Stacy bit her lower lip and knitted her hands together on her knee. "It actually involves my father, and even the dinner last night. But before I tell you, you have to swear never to tell anyone. Not even your own mother."

Lehigh looked away for a moment and rubbed his face. "Stacy...my mother and I...we don't talk anymore."

Her eyebrows arched, eyes wide. "But...you two were always so close."

He shook his head. "Used to be. Not for twelve years."

Stacy cocked her head to one side. "Since you and I..."

He nodded.

"But why?"

He shrugged. "For a year after we split, neither one would talk to me. Said if I couldn't give 'em grandkids, I was no use to 'em. Pappy came around, but Maw...she's not...*right*. I think it's dementia, but she won't get checked and Pappy won't make her."

"I'm sorry."

He swallowed, cleared his throat, and waved it off. "Anyway. We're getting distracted from our main point. Namely, you telling me about your relationship with Downey and how it all ties with your father and last night."

She pointed a finger at him. "You have to swear to never tell. Secret forever."

He spit into his palm and rubbed it in. "Sure, sure. Now, tell me of your sordid past."

"It's not so bad as all that." She smiled at half-mast and avoided looking him in the eye. "Unless you're into politics."

"Which I'm not. But neither are you." He rested an open hand on her knee.

"But my father is." Now her eyes met and held his, and she picked his hand up toward her chin. "That's why you have to promise never to tell."

He stared into her eyes. The grip on his hand tightened. He returned the squeeze. "Okay. I swear."

She reached her arms around his shoulders. He allowed her a stiff hug. She pulled back. "You're still mad about last night."

"A little."

"I can explain."

"Please do." He spread his arms, indicating the room.

She shook her hair back. "It's all part of the same story. You see, Daddy and Mr. Downey are old friends. It goes back to their high school days. They were roommates in college one year and even went into business together, selling replicas of the official university football uniforms."

"Let me guess. They lost their shirts."

Stacy moped a sour grin. "You and the Senator have the same punny sense of humor." Her expression grew serious again. "After college, Daddy went to law school, but Mr. Downey came back to Clarkesville and went into business. Well, lots of businesses. This club here is just one of many."

"Doesn't Downey own the land under the shopping center?" Lehigh asked.

She nodded. "He got it in a land swap with the state, when they wanted to build that new Health Services building."

"Let me guess. Senator McBride helped organize that trade. With help from Speaker Ramsey."

A shrug. "A man has to take care of his campaign contributors."

Lehigh leaned forward and took her hand again. "Of course I'll keep my promise," he said, "but so far you haven't told me anything that isn't public knowledge or soon will be. Land deals are public record, as are campaign contributions."

"Mr. Downey is a clever and powerful man." Stacy turned away again. "He likes to keep his business dealings quiet." She looked back at him. "And his politics."

"I'm sure that suits the Senator's interests as well."

"Of course, some of Mr. Downey's businesses—like this one—are not the kind most politicians want to be associated with."

"Ah," Lehigh said. "But some were. Let me guess. Some of the money coming to the Senator's campaign coffers comes from businesses of that kind. Right?"

"Right. That's where I come in. And...the real purpose of this room."

CHAPTER 9

"Why don't we start at the beginning?" Lehigh sat next to Stacy on the soft leather sofa, sipping coffee in Wedgewood china cups lightened with real cream from·the fridge and sweetened with orange blossom honey.

She edged away from him, but his scent—a musky after-shave she'd always adored—followed her across the couch. "Before you and I dated," Stacy said, "I worked in one of Mr. Downey's establishments, serving cocktails. Summers off from college at first, and then full-time for a while afterwards. My father hated me for it, but we weren't really talking much then anyway. I wanted to be independent—he'd say rebellious—and it paid well enough that I could live on my own."

"Which place was it?" Lehigh asked. "Not that I'd know it. I ain't never been much for bars."

"It was called Montgomery's, that upscale place by the hotel on the Gorge. Ten dollar drinks even then. I can't imagine you in there."

Lehigh shook his head. "I can't imagine *you* in there. Did you have the skimpy outfit, low-cut dress, all that?"

"The works." Stacy's face grew warm and no doubt as red as her lipstick. "Oh, God, sometimes I can't believe it all myself."

"So, you were what, a pole dancer?"

"Lehigh Carter! Don't be ridiculous."

He held up both hands in surrender. "Sorry. So, how does this all connect with the Senator?"

"As a newly elected legislator, Daddy crusaded on a whole host of 'morality' issues. He sponsored a bill to close 'gentlemen's clubs' in cities under 30,000 people. Mr. Downey would have lost a fortune. But rather than losing in open war, he used his secret weapon."

Lehigh narrowed his eyes. "You?"

Stacy nodded, amazed at how these memories never faded—the ones she wished would go away forever. "One week, there was a 'bonus' in my paycheck, and an envelope for Daddy. I was supposed to hand-deliver it, but not open it."

"Did you?"

Her gaze dropped to her lap. "Yes to both. It was a big donation to Daddy's re-election bid. Ten thousand dollars, which was a lot back then for a legislative race. Daddy was facing a big challenge from that sleazy TV news guy, Bruce Bailey."

"I remember him. He got exposed as a tax cheat right before the election, didn't he?"

Stacy barked out a haughty laugh. "Guess how that came about? Daddy's morality bill died a quiet death in committee, and a certain regular customer at Montgomery's, who happened to be Bruce Bailey's accountant, somehow had his office burglarized two weeks before the election."

Lehigh let out a low whistle. "These guys play dirty."

"It gets worse. And—this is the hard part." She swallowed a deep gulp of coffee. It tasted like concrete blocks going down. She fought tears, willed them back into her eyes. *Steady. Be strong.*

Lehigh reached for her hand. "Go on. I need to know, even though I ain't sure I want to. But your secrets are safe with me."

"Thank you." His gentle voice calmed her. She leaned back and shook her hair about her shoulders. "Nothing stays secret forever, I know. But this needs to stay secret, at least for now, until the election next fall. If it ever got out–"

"It won't. At least, not from me."

She squeezed his hand, took a deep breath, and chose her words carefully. "I...quit the waitress job and...later, I went to veterinary school. It was tough going. As you know, I never actually finished."

Lehigh nodded. "I never held that against you."

"No, you've always been very supportive of me," she said. "But when you know how it all got paid for, you might never want to see me again."

***

Lehigh and Stacy had dated for two years in their mid-twenties. At one point he'd considered proposing to her. He'd known her since high school, when they were both fifteen. He thought he knew everything about her, except for whatever had happened in the last twelve years. To discover secrets now about what she did just prior to their earlier courtship—secrets that could change his opinion of her forever—went way past disturbing to the downright scary and infuriating.

He crossed his arms and legs and sat back on the couch, studying Stacy's face. He licked his lips, started to speak, then stopped. He stood, paced, and waited. A loud exhale, a stammer, a cough.

To not know would be even worse.

Finally, he said: "Well, I reckon you oughta tell me then."

Stacy's gaze locked onto a clear glass ashtray resting on the center of the coffee table. She spoke in a monotone, as if reciting a memorized passage.

"You remember I told you I got a scholarship from the local Rotary Club? Also from 4-H, Kiwanis, a few other places."

Lehigh nodded. "Vaguely. What's wrong with that?"

She reddened. "Mr. Downey was on the board of directors for most of them. As for the others, he might as well have been. Speaker Ramsey was on the ones Downey wasn't on."

Lehigh shrugged. "So? He put in a good word for you."

She frowned. "More than a good word. He basically controlled their decisions. Still does, when he wants to." She looked away from Lehigh. "Say what you want about strip clubs. They're very profitable."

"How much money we talking here?"

Stacy sighed, and her moist eyes met Lehigh's. "The scholarships paid for everything. It was tens of thousands of dollars a year. More in my three years of vet school than they'd given in the previous twenty years of scholarships to all students, combined."

"Jesus." Still, it was only money...Lehigh bit his lip. "Okay. So he liked you, you were deserving. What's the problem?"

"Lee, Mr. Downey doesn't do things for people out of the goodness of his heart. Never."

Lehigh cocked his head and squinted one eye. "He wanted something in return?"

She nodded, gestured toward herself. "Favors—from both me and Daddy. Actually, from Daddy it wasn't so much favors as blackmail. He threatened to expose the illegal contributions and claim they were forced out of him if Daddy didn't toe his line in the legislature. And now that he's running for Governor..." Her voice cracked.

He pursed his lips. "I still don't see what's so irregular about the scholarship."

"Lehigh, how could you be so thick?" she said, almost a shout. Lehigh took a step back, away from the force of her words. Damn her, if she's going to yell at him–

"Besides the sheer amount of his own cash he funneled my way," she said, "he coerced the Boards to give their money to me, for his own benefit."

"His benefit? How did it benefit him?"

Tears crept down Stacy's face, dripping brown mascara over the light rouge on her cheeks. She wiped the tears away with her fingers, creating a dark smear on either side of her nose.

"He wanted favors, Lehigh," she said. "You know? Favors. For himself, for his friends, his connections...like Speaker Ramsey."

Lehigh sat next to her again on the couch, hesitated a long moment, then cleared his throat. His voice sounded tinny in his ears as he asked, "What kind of favors, Stacy?"

The tears flowed freely now, far beyond Stacy's ability to wipe them clear. "The kind of favors that a dirty old man can't get any other way," she whispered, "except by blackmailing a scared young girl. One who has no money of her own and won't get from her father because of her stupid pride. A pretty girl, Lehigh...I used to be pretty..."

Stacy curled into a fetal crouch on the sofa, hugging her

knees and crying into her arms. She rocked back and forth on the couch, emitting a high-pitched whine from her vocal chords as tears drenched her cheeks.

Lehigh brushed her hair away from her face and lifted her chin until their eyes met. "You're still very pretty, Stacy McBride," he said. "And you have nothing to be ashamed of."

She leaned into his open arms, and they lay still for what seemed like a very long time.

***

Stacy's cell phone chimed. Twice. Three times.

"You going to get that?" Lehigh murmured. Stacy shook her head. The phone rang a fourth time, then went silent. A minute later it emitted a single loud beep.

"They're probably done with Lucky back at the clinic," Lehigh said. Stacy squeezed his ribs. He held her a little tighter, too.

"Tell me about Paul," he said. "Why does he think you two are engaged?"

Her hug melted away and her body sagged. She took a deep, noisy breath and leaned forward with her head in her hands.

"Paul and I talked about getting married once, about a month ago. He never actually proposed, though, and if he had…well, I don't know."

"You don't know? As in, maybe you'd have said yes?" Lehigh leaned forward next to her and dangled his hands between his knees.

Her cell phone beeped again. Still she didn't respond.

"How serious were you?" he asked.

"I don't know, Lehigh," she said. "He's very devoted to me, and he's so safe in some ways…but in other ways, so dangerous." She turned to face him. "If Daddy had his way, I'd marry him."

"What's their deal? Seems like they're closer than you and Paul are."

She chuckled and touched Lehigh's arm. "Too true. Paul is the son of one of Daddy's oldest friends and political allies. He practically grew up in the back hallways of the legislature in Salem. When Paul's father died, Daddy sort of adopted him, in a professional sense—if you consider politics a profession. That was about ten years ago.

"I've known Paul almost my whole life. But I'd never thought of him romantically until about a year ago, when he came to Clarkesville to work on the campaign. He's a decent, caring man, but there's something about him I can't pinpoint. He's, I don't know…dark, and mysterious. It's hard to get close to him, really."

Lehigh grunted. "Sounds like you don't trust him."

"You know," Stacy said with a snort, "My mother never liked or trusted him. Nor did she trust his father, for that matter. I think because they're so involved in politics, particularly fundraising. She views those types as unprincipled prostitutes."

"Wise woman."

Stacy grinned and leaned her head on his shoulder. "Mutual admiration society. She always liked you, too."

Lehigh smirked. "That's because I always complimented her cooking."

"I know." Stacy play-punched his ribs. "What's up with that? My mother's cooking sucks."

"It's better than mine." Lehigh grinned. "And she knows some great caterers."

"Oh, you!" Stacy's fingertips flew over Lehigh's abdomen, knowing exactly where to touch him to get the maximum tickle from his sensitive skin.

"Stop it!" Lehigh giggled like a child and chased after her hands with his own, but her fast hands always danced a step ahead. He changed strategies, returning the tickle to her own flat tummy, and ribs, and breasts…

Then his mouth covered hers, and their hands stopped tickling, but kept roaming, feeling, groping, then tugging at buttons, straps, and clasps. Clothes piled up on the floor, then formed a sprawling path from the sofa to the bedroom door, which closed with a click behind them.

***

Stacy's phone rang five or six more times before they left the apartment some twenty minutes later. "You drive," she said, and tossed him a set of keys. She got in the car, then checked the phone for missed calls. She cursed under her breath and shoved the phone back into her purse.

Lehigh pulled into traffic and nodded once in her direction. "Aren't you going to answer your voicemails?"

She blew air out between tense lips and shook her head. "That can wait."

"I guess we'll be back at the clinic in a few minutes anyway." He shrugged. "You know, it's strange. They never called my phone to let me know that Lucky was ready to go."

Stacy's voice was distant. "She might not be."

Lehigh cocked an eyebrow. "So why would they keep calling you?"

She looked out the passenger-side window and worried her bottom lip between her teeth. "Only the first call was from the clinic. The rest were from Paul."

Lehigh gave a slow nod and mouthed "Ah." They drove in silence for a few minutes. Stacy lowered the passenger-side visor and freshened her makeup in the mirror.

"You look fine," he said.

"I'm a mess." Dab, dab, brush.

"Really. You look terrific."

"Uh-huh. Nothing a little blush won't cure." She followed the blush with lipstick, eye shadow, and a brief consideration of eyeliner before the road's bumpiness forced her to give it up. She stole one final glance in the mirror as Lehigh pulled into the clinic's parking lot and declared, "I'm a wreck. A total flipping wreck."

"You are not," he said. "Besides, I like–"

"Crap!" Stacy's phone chirped again. She pulled it out of her purse, stared at the screen a moment, then clicked it into silence. She leaned back in her seat with a heavy sigh and closed her eyes.

Lehigh killed the engine. They sat still for several moments. He tapped the steering wheel, waiting. Finally, he broke the ice. "I guess we'd better get inside."

She nodded, eyes still closed.

"Stace, it's okay. Nobody knows—"

"Lee, please." She opened her eyes and stared hard at him, worried. He reached out to take her hand, but she pulled it away.

"What's the matter?" She flinched. He hadn't intended so much heat in his voice. He gestured toward the clinic. "Afraid they'll see?" She didn't reply. "Is that it? Are you—Stacy, are you ashamed of me?" Now the heat was intended.

She looked away, nibbling her knuckles. "No, Lee. It's just that—"

"What? You're afraid it looks bad? Afraid someone will find out we're a couple? Afraid—"

A knock on Lehigh's window interrupted his rant. He lowered it, and a tall, black-haired man squinted at him.

"Get out of the car," Paul said.

"Lee," Stacy said before Lehigh could react, "would you give Paul and me a minute?"

"Sure," Lehigh said. "I've got to go get my dog anyways." He gestured to Paul, who stepped aside so Lehigh could open the door.

Just as Lehigh's feet hit the pavement, Paul pressed his face close to him and wagged his index finger an inch from Lehigh's nose. "Stay the hell away from my fiancée, Hayseed," he said, "if you know what's good for you."

"Talk to the girl," Lehigh muttered back, taking a step to his left. He pressed the "lock" button and slammed the door shut. "If you're man enough."

"Don't mess with me." Paul spat. "And whatever you do, don't mess with her."

Lehigh suppressed a smile. "I've known her a long time, Paul. I know better." He narrowed his eyes and leaned forward. "How well do you know her, really?"

Paul snorted. "Go get your damned dog."

***

"Paul, we do need to talk." Stacy faced him, hands knitted at her waist. She planted her legs shoulder-width and pressed her butt against the front grill of Lehigh's pickup.

"I'd say," Paul replied. "It's the least that a soon-to-be-married couple should do."

"Stop saying that!" Stacy turned away from him just a bit. "You shouldn't go around telling people we're engaged."

"Why not? It's the truth."

"It is not!" She turned toward him again, and closed the gap between them a half-step. She glanced over her shoulder to make sure Lehigh had gone inside. The lot behind her remained empty. "Talking about maybe getting married someday is not the same as being engaged. You never proposed and I never accepted. And now—"

"I did too propose and you did too accept. Or have you forgotten our conversation at the Gorge overlook?"

"That wasn't a proposal. It was more like a business lunch. And all I said was that we'd both be financially better off living together than apart."

"And you said you couldn't live with me unless we were married. So I said okay, and you—"

"That isn't a proposal!" Stacy nearly shrieked. She lowered her voice. "And what's more, no matter what else we've discussed, I have to tell you—it's not going to work between us, Paul. I'm going to have to break it off."

"What? Stacy, no! Why? That's—I don't—" He glared at her, a deep crimson flowing upward over his face. "It's that Lee Carter guy, isn't it? You're getting back together with him, isn't that right?" His voice cut like a steel blade.

"Paul—"

"I tell you, Stacy. He's not right for you. He's not good enough, for one, and second—well, he's just not right. You already know this, from before. He's a wishy-washy tree farmer, an oaf. You'll waste years on him again and then he'll never do right by you. You need a real man—one with the strength of his convictions, one who adores you and will stand up for you. One—"

"Paul, listen. It's simpler than that. I don't love you anymore. We're not a good match. We're through."

"Stacy!" He fumed and spun his body in a circle on the gravel. Then he peered in closer, his eyes wide and mouth set in a line. In a quiet, steady voice, he asked, "Are you cheating on me?"

"No, Paul," she said. "I'm breaking up with you."

Paul sneered and pointed toward the clinic. "Lehigh Carter," he said, turning on his heel, "is a dead man."

CHAPTER 10

Anne-Marie pushed open the door from the recovery area into the clinic's modest lobby, holding Lucky like a baby in her arms. The dog wiggled out of Anne-Marie's embrace as soon as she spotted Lehigh. Lucky stumbled, still groggy from anesthetic, and nearly fell sideways in her attempt to bound across the room to Lehigh's open arms.

"We had to sedate her, because she wouldn't sit still for the suture removal," Anne-Marie said. "We tried calling, but we only had your home number."

"It's okay." Lehigh gulped at the bill. Damn. This was a spendy morning.

He glanced at the frisky pup and smiled. Ah, well. It was worth it.

"I'll have to put this on Visa." He reached down to pet Lucky, pressing herself hard against him. "You're going to send me to debtors' prison."

Lucky panted in an open-mouthed grin and licked at his pants leg, then sniffed his crotch.

"Get away from there." He pushed her snout away. Anne-Marie blushed and busied herself with his charge slip. Lucky sniffed at him again, this time earning a gentle swat on the nose.

"Here you go," Anne-Marie said in too loud of a voice. "Just sign here, and that's your copy."

He scribbled across the bottom of the form and pocketed his receipt, again pushing Lucky's nose away from his privates. "Let's go, girl." He clipped a leash to her collar.

The front door slammed open, and Stacy rushed through it, face flushed.

"Hey," Lehigh said, "We're all set. She–"

"We need to talk. Right away." Stacy glared at Anne-Marie, who no longer pretended to hide her nosiness. Lucky sniffed at Stacy's crotch, and Anne-Marie turned a darker shade of red.

"Why don't I put her in the truck and–"

"No!" Stacy grabbed his arm and lowered her voice to a whisper. "Paul may be waiting for you outside. He's very angry. Lehigh—I don't know what he might do to you, or to Lucky."

Lehigh nodded, his face darkening. "Okay. Where to?"

They sat in Stacy's office, she in her chair, Lehigh on the edge of her desk, and Lucky on the floor at his feet. Stacy recounted the confrontation with Paul and added, "He has an awful temper. It's one of the reasons I haven't wanted to commit to him. Now he sees you as the man who stole me from him."

Lehigh grimaced. "I reckon I see his point."

Stacy's face softened, her worry gone for a moment. "I don't feel stolen. If anything, for the first time in a long time, I feel that I've given myself freely and fully to the man I want." She took his hand. "A long time, Lee. Twelve years, to be exact."

They sat for ten, fifteen minutes, holding hands. At length Lehigh squeezed her hand between both of his and stood to leave. Lucky scrambled to all fours, wagged her tail and tugged at the leash, nose pointed at the floor. "I'd better get her home," he said.

Stacy's face fell. She loosened her hold on Lehigh's hand and let it fall away. Lehigh let his dangle mid-air between them, then eased it back to his side.

"I guess we can discuss this all later," she said.

"Stacy, I–"

"No. Please." She held up one hand to silence him and turned her pained expression to one side. "I don't want to push you into anything. I just thought...I don't know. I don't know what I was thinking."

"I do."

She jerked her face back toward his, a flash of annoyance crossing it until she met his gentle gaze. "You know what I think?" she asked. "Do you?"

"That's not what I meant," Lehigh replied. "What I meant was, I know what I think, and what I want." His hand curled around the back of her neck. His thumb massaged her tense shoulder muscles, the way she always liked it.

"What's that, Lehigh?" she whispered. "What do you want right now?"

Lucky tugged again at her leash. Lehigh tugged back and pointed at the floor, her command to sit. With a sad stare of reluctance, the dog obeyed.

Lehigh turned his attention back to Stacy. "What I want right now," he said, "is–"

Stacy's desk phone rang. Lehigh waited. It rang again. He gestured toward it. "Do you need to get that?"

She shook her head. "It can wait." A third unanswered ring split the air, then a fourth, then silence prevailed until a red light blinked on the handset. "It went to voicemail," she said. "Now, you were saying?"

He cleared his throat again. "Twelve years is a long time to wait," he said. "A long and lonely time."

Still seated, Stacy pressed her hands onto her knees and drew in a deep breath. "Is that all this is to you? Relieving your loneliness with the comforting presence of an old flame?"

"You're not an old flame anymore." He patted his chest. "It's a brand-new flame. And it's hotter'n'hell." He reached both hands to her, lifting her out of her chair. She rested her hands on his forearms, their faces now just inches apart.

"Flames of lust...or something more?" She edged even closer.

"Flames of...everything. Lust, love, you, me. Stacy, what I'm trying to say is, I want you back. I don't know why, and I may well be crazy, 'cuz everything was just fine before I saw you a week ago, but–"

"Hush." She enforced her order by covering his open mouth with her own.

***

Paul had vacated the clinic's parking lot when Lehigh entered the late morning sun, Lucky in tow. Her ginger walk slowed their pace and he had to lift her into the pickup. He climbed into the driver's seat. "Sleep it off, girl. We'll be home soon."

He drove slowly to minimize the bumpiness of Clarkesville's uneven streets, but it seemed that every stretch of road had a pothole he couldn't miss. A few actually rattled Lehigh's teeth together. After hitting one particularly bone-jarring divot, Lucky lifted her head in a sad, complaining stare that seemed to ask, kid-like, "Are we almost there yet?"

Finally they reached the smooth surface of the state highway, and Lucky relaxed into a sleepy curl. Lehigh petted her head to help calm her. It helped calm him, too. "Good girl," he said. With few cars to pass on a quiet weekday morning, he held the wheel and the accelerator steady, and stole long gazes at her while she slept.

"I wasn't sure about you at first, old gal," he said after a time, "but you're a charmer." The dog yawned but kept her eyes closed under his gentle caress. "Besides," he said, "you brought Stacy 'n' me back together. That's a good thing, I reckon." He checked the road again—straight and empty—and his speed—a cautious fifty-five—and turned back to her. "Yep," he added, "you done real good."

Lucky responded with a satisfied snort and stretched her legs out further. Lehigh watched her a moment longer, then turned back to his driving–

Just in time to avoid a collision with a careening black BMW!

The car had come from nowhere, cutting in front of his pickup at high speed as it passed him. It pulled into the lane just ahead of him and slowed to forty miles per hour, then thirty-five, then thirty.

"What the hell are you doing, mister?" He assumed it was a man. Probably that idiot Paul, but because of its darkened glass, he couldn't tell for sure.

When the other car slowed further, he signaled left and veered into the empty oncoming lane to pass. The BMW edged left, straddling the dashed yellow center line ahead of him and sped back up to forty-five.

Lehigh shook his head. "Would you make up your mind?" he muttered, and pulled back to the right. The BMW edged back into the right-hand lane and slowed again. Lehigh slowed with him, and braked a little harder to maintain some distance between them. When their speed dipped below twenty-five, he dropped the truck into low gear, gunned the motor and swept around the BMW to the left.

The BMW sped up and veered left again, forcing Lehigh across the lane and onto the shoulder. "Maniac!" he yelled at the driver. He skidded to a stop, sweating and cursing, nearly knocking Lucky off of the front seat. She yelped and gave Lehigh a forlorn look. Lehigh took a few deep breaths and petted the dog on the head. "Easy, girl," he said.

The BMW stopped about a hundred yards ahead of him and began to back up.

"What the hell?" Lehigh said. The car continued toward him in reverse, swerving and fish-tailing along the side of the road, its engine whining in angry protest of its high speed. "Hang on, girl." He readied the wheel.

The BMW swerved to a halt a few yards ahead of him, its nose jutting over the solid yellow stripe dividing the traffic lanes. The driver door opened, followed by the passenger door. He recognized the driver, a clean-cut thirty-something man, and cursed. Paul. The passenger, a heavy-set younger man with brown hair, did not look familiar, but he carried a crowbar in both hands.

Lehigh cut the wheel hard right and punched the accelerator. His tires spit gravel. The pickup lurched toward the pavement. The heavy-set man leaped toward the passing pickup and swung his crowbar like a baseball bat. Lehigh swerved, but not fast enough.

Crack! The end of the bar hit the windshield, sending a thick spiderweb of cracks across the glass. Lucky yelped and sat up in her seat. A moment later she slammed against the seat back when Lehigh gunned the accelerator harder. The pickup sped across the empty oncoming traffic lane, then swerved back onto the right side. He hit highway speed in record time, praying that no other cars would appear. He could barely see through the damaged windshield, but he had no desire to slow down.

He checked the rear-view mirror. As expected, the BMW resumed its chase. Cursing, he speed-dialed his phone.

"Lee!" Stacy answered. "I'm glad you called. Paul is—"

"Chasing me down Highway 279," Lehigh cut in. "His buddy's already smashed my windshield. But if they get that close to me again, there's gonna be a pickup-sized indent in that pretty little car of his."

"He's chasing you?" she asked. "What's that about your windshield?"

"They busted it with a crowbar. Look, you'd better call him and let him know, if he don't get off my tail like right now, he and his fat little friend are gonna get hurt. My next call's to the highway patrol." He checked his rear-view mirror, confirming their continued tail, and then his speedometer. Seventy-five. Not good on this cracked, gravel-dotted pavement.

"Don't do anything rash."

"Rash, like run me off the road? We're way past rash. We're well on the way to stomping his ugly smirk under my boots. If you still have any influence over him, you'd best call him now." He slowed for a curve, then downshifted and punched the accelerator to regain his speed on the highway's steady uphill incline.

"If I called him now, it'd only make him madder."

"Well, someone oughta tell him that in the event of a collision, the repair bill's a lot higher for the Beemer than a rusty old Ford pickup. Hell, I gotta go. He's getting close."

"Don't—"

He couldn't hear the rest, as he'd tossed his phone to the floor. He goosed the gas pedal just in time to avoid being rear-ended.

"Okay, ass-wipe. You wanna play rough, we'll play rough." He slowed the truck to 70. When the BMW closed to within a car length behind him, he braked hard. The BMW's tires squealed and its front grille nudged his rear bumper. Lehigh downshifted and floored it. The truck jetted ahead and he steered it to the right side of the highway. In the distance, a car approached in the opposite lane.

"Help me out, here, pal," he muttered. Lucky lifted her head from between her paws, her eyes just slits, her body as flat as a snake's to the seat. "You too, girl," he said. The dog whimpered and licked her lips, then rested her head again.

As expected, the BMW accelerated and veered left, as if preparing to pass. Lehigh sped up again too—85, 90. The BMW stayed in hot pursuit. Lehigh edged the pickup further right. His tires kicked up loose glass and gravel from the shoulder of the road. He jammed the gas pedal to the floor. The truck sped to a steady, bone-jarring 95 miles per hour. His teeth felt about ready to fall out of his jaw, and the roar of his eight-cylinder engine drowned out all other noise.

The BMW's front grill pulled even with Lehigh's tailgate. The oncoming car would reach them in a matter of seconds. Lehigh edged further right. The center of his truck straddled the white line on the highway's shoulder. Inside the BMW, two shadows shouted and gestured. No doubt Paul's passenger wanted no part of this game of high-speed chicken.

The highway widened. Lehigh pulled his truck further right, taking advantage of the extra pavement. The BMW pulled up almost even and stayed close beside him. Only its left headlight remained across the yellow centerline. The oncoming car angled to its right to give the BMW more room. The Beemer edged closer–

"Party time!" he yelled, cut his wheel left, and braced himself. The BMW's passenger-side mirror snapped off and tumbled to the highway. The Beemer's nose turned away and braked. The combination sent the car into a spinning skid, tires screeching as the car spun across both lanes, barely missing the hind end of the pickup. The oncoming car's brakes squealed it to a stop on the far side of the road.

Lehigh couldn't see the rest, as he'd slowed to a calm and reasonable sixty-five in time to exit onto Brady Mountain Road, humming an old country song and petting Lucky to sleep.

CHAPTER 11

"Young lady," the Senator's voice boomed across his spacious living room, "just what in the hell do you think you're doing?" He stood over Stacy's slouching figure, fists clenched. His white hair rose like wisps of smoke from the fire of his round, flushed-red head.

"I thought you wanted me to be happy, Daddy," she said in a meek voice.

"Don't give me this girly-girl nonsense in the middle of my campaign!" he yelled again. "Do you know what this is going to do to my fundraising efforts? Paul is my campaign treasurer. His job is raising money. But today he called to tell me he's resigning—because my two-timing daughter has called off the wedding!"

"Well, I'm glad that registered, at least." She stood taller. "Not that there ever was a wedding actually being planned. I mean, we never actually set a date, or even decided to really do it."

"Of course you had," Senator McBride said, calmer now. "Paul and I talked about that. August of next year is a slow news month for the campaign, so we thought it'd be a great time for a story in the society pages. And Paul would have a little free time for–"

"Wait!" Stacy's voice shook. "You and Paul set a date for my wedding? To benefit your campaign? Daddy, how could you?" Stacy paced the floor, fists clenched.

"It's not exactly like that," he said. "We just wanted a time when the focus could all be on you, Precious, rather than me." He reached out for her shoulders and gave them a squeeze. She twisted away from his grasp.

"Don't lie to me and don't patronize me!" Her eyes welled with tears and she made no effort to stem their flow. "I can't believe you'd use my wedding and my life as a publicity stunt for your political ambitions. Daddy, I am disgusted."

"Precious, don't–"

She batted his outstretched arms away and took a step to the side. Never back away, he'd taught her at a young age. "Don't 'Precious' me. We had an agreement, you and me and Mom. We'd never let the outside world interfere with our family. Family first, remember?"

"This is about family." He turned to face her again. "Right now, Stacy, I need your support in what's going to be the biggest thing that's ever happened to our family. I'm running for Governor. State-wide office. Do you know what that means for us if—I mean, when—I win? Everything changes. For the better. For all of us."

Stacy glared at him with crossed arms, then narrowed her eyes. "I'm not so sure. Maybe for you. But if this is how I'm going to be treated–"

"Stacy, listen." He touched her arm and kept his soft gaze locked on hers. "I'm sorry about how this all appears. It's not that way, really. But I need Paul on my campaign. To lose him now—well, I'd have to start all over, and if I did that I might as well quit. Plus, with all of our history…I'd appreciate it if you can at least stay cordial with him."

She snorted. "I am cordial with him, Daddy. I just don't want to marry him."

The Senator sighed. "As for Lehigh Carter…"

She tapped her foot a few times. When nothing further came, she asked, "As for Lehigh, what?"

McBride scowled at his daughter. He pursed his lips, narrowed his eyes, let out a breath, then refreshed it. Finally he spoke. "He's not family."

Stacy's face flushed red, her mouth set on a line. Her eyes blazed. "Are you trying to tell me who I can date now?" She leaned in to him. "Are you saying that my social life has to take direction from your campaign?"

"I should hope it wouldn't come to that," McBride said. "Being my daughter, I'd think you'd want to do everything you can to support me in this. You do support me, don't you, Precious?"

Stacy seethed. Tiny bits of spittle sprayed from her clenched teeth as she spoke. "Of course I hope you win," she said. "But not if it means the end of my privacy and independence. Let me make this very clear to you, Daddy. I love Lehigh—and I choose him, not Paul. I don't care what that does to your campaign."

She turned on her heels and walked toward the kitchen. McBride stopped her with his voice. "Stacy."

She faced away from him, her hand on the doorway.

"My daughter. My most precious daughter. I—I'm not good at these sorts of things…"

She half-turned toward him. "What sorts of things?"

McBride swallowed hard and bowed his head. His voice dropped a register.

"Asking for help," he said.

Stacy waited as long as she could, but she knew he could outwait her. "I want to help, Daddy. You know I do."

He lifted his eyes to hers. "Then please—talk to Paul. I'm not saying you have to marry him—although I wish you would. God knows you've never done a single thing you didn't want to do, just because I said so."

"Not true. I got braces in eighth grade."

McBride smiled. "That was your mother's doing. I thought your teeth were fine."

Stacy managed a wan smile too. "So did I. Look, Daddy. What you need from Paul on your campaign has nothing to do with his status with me. It has to be that way."

"But it's not."

"But–"

"It's not!" The Senator's booming voice silenced her. More quietly, he went on. "Look. This governorship is good for all of us. To get there, I need money—the kind of money that only Paul can raise for me. His connections mean everything right now. But if he thinks he has no chance with you—well, then I have no chance. Understood?"

"I don't see the connection."

"It's simple. He's taking valuable time off from his career to help me because he loves you, and thinks you love him. He views this as supporting the family—the family he wants to be a part of."

She shook her head. "I want to support the family too, but not at the cost of marrying the wrong man."

He clasped his hands together, pleading. "If family is important to you, then do this for me. Tell Paul...I don't know. Tell him you want to wait a year. Tell Lehigh Carter the same thing. After the election, you can do anything you want, with my blessing."

Stacy peered at him with new understanding. "And until then...?"

The Senator's face darkened. "I don't want to even hear the name Lehigh Carter spoken in my household." He turned on his heel and left the room.

***

The telephone rang on the Senator's desk at the appointed time. The number appearing on his phone's LED screen confirmed the caller's identity. He lifted the cradle to his ear and said, "Mission accomplished."

"Really?" the caller said. "He's staying on?"

"He will," the Senator replied.

"You've confirmed this?"

A pause. "I am convinced of it."

The caller snorted. "Don't use politician-talk on me. You have either confirmed it, or not. I'm betting not."

"It all hinges on her. And I know what she'll do."

"You know nothing!" The caller's voice was angry and hoarse, as if trying to shout and whisper at the same time. "The end of her first marriage proves this. Your ignorance of her current whims confirms it further."

"All women have whims. They mean nothing. She's been

through this before, and nothing came of it. I saw to that. The same thing will happen again, I promise you."

"In the meantime, we have nothing."

"No. We're doing well. Money is still flowing in, and more will come. This whole event is just a minor blip. We've had bigger ones and we will again."

"We can't afford blips!" The caller's voice went shrill. "This isn't some local podunk popularity contest, Senator. This is the governorship. The whole state. You need to convince people you've never met to support you. People in big cities, savvy people. Cynical people, who have other options. People who look for chinks in your armor, reasons not to support you. Mistakes you've made. You understand?"

"Don't patronize me," the Senator growled.

"Why not?" the caller said. "Am I not your patron?"

A long moment of silence ensued. Finally the Senator spoke. "What would you suggest I do?"

"That's better," the caller said. "Asking for advice from your advisers is a very good sign."

McBride gritted his teeth and waited.

"You need to ensure that this fling of hers with the mountain man is over—at least, out of eyesight. And you know whose eyesight I mean."

"I can't follow her around–"

"No, but you can hire someone who can."

"Which is why I reached out to you," McBride said. "I'll need some walking-around money."

"You mean, stalking around money."

"Don't be crass. It needs to be cash. And it needs to be completely separate from the campaign."

"And anonymous, I presume?" The caller's voice dripped with disgust.

"Why else would I insist on cash?" The Senator took deep breaths to stay calm. McBride had learned at a young age that politics required the patient suffering of fools—especially rich fools.

"I'll insist on some, shall we say, greater firmness in your public statements on certain matters."

"Public statements? Now? Wouldn't things I do later—after the election—matter more?"

"We want assurances now."

McBride considered this. "You'll get what you want. Now, let's not speak of this again...directly."

"You're right," said the caller. "The rest should be handled discreetly. Through a subsidiary—a contractor."

"Have your man get in touch with my man. You know who I mean." McBride hardened his voice. "But whatever you do, keep her out of it. I don't want her hurt—at all."

A light cackle in his ear froze the Senator's spine. "You should learn to trust me more," the caller said, and hung up.

CHAPTER 12

Another hang-up message. Of the five calls recorded by Lehigh's answering machine, only one contained an actual message—a client inquiring about the state of a troubled tree stand. The others: clicks and a dial tone, or on several occasions, dead silence.

Wrong numbers, he told himself, but didn't believe it. Innocent misdialers ask for their intended party and apologize before hanging up. This caller—or, these callers—waited until he or the machine answered, then hung up without a word. Today it happened about once an hour. Not exactly on the hour, so a human made these calls, not some auto-dialer. But who? And why?

Three theories sprang to mind. One—a prank dialer, someone trying to get his goat. Kids, probably. If so, they'd soon tire of this game and quit. Pranksters would want to get some angry reaction from their victim. Lehigh gave them nothing of the sort—just a calm "hello" or two, and patience until the caller ended the connection.

The second theory: Paul van Paten. But that didn't seem likely. A busy guy like that, with so much to lose, wouldn't resort to such childish pranks.

Theory three: someone, somehow, knew he'd adopted Lucky and wanted her back. Maybe they got access to records at the clinic. Stacy said that they enter all their client files onto a new computer system. They had an Internet connection. Maybe one of those hacker types–

The phone rang. He picked up the receiver. "Carter Forest Management."

One second went by, then another. After five seconds, Lehigh repeated: "Hello. Carter–"

"Lehigh?"

Relief at Stacy's familiar voice.

"Sorry," she said, "my cell phone reception is bad here. Listen, we need to talk in person soon. Things are…well, things are weird."

Lehigh's throat constricted. "What sort of weird?"

"It's just—well, I'd rather wait until we can talk in person."

"I'd love to see you tonight," he said. "I bought some shrimp for dinner, and maybe we could watch a movie."

"Can't tonight," she said. "Daddy has another campaign event he needs me for. How about tomorrow?"

Damned campaign. He checked his desk calendar. "I can't tomorrow," he said. "I have to go into Portland and may even stay overnight. Forestry Council meeting. In fact I was hoping you could look in on Lucky for me."

"Uhhh…sure. Leave a key. Well, we'll have to figure this…" Static filled the line until it went silent, then dead.

***

Lehigh left several voice mail messages on Stacy's cell, work, and home numbers all afternoon, but never reached her in real-time. At five o'clock, obsessed with the need to hear her voice, he picked up the phone and dialed the private home number of Senator George McBride.

The first six digits, anyway. Then he hung up. He took deep, even breaths, each slower than the one before, and his heartbeat slowed. When he'd calmed enough he re-dialed. Once again he hung up, unable to maintain his usual placid demeanor long enough to punch in the numbers.

It took fifteen minutes and three more tries to complete the call. He gripped the receiver with clammy hands. One ring, two. Come on, pick up. The line rang a third time. He wiped sweat from his brow. Four—

A strange female voice answered. "McBride residence. How may I help you?"

Lehigh's throat tightened and he coughed once to clear it. He'd expected Stacy's mom or perhaps Stacy herself to answer. The strange voice threw him.

"Is anybody there?" the voice asked, with a hint of a Southern accent.

"Um, yes…this is Stacy's, um…boyfriend."

"Oh, Mr. van Paten! I didn't recognize your voice. This here's Suzie from Honeycut Caterers. Are you coming over for tonight's dinner?"

"Um…not sure." Lehigh reddened. Van Paten. As in Paul van Paten—the man everyone still thought of as her boyfriend. Or fiancé.

"Oh, you'd better, Mr. V," she said. "I made those prawn pies you love. Anyway, do you want to talk to the Senator? Stacy's not here yet. We don't expect her until seven—you know how she hates these campaign fundraisers. Oops, I'm sorry. I don't mean to offend."

"No problem." Lehigh coughed again. "I'll call back another time."

"Well, you'll see her in less than two hours. Are you okay, Mr. V? You don't sound so good."

"I'm fine," Lehigh said. "Thanks, Sally."

"Suzie!" she said. "Hey, wait a minute. This isn't Mr. van Paten, is it? I see him on the front lawn right now. Who is this?"

Lehigh hung up and stared at the phone on his desk. Moments later it rang, startling him. Holding the phone again to his ear, he answered in a raspy voice. "Hello?"

"Hello, Mr. Whoever-You-Are." Suzie's southern drawl whipped his ear. "I've got your number on Caller ID and if you ever call here again, pretending to be someone else–"

He hung up again, jumped away from his desk, and dashed into his bedroom. Two minutes later he emerged, wearing his one and only suit, which, thank God, still fit. "Come on, Lucky," he called to the sleeping dog. "We're going to crash a party." He ignored the ringing phone and locked the door behind him.

***

"They're just confused," he explained to Lucky while he drove. "Stacy just hasn't told them yet about me." Lucky yawned and lapped at her new stitches. Lehigh nudged her mouth away from her belly. She'd torn the protective cone off minutes after it went on, and he hadn't had the heart to replace it. "The question is, why not?" Lucky batted her tail a couple of times on the seat and gave him her most sympathetic stare, then laid her head back down on the seat.

The truck chewed highway miles. After a bit he glanced back at Lucky. She'd resumed her usual vigil in the shotgun seat, two paws on the base of the open window and both yellow ears flopping in the wind.

"Why can't I be more like a dog?" he asked. "Simple, carefree, no women problems. Just eat, sleep, and do my job."

Lucky opened her mouth wide and sucked in the rushing highway air.

Lehigh sighed. His life had been simple and woman-free a few weeks before. He couldn't claim that he'd been particularly happy then, either, though.

He turned into the McBrides' long driveway. Several cars clogged the parking area near the house. A few guests milled about. One seemed to watch him as he approached.

A turnoff from the long driveway led to an easement on a small private fishing lake at the edge of the property. On impulse, he took the turn and drove into the thick patch of forest until he could be confident the guests could no longer see his truck from the house.

"Stay, Lucky." He got out. The dog stared at him.

He called Stacy's cell. No answer. He left a quick message. "Stace. Lehigh. I'm here, at your folks' place, on the lake road. We gotta talk."

They'd been down this path on foot a hundred times in their twenties, seeking privacy and respite from the Senator's disapproving comments about him—often in Lehigh's presence. Snide comments about his humble clothes, his gruff appearance, his simple vocabulary. It amazed Lehigh that a man so impolite could get elected to anything, until he noticed that the Senator didn't subject anyone else to such abuse. Stacy assured him that McBride treated previous boyfriends the same way, but that didn't make him feel any better. He doubted the Senator subjected Paul van Paten to that treatment.

Footsteps shuffled through leaves and underbrush to his right. Moments later Stacy popped into view. She wore a formal light-blue dress and two-inch heels, but when she saw him she broke into an awkward run. She reached him in moments, clutched him, and kissed him desperately and out-of-breath. "Lehigh, what are you doing here?"

He wrapped his arms around her and lifted her off the ground. They kissed again. He pressed his head to hers and drove his tongue hard into her mouth. She slid down his body until her feet touched the ground, still kissing him, leaning against him. They groped at each other, hands and lips and tongues moving with force and speed into now-familiar places, heat building–

She broke the embrace, pushing his chest away with her hands. "You shouldn't be here," she whispered.

"Neither should you," he whispered back.

She melted back into his arms, burying her face in his neck and shoulders. He held her close. Really close. Close enough to feel her heartbeat, pounding like race car pistons at first, fading over time to a firm, steady drumbeat as she calmed down.

"I hate these people, Lehigh," she said.

He squeezed her closer for a moment, then loosened his grip. One hand caressed the small of her back. The other combed through the long black locks decorating her neck. "I hate them even more," he said.

She kissed his shoulder and squeezed him in a side-to-side rocking motion before leaning away again. They looked into each others' faces for several seconds, then brushed their lips together. She slid to his side and they leaned arm-in-arm against the front fender of his pickup.

"I should get back," she said. "They're going to wonder where I went off to."

"Why do you even have to be at this party?" he asked.

"Appearances. Daddy wants his pretty little daughter here to show off his happy little family. God, politics can be so awful."

"I just...I don't know."

"You just what?"

He grimaced and turned his face away from her. "Why does he have to be here?"

She sighed. "Paul's the campaign treasurer. It's a fundraiser. He's here to collect the checks and encourage people to dig deeper into their wallets. He's pretty good at it, actually."

"I see. Is that all?"

She bowed her head. "No," she mumbled. "Daddy wants us to keep up the facade of an engagement. It's better for the campaign, somehow."

"How much of a facade?" His voice was thin. Clearing his throat didn't help.

Head still bowed, she shrugged. "For me it means doing events like this, some public appearances with him. For Paul..." She paused. Long seconds passed.

"For Paul?"

She sighed and stared into Lehigh's searching brown eyes. "For Paul...it's not pretend."

"He still considers you engaged?" Surprise and a hint of anger edged his voice.

"He doesn't accept my break-up with him. He says that I'm just confused, that it's because he wasn't spending enough time with me. So now he wants to spend every waking moment together."

"What do you want, Stacy?"

She shook her head. "I don't want to be around him at all. Him, or any of these people. I just want to be with you."

Lucky yawned at them from the car window. Stacy grinned at her. "And with you, of course, Lucky."

Lehigh turned toward her. "So, Stacy. Let's go somewhere right now."

"I can't, Lee. I—I just can't."

"Come on. You hate this. These dinners, the fakey people, the politics."

"You're right, I do. I'd love to leave with you right now. But Daddy would…well, he wouldn't understand. And Paul– "

"Gah!" Lehigh spit into the loose pine needle carpet covering the forest floor.

Stacy looked away, eyes closed, her lips curled down. "I have to get back." She held out her hand. He took it, then pressed his free hand on the small of her back.

"I'll walk you out," he said.

"No." She stepped away from him. "We shouldn't be seen together—especially not here."

"What the hell?" Lehigh's eyes flashed, his arms spread wide. "I can't be seen with my own girlfriend? What do I—"

"Lehigh!" Stacy stared at him, open-mouthed, a shy smile forming at the corners of her lips. "What did you just call me?"

He blanked, motionless. "Well, ah…my girlfriend, is what I recall saying."

Stacy's smile broke into a broad grin. "Really? You think of me as your girlfriend?"

"Well…shouldn't I oughta?"

She folded back into his arms and sandwiched his body between hers and the truck. "Of course you should. I just wasn't sure that you did."

He held her, kissing the top of her head over and over again, until she broke his embrace several minutes later. With a wordless smile she retraced her path out of the woods.

A wistful joy crept into his cranky mood. Girlfriend. He mulled it over. Sounds good. What's more, she seemed happy about it, too.

***

The curly-haired man leaned forward against the back end of his car, steadying his apple-shaped body, and peered through his binoculars at the tall, lanky man in the suit and the slender, dark-haired woman some eighty feet away. At that range, binoculars were overkill, perhaps. But he needed to be sure.

"Is it him?" asked his companion, a burly blond named Brockton.

"Sh! Keep your voice down." He looked again. The man's back was to him, facing the dark-haired woman, whose hands hid the side of the man's face. A long pony tail emerged from the man's baseball cap, a stupid look if there ever was one. But that's a Portlander for you. Funky for its own sake.

"I wish they'd turn, so we could see his face," Brockton said in a hoarse whisper, for lack of anything else to do. Not that seeing the man's face would help. He didn't know what the guy looked like in the first place, other than a general description of tall, fit, and probably well-dressed. And this guy fit that bill.

"It's definitely her," Thornburgh said. "McBride's daughter. I recognize her from the pictures in the paper. And the way they been smooching—it's got to be him. They're engaged, right?"

Brockton grunted. "Unless she's a cheater."

Thornburgh wiped damp curls away from his forehead, sweaty despite the chill autumn air. "Maybe we ought to take some pictures, just in case. Get the camera."

"You get the camera. I ain't your gopher."

"Come on, get the stupid camera!"

Brockton spit. No way he was going to let Thornburgh boss him around yet again. "Let me look first." He reached for the binoculars.

Thornburgh held them out to his partner, then stopped when the strap got caught around his ears. "Dammit! Wait. Let me get this off my head." He pulled the strap over his head and surrendered the glasses to his muscular friend.

Brockton squinted through the sights, then lowered them. "I hate these things. I always see double. How do you adjust it?"

Thornburgh snatched the binoculars back from his partner. "No way. I just got them all set up for me. I ain't gonna let you mess 'em up now."

Brockton grimaced. "Then how'm I supposed to tell if it's him or not? We both gotta give a positive I.D. Boss said so. That's why he sent two of us."

"Yeah, well. You do it without these. I need 'em more than you do. Besides, we both know the real reason why you're here."

"Yeah? What's that?"

Thornburgh grinned. "It ain't for your brains. And it sure as hell ain't for your looks." He peered through the lenses again to find the couple making out again. "Damn, get a room."

Brockton snickered. "I always liked the woods, myself."

"You would. Hey, maybe when she's done with him, we can take a turn?"

Brockton laughed under his breath, a guttural sound. "Yeah, that'd be real nice."

Thornburgh held out a hand. "Wait a sec. Looks like she's leaving. Yep, she's going back to the house."

"He's staying, though," Brockton said. "As if he's expecting to meet someone, eh?"

Thornburgh nodded. "I think you're right. Let's go. We got a deal to make." He stood, grabbed the briefcase propped up against the tires of his SUV, and walked toward the long-haired man, whose back was still turned.

"But what if it ain't him?" Brockton followed Thornburgh, one step behind.

Thornburgh smiled. "I got a plan for that."

"A plan? What plan?"

"I'm gonna ask him a few questions. If he answers right, we do the deal. If not…well, we just gotta make sure he don't go blabbing to all those other suits inside. You get my drift?"

Brockton grinned. Yeah. That's exactly why he was here.

***

Lehigh ambled around to the driver's side of the truck and opened the door to get in when a movement in the woods stopped him. Two men dressed in dark blue suits approached from the path opposite the direction Stacy had just gone. Briars tugged at the baggy slacks of a short, overweight, sweaty-faced man wearing a fedora over black curls. His taller, once-athletic companion, blond and sunburned, trailed behind.

"Thought you two would never stop making out," the curly-haired one said. "Did you forget about our appointment?"

"I only made one appointment for tonight," Lehigh said. "And I was stood up."

"We, uh, well, we got a little held up." Curly glared at his partner, who looked away.

"Remind me," Lehigh said. "Where have we met?"

"Well, we haven't actually met in person. Our boss talked on the phone with you about finding a quiet place for us to chat before dinner." Thornburgh smiled, but nerves made it a sickly grin, almost a grimace.

"I talk to a lot of people. What's your boss's name?"

"He'd rather not...I mean, we'd rather not mention his name out loud, in case anyone's around, you know what I'm saying?" Thornburgh's smile faded. Brockton puffed out his chest. Lehigh rolled his eyes.

"Look fellas, I've got to get going. What did you want to discuss?"

"Of course, of course. No doubt you have several 'meetings' planned tonight, busy man like you. I'm Thornburgh. This here's Brockton. Cal-Tex Lumber. Ring a bell, Mr. van Paten?"

Lehigh grinned. How many people could possibly confuse him for Paul in a single day? Might as well play along. "Sorry," he said. "I get so many calls."

"Well, I won't keep you long," said Curly. Thornburgh. Whatever. "We brought what you wanted. Show him, Brock."

The blond lifted a briefcase into full view and opened it. "Fifty G's, cash, like you said. But first, we need assurances." He closed the briefcase and furrowed his brow.

"I understand." Lehigh stared at the cash and wondered if it were real.

"What we're saying is, we wanna know what we're buying," Brockton said. "Is McBride gonna be more timber-friendly than those current yahoos in there?" The "th's" were "d's" in Brockton's pronunciation: "den dose yahoos in dere."

"That goes without saying," Lehigh said. "But I suspect you want something more specific than that for your money." He crossed his arms. He had no idea how well he played the part of Paul, but he didn't care. Their mistake, not his.

Of course, if they discovered his ruse, he could be in a heap of danger.

"You're a smart man," Thornburgh said. "We do have a few specific things in mind. As we discussed."

"Of course," Lehigh said. "But again, I talk to a lot of people. Refresh my memory. What did we discuss?"

Brockton gave him a suspicious look, but Thornburgh seemed unfazed. "We're losing money on state and federal cuts," he said. "My superiors require a more, ah, open policy on public forests."

"Clear-cuts, you mean? Salvage logging?"

Brockton relaxed his worried brow and nodded. "Yes," Thornburgh said, "but also a more industry-friendly pricing policy, rather than the tree-hugger nonsense they got in there now. You know what I mean?"

"I know what you mean." Lehigh hoped they would interpret his smirk as co-conspiratorial rather than ironic. "I can assure you that Governor McBride will look much more favorably on those practices than the current administration. But, you realize, he has no authority over federal lands—only state. The U.S. Forest Service dictates policy on federal land."

Brockton's eyes narrowed. Thornburgh held up one hand. "True," he said, and Lehigh suppressed a sigh of relief. "But the state has influence over the feds. I want to hear you say: Governor McBride will support clear-cuts as sound forest management practice on public lands." He pointed to Brockton's briefcase. "No promise, no money."

"Governor McBride will support clear-cuts as sound forest management practice on public lands," Lehigh parroted. Probably true, anyway.

"You're certain you can deliver him on that?" Thornburgh said.

"Absolutely."

"We'll hear him say so, in a speech? Soon?"

"At his earliest opportunity."

Brockton held the briefcase out to Lehigh. Thornburgh stopped him. "Maybe we should wait until we actually hear the speech."

Lehigh shrugged. "Suit yourself. If you don't want his

support on your issues, save your money. I'm sure we'll get by just fine. Lots of other opinions out there. Lots of campaign money." He tugged on the truck's door handle.

"You're a very cool operator, van Paten." Thornburgh nodded to Brockton, who pushed the case forward, within Lehigh's reach.

Lehigh glanced at it, held out his hand, and waited.

Thornburgh scowled at him. "And…you'll take care of that other problem?"

Lehigh sighed. "Do we have to repeat everything we've ever discussed?" He moved toward the truck.

"Give it to him, Brock." Thornburgh waved at Brockton, who hesitated. Finally he shoved the case forward.

Lehigh opened the truck door, took the case, and tossed it behind the seat. "I don't suspect you'll need a receipt."

"What, are you freaking crazy?" Thornburgh stage-whispered.

"Much obliged, gentlemen," Lehigh said. "We'll be in touch."

***

Lehigh waited in his truck until Stacy entered the little apartment, turned on lights and closed the door before speed-dialing her cell. She answered on the first ring.

"Come on inside," she said. "I'll make coffee."

"Better make it an Irish coffee," he said.

"Bushmill's okay?"

He couldn't tell if she was kidding or not. He wasn't. "Bushmill's is fine. Two shots." He gave Lucky a final pat on the head and a dog biscuit. Her box of treats had served as most of her dinner. That, and the second half of his cold roast beef sandwich. She liked it more than he did.

He approached the door, holding the briefcase close, wishing he could hide it. The darkened parking lot added to the cloak-and-dagger ambiance. A rash of cars clustered around the front and sides of Downey's place, but here in back, his and Stacy's vehicles stood alone.

She'd left the door unlocked. He entered and discovered that Stacy had been serious about the whisky. An open bottle of 14-year-old Irish rested on the kitchen counter next to the sputtering coffee-maker.

"Stacy?" he called.

"In the bathroom," her muffled voice replied.

He set the briefcase on the floor next to the bar and sat across the room on the couch. He wished he could sit further away.

The toilet flushed, then water ran in the sink. After what seemed like eternity, she emerged into the living room. She ran to him and wrapped her arms around his back in a tight hug, knocking half the wind out of him. "I'm so glad you came," she said. "What an awful night."

He patted her back and they swayed a little as they hugged. "Worse than usual?" His eyes drifted again to the briefcase. He forced himself to look away.

"Horrible." She hugged him tighter. "Paul behaved like a perfect ass all night to me. Then he pulled me aside and accused me of cheating on him. Never mind that I broke up with him. That idiot!"

"He doesn't seem to get it."

"It's worse than that. He apparently has this sick notion that since I'm pretending to be his fiancée for appearances sake, that I should…well, do more than just pretend."

"As in…?" Lehigh leaned back so he could see her face.

"As in—yes. He wanted sex from me tonight!"

"That sumbitch. I'll cut his manhood off if he touches you!"

She giggled. "It'd sure serve him right. But don't worry, I can handle him when it comes to that. What gets me is all the 'honey' this and 'darling' that and the little displays of affection—stuff he never did while we were actually a couple. But now that it's all for show, he's Mr. Romantic."

"Maybe he should've been an actor instead of a fundraiser."

"He makes me sick." She buried her face in his neck.

"Well, if it's not bad enough yet, I've got something that'll make it worse. Maybe even make you hate him outright."

She broke their embrace and stepped back from him. "I don't understand. He was with me from the time I left you until now. How could he...?"

"He didn't need to be there. His friends were. Right after you left, they came out of hiding, called me 'van Paten,' and made me promise to convince your father to support some industry give-aways—in exchange for cash. A lot of cash."

"Cash? But that's completely illegal."

Lehigh nodded.

Stacy's mouth formed an "O" and she gasped. "That explains it, then."

"Explains what?"

She turned toward him, eyes focused now, hands on his knee. "Tonight, Paul said that someone saw us together. I thought that was what bugged him, but halfway through the night his mood got even uglier. I couldn't figure out why. I bet he realized he missed that meeting with them. Oh, God." She draped an arm across her brow. "This could get ugly, fast."

Lehigh pressed his hands on his thighs, preparing to rise. "I should go to the authorities."

"No!" Stacy's eyes grew wide and she gripped his arm. Her fingernails dug into his skin through the flannel shirt. "Lehigh, you can't. That'd be the end of Daddy's campaign, maybe his whole career."

"Sounds justified," Lehigh said. "Wouldn't that simplify your life, too? This campaign's been nothing but a pain in—"

"No! I can't do that to Daddy," she said. "It's not his fault. Paul's the one taking the illegal donations. I'm sure Daddy's not even aware of it."

"Hmm. I doubt that. You told me yourself, he's got a history of shady deals." He waved his arm around. "Isn't that why we're here in the first place?"

Stacy expelled air between her lips and collapsed back onto the sofa. "You're right. God, I hate to think that he's sunk so low."

"Typical politician," Lehigh said. "The higher his ambitions, the lower his morals."

"Don't judge him!" She gripped his knee. "He may be a sleazy politician to you, but he's still my father."

"Okay, fine. Sorry. But what are we gonna do?"

Stacy shrugged. "Maybe I should talk to Daddy."

"Bad idea. That soils his hands. This way, at least he can claim no direct personal involvement."

"Well, we have to do something!" She got up from the couch and poured coffee for each of them and added a double shot of whisky to each cup. "Once Paul figures out what's happened, he'll come after it. And he'll come after you."

Lehigh waved her off. "I ain't afraid of him."

"Oh, I don't mean him personally. He'll probably send goons—people you should be afraid of."

"Like, cut-off-your-thumbs sort of goons?"

"Or worse." She set the coffee cups on the low table in front of them. "Once he finds out, he'll hound you—and me—until we–"

"Stacy! 'Hound'—that's it!" He set his coffee down with a clatter. Hot brown liquid spilled onto the table.

"What do you mean? What are you thinking?"

A wicked grin split Lehigh's face. "Heh. I shouldn't tell you. Best that you don't know. Oh, but you'll see. This is great!" He stood and fished his keys out of his pocket, then bent to kiss her. "Don't you worry about a thing. I've got an idea that'll guarantee that Paul won't get his hands on that money—ever." He grabbed the briefcase and headed to the door.

"Where are you going?"

"I've got some work to do," he said. "I'll call you tomorrow. Um, do me a favor though, okay? Go in to work late tomorrow morning?"

She flashed him a demure smile. "Come back here tonight and I'll guarantee it."

A wistful grin betrayed the temptation, but he shook his head. "It's better if I don't," he said. He grabbed the briefcase, and a moment later, the door banged shut behind him.

Only after he'd gone did it occur to her: Lehigh never carried a briefcase. Why, all of a sudden, had he started now?

PART 3

Money Changes Everything

CHAPTER 13

Anne-Marie parked her three-year-old silver Pontiac Coup de Ville in her usual spot—three spaces from the front door of the clinic. She could have parked closer, but no. She knew her place in this world. Besides, Jesus said we should be humble. Philippians 2:3: "Do nothing out of selfishness or conceit, but in humility consider others as more important than yourselves." Surely there were at least three others more important than her, such as the day's visiting vet, and of course Stacy, and the day's first client.

She shuffled to the door in flat, comfortable nursing shoes, key in hand. Her foot brushed against something—a brown paper grocery sack.

"What's this? A package?" Clearly it wasn't a Federal Express or UPS delivery. She peered closer. Somebody had folded the top of the bag shut, stapled an envelope to it, and typed on the front of the envelope: "Clarkesville Animal Hospital, Lucky Companion Foundation."

Lucky Companion Foundation?

She unlocked the door and brought the package inside. She removed her coat, turned on lights and computers, made coffee, and heated water for tea. Only then did she return to the counter where the package begged to be opened.

She stared at the package for several minutes, listening to dogs yapping over the sputtering gasps of the coffee maker. "Maybe I should call Ms. McBride," she said aloud. But Stacy had called her at home to say that she needed to run errands this morning.

"You take care of opening up," Stacy had requested. Well, this was part of opening the clinic, wasn't it?

Another minute of staring, and her hand crept to the envelope. She detached it, and the top of the bag fell open. She looked inside, and gasped.

***

The press arrived within a half-hour, minutes ahead of Stacy. "No comment until I see the note," she said in response to their shouted questions. And until she got some damned coffee.

"Do you have any idea who the anonymous donor might be?" a reporter asked. Bruce Bailey from Channel Seven, the guy her dad had beaten in the state Senate race years before.

"What part of 'No Comment' was unclear to you?" She pushed his microphone from her face.

"When will you be available for comments?" Bailey asked. Behind him, a camera floated on the beefy shoulders of a sweaty man half his age.

"Not sure yet," she said. "Maybe in an hour or two."

An audible groan rose from the dozen or so media types gathered on the clinic's steps. Clarkesville had only two local TV stations—Channel Seven was a network affiliate, the other was a public station—and one weekly newspaper, plus a couple of radio stations. But she noticed logos on jackets for various radio and TV outlets from as far away as Portland, Bend, and Salem. Statewide coverage!

She muscled her way through the group to reach the entrance and locked the front door behind her. Anne-Marie rushed toward her, waving the note. "Oh, Ms. McBride," she said. "It's been so crazy here!"

"Don't worry, Anne-Marie." Stacy gave the older woman a reassuring hug. "It'll all be fine."

"Oh, it'll be much more than fine!" Anne-Marie practically danced on her tiptoes. "You should see it. All that money, in cash! I've never seen so much money before."

"You didn't touch it? The actual bills, I mean?"

"Why, no, ma'am. I wouldn't do that. It's for the animals."

"Let me see the note." She took the single typewritten page and scanned it.

```
To whom it may concern:

I have long admired your work caring for
animals in our community, especially your
charity work. Pets can be a man's best
friend—or a child's.

To reward your great work, and to further
the cause of finding homes for pets and pets
for homes, I hereby donate $50,000 cash to
your clinic. I would like it to be used to
set up a special fund. I suggest you call it
the Lucky Companion Foundation, to pay the
costs of caring for strays and finding them
good human companions. Poor people need
pets, too.

I prefer that people not know the source of
this money, so I am making this donation
anonymously.

Sincerely,

Your Patron
```

"Do you have any idea who it's from?" Anne-Marie asked.

Stacy shook her head. "No idea." But she couldn't stop grinning.

***

Stacy's cell phone chimed on the way to her office. "Hail to the Chief"—Daddy's ring.

"I heard about your good fortune," Senator McBride said. "Congratulations."

"Word travels fast." She shrugged off her coat and closed the office door behind her. "You're not angry, are you?"

"Angry? No, why ever would I be angry?" True puzzlement rang in his voice.

Relieved, her voice took on a lighter tone. "Oh, I don't know," she said. "I'm kind of stealing the limelight from you a little."

"Oh, heck no," he said. "I'm happy whenever a McBride is doing well. Rising tides lift all boats, particularly when it comes to family. Don't you think?"

"Sure, Daddy." She took a deep breath. His silence convinced her. "So, what do you want this morning?"

"Want? Well, I don't really want anything," he said. "I mean, uh, I just wanted to share in your moment of good fortune, that's all."

"Uh, huh." She sat at her desk, turned on her computer, and counted the number of flashes on her voice mail indicator. She stopped counting at twenty. Still, silence reigned on the Senator's end of the phone. She sighed. "We have a fair amount of press here," she said.

"That can be a blessing, or a curse," he replied.

"I'm not experienced with handling the press," she said.

"Do you need some help from an old pro?"

She could almost hear him beaming. "If you can keep it about the animals, Daddy, and not the campaign–"

"I'll be there in fifteen minutes," he said. "Write me up some talking points. Don't take any questions until I get there. If you can, write up a few remarks to kick things off—how many animals this will feed, blah, blah."

"We're a hospital, Daddy, not a shelter."

"Well, you know what I mean. Get me some facts and figures to work with–"

"Whoa, whoa, whoa. Get you some facts and figures? Whose

press conference is this?"

"You are so right," he said. "My apologies. You know I get so carried away, I lose my head sometimes. I should shut my big fat mouth before my foot takes up permanent residence there."

Stacy laughed. "Senator McBride, you don't go humble often, but when you do, you go all out. Now look, I need your advice, and I don't mind you getting a little free press out of this, but it's not about you, okay? Nor me, nor the clinic. It's about the animals. Okay?"

"Write that down: it's about the animals," he said. "That's the message we want to stay on. Hey, I just had a great idea. You know who's great at this sort of thing? Paul. You should give him a call—"

"No!" Stacy's voice shrilled. An anxious moment of silence followed. She calmed herself. "I mean, I'd rather not bring Paul into this. Let's just keep this one in the family, okay?"

"Whatever you say, my dear," McBride said, still buoyant. "I'll see you shortly."

Stacy called Lehigh next. "I hear you came into some good fortune," he said without a greeting.

"Oh, you heard, did you?" She laughed. "And how is it you heard this?"

"A little birdie told me."

"The little birdie could have told me last night that he actually had the money in his talons, rather than let me believe you only heard about it."

"Best I didn't tell you. Loose beaks sink ships, and I didn't want the buzzards to find out."

"You're incorrigible!" She leaned back in her chair, feeling warm.

"Such a big word. Remember, I went to a state college."

"Should I use all four-letter words, then?"

A brief silence, then: "Are you angry with me?"

"No." She shook her shoulders and rolled her neck. "I'm just tense, that's all. When Paul finds out, he'll—"

"Do nothing," Lehigh said. "I thought of that. Once the press gets there—"

"They're here. " She leaned forward and planted her feet on the floor. "They're crawling all over the building. But that won't stop his temper."

"He can't do anything to you. He can't risk exposing himself—and your father. Sure, he'll be mad, but you wanted to be rid of him anyway, right?"

Stacy put her head in her hands and shook her head as if in pain. "There's just one hole in your strategy in all this. You didn't protect yourself."

"I'm not worried."

"You should be. He'll connect the dots pretty quickly. He won't be happy, and he's dangerous when he's mad."

Lehigh paused, a long few silent moments. "Stacy. Did he ever hurt you?"

Her turn for a long pause. "This isn't a good time to discuss it."

"I tell you what." Lehigh spat out the words. "It's not me that should be afraid. Next time I see that sumbitch I'm gonna kick his balls in."

"Oh, for heaven's sake." Stacy rubbed her neck, now a mass of steel cable. "Don't go picking a fight with him. Why do men always have to hurt someone to show that they care?"

"Is that how he justified hitting you? He was showing that he cared? That rotten, no-good–"

"I said I didn't want to discuss it right now. I have to get ready for this press conference. Daddy's on his way over and I need to prepare some talking points for the press. I'd better go."

"Your dad's going to be there? I love it!"

"Me too. He's pretty good at this."

"No doubt. It'll completely neutralize Paul."

"Neutralize? Big word, State boy."

Lehigh chuckled. "Once his boss smothers this with his seal of approval, Paul will have no choice but to drop it."

"You don't know Paul."

"I'm beginning to consider that a blessing."

Stacy leaned back in her desk chair, rubbing her temples. "Hopefully you'll remain so blessed. But don't count on it. He'll be plenty mad and he'll blame you. So be careful." Her phone beeped—call waiting. She sighed. "Speak of the devil."

"Don't answer it," Lehigh said.

"He'll just keep calling."

"Turn off your phone after we hang up. If I need you I'll call you at work."

"Don't you think he knows my work number too?" As if on cue her desk phone rang. "Jeez, it's like Grand Central Station in here." It rang again.

"I'll let you go so you can prepare. Good luck at the press conference."

"Thank you." Her cell phone double-beeped, indicating voicemail, and her desk phone rang for the third and fourth times. Two quick rings with a long gap between sets—an internal call.

"You're welcome," Lehigh said. "Knock 'em dead. I'll watch you on TV."

She cut the connection and picked up the desk phone. "Your father is here," Anne-Marie said. "Should I send him back to your office?"

"Give me a minute." She clicked open her word processor and banged a few sentences in before calling her back. "Okay," she said with a sigh, "send him in."

***

"This donation exemplifies the generous spirit we find throughout our community, and all over the great state of Oregon," Senator McBride crowed to the press in the clinic's parking lot some twenty minutes later. "It's one of the reasons I first ran for public office many years ago—to give back to this community, which has given so much to me and my family."

Stacy suppressed an eye roll, thanks to years of practice. She hadn't wanted this to become a campaign event for her candidate father, but she couldn't stop him now.

Besides, he really did excel at this. And the irony was so rich.

"How would you respond to critics who say that this money could have been used to help people?" Bruce Bailey asked.

"Aren't people more important than animals?"

Stacy glared at him. That sort of attitude frosted her. Morons like him always reduced everything to an either/or proposition.

Candidate-for-Governor McBride took a different tack. "The way I see it, it is about people. The money will help families adopt and care for dogs and cats who otherwise couldn't afford it. Pets bring great joy to many people, especially young children. Who are we to deny those people—those children—their happiness? Should only rich kids have dogs?"

The small crowd surprised Stacy by applauding. "How many of you here today have pets at home?" the Senator asked the crowd. A clear majority of those present—including Bailey—raised their hands. "There you have it. Clearly our generous donor knows something about the human spirit."

"Will you try to identify the donor?" someone asked.

Stacy stepped to the microphone and squinted into the bright sunlight. "No. We wish to respect the donor's privacy. In fact, we wish more people gave without seeking attention for themselves. Isn't that true generosity?"

As the crowd applauded her response, she mouthed another "thank you" to her father. He'd coached her well. Maybe politics could benefit the entire family after all.

CHAPTER 14

Lehigh returned from his morning errands exhausted and starving. He'd stayed up late to set up Stacy's morning surprise and rose early with only coffee for breakfast. The noon hour approached with him ready for a meal and a nap.

He missed having Lucky ride with him. She'd become quite the fixture in the shotgun seat of his pickup lately. But with fresh stitches in her belly and all the adventure of the day before, he'd let her sleep late and left without her.

He drove with the windows down, enjoying the sunny October day, and fiddled with the radio, searching for the all-news station. He really wanted to catch the midday news report so he could hear how Stacy handled the press earlier that morning.

Then he smelled it. Smoke. Burning wood. Fresh, green wood.

He pulled to the side of the road. A light, steady wind blew out of the east, swaying the upper branches of the canopy overhead, a mix of Lodgepole pines, Douglas firs and the occasional yellow-leafed alder. He slid out of the truck and crossed the road so he could see more of the eastern horizon. Sure enough, a column of dark gray billowed up from the treetops, some three or four miles away…in the direction of his property.

He jumped back into his truck, cursing, trying to remember: had he left anything on at home? A coffee maker, the stove, the portable heater? He didn't think so. Maybe Lucky bumped something over? He wished again he'd brought her with him. If anything happened to her–

"Stay calm," he muttered, and pulled the truck back onto the old muddy road. "We can't assume anything yet."

He drove too fast down the old road, a relic of logging's glory days, back when roads were built for short-term use. No need to over-engineer a road that's just going to serve a single clear-cut and replanting. The trucks traversing this road fifty years ago would have dwarfed Lehigh's pickup. The road they left behind reflected that: crumbling asphalt, huge potholes, and unrepaired cold heaves. Try as he might, he couldn't go much above thirty for very long without having to slow back down for the next road hazard.

Finally he reached the highway. He headed east, toward the smoke, through light traffic. He pushed his truck's speedometer up to eighty. Please, no cops.

The smell of smoke grew stronger. He exited the highway and turned onto the local road that brought him closer to home. A quarter-mile before reaching his property, fire trucks formed a roadblock across the highway. Behind it, a pillar of black smoke thickened the sky.

He parked on the side of the road and ran up to the yellow-jacketed official staffing the roadblock. "Where's the fire, exactly?" he asked.

"Along this road, some four or five hundred yards up," the firefighter replied. "It looks pretty contained, but it'll be a while. You'll have to drive around if you need to get through. Try the Interstate."

Lehigh shook his head and pointed. "That's my property. Tell me, is it just the trees, or is it close to my house?"

"This is your place? You're—" He checked a clipboard. "Mr. Carter?"

"That's me. How bad is the fire? Is my house at risk?"

The firefighter's long, sandy-colored hair couldn't hide the transformation of his gritty face into a wrinkled frown. "Afraid so, Mr. Carter. Fact is, the fire probably started there, from the looks of things, then spread to the trees nearby. Was anybody else home that you know of?"

Lehigh cursed and spat. It took him a long moment to reply.

"Nobody else lives there, except my dog. You didn't happen to spot her, did you? A yellow hound/lab mix, about three years old."

"Nope. But to be honest, we didn't have much opportunity to check. By the time we got there, the house was pretty much a goner. We've mostly been trying to stop the spread in the trees. Given how damp it's been, that shouldn't be a problem. You'll probably lose twenty, thirty acres, though."

"Damn. Damn, damn, *damn!*" He threw his hat to the ground and stomped around for a few moments. So much for going to Portland tonight. Hell, so much for just about anything. What a mess. He glanced up at the smoke again, billowing up into the clouds. Thirty acres of prime forest. And his house. His *house!* He swung his leg back, then kicked the rear tire of his truck. His foot rebounded hard and spun him around, nearly toppling him over. Great, now his damn leg hurt, too. Stupid, stupid, stupid. He kicked his hat into the side of the truck. Why didn't any of this make him feel any better?

The sandy-haired firefighter regarded him with what appeared to be a mix of sympathy and detached amusement. Lehigh realized how his tantrum must look and took a few deep breaths to calm down. After all, it could have been worse. At least it hadn't started while he slept. He picked up his hat and dusted it off, then walked back to the fireman, forcing himself to remain calm. "I suppose all of my stuff inside burned too?"

The fireman shrugged. "Hard to say, Mr. Carter. But given how fast it went up, I'd say most of it's lost, yeah."

Lehigh took another deep breath, and coughed it back out. "Wind must be blowing this way."

"You can grab one of those masks from my kit over there if you plan to stay nearby," the firefighter said. "I'm Dale Hansen, by the way."

"Pleased to meet you, Mr. Hansen. Although I wish it were under better circumstances." Lehigh retrieved one of the white paper masks from Hansen's oversized tackle box, slipped it over his face and adjusted the elastic straps. He couldn't make it comfortable, no matter what he did. No matter. He had things to do, things to think about. He approached the firefighter again. "Say, Mr. Hansen, when might I be able to get to the house? I'm worried about Lucky."

"That's your dog, Mr. Carter? And please, call me Dale."

Lehigh nodded. "Call me Lehigh."

"You probably can't get in there until morning, the earliest. Maybe a few days, depending on the investigation as to cause. Did your dog have a way out? A dog door, an open window?"

Lehigh shrugged. "I may have left a window open—it was warm last night." Another heavy sigh. "I hope so."

"Me, too. She wouldn't have had much time. The house went up pretty fast, I'm told."

Lehigh took a quick step closer to him. "Really? How fast, do you reckon?"

Hansen held up his hands. "I didn't see it. I'm probably telling you too much as it is. Captain McBride will probably chew my ass out for saying this much."

"Hold on. Did you say 'Captain McBride'?"

Hansen nodded. "Henry McBride. You know him? His brother's that politician. State legislator or something."

"I met him, a long time ago. I'm dating the Senator's daughter, Stacy."

Hansen grinned. "You lucky dog. She's a looker." Lehigh glanced away. "Sorry," Hansen said. "I meant no disrespect."

"No, no, it's not that." Lehigh waved his hand. "It's Lucky. Lucky the dog."

Hansen turned his head toward the billowing smoke rising from the trees behind them. "Let's hope she is a lucky dog, Mr. Car– I mean, Lehigh."

Lehigh smiled behind his mask and clasped Hansen's shoulder. "Thank you, Dale. I hope so, too."

Hansen's radio crackled from its holder on his belt. He listened intently for several seconds to what sounded to Lehigh like nothing but static and gibberish, then held it to his mouth. "Roger that, Green Team. I'll relay the word." He lowered the radio. "The wind has pushed the fire further than we'd like. I'm sorry, Mr. Carter, but it looks like you're going to have to leave after all."

Lehigh drove his pickup away from the roadblock. Black smoke climbed skyward in his rearview mirror. He pounded the wheel.

Why did this happen to me?

***

Two hours of searching the woods upwind of the fire turned up no sign of the missing dog. The mix of rolling hills, deep ravines from dried-out stream beds and thick columns of trees made for a slow, laborious investigation, covering far less ground than Lehigh had hoped. He began to doubt that Lucky had escaped the burning house, and expressed that view to Stacy, who'd insisted on helping. "We won't know for sure until I can get into the house," he said, "but I'm afraid the news'll be bad."

"Hush!" Stacy said through her soot-stained mask. "I'm not giving up until we find her—dead or alive."

"We'll have to quit soon for the day." He pulled his mask onto the top of his head. "We're losing daylight, and if I don't get some clean air soon I'm going to puke."

"But what if Lucky's alive, trying to breathe in this smoky forest, too?" Stacy asked. "We owe it to her to keep looking." She slipped on a thick bed of loose pine needles, but righted herself before Lehigh could catch her.

"So long as she ain't hurt, I doubt she'd stay anywhere near the fire," he said. "I reckon she'd run until she was completely out of range. That's survival instinct—and Lucky, if anything, is a survivor."

"You're right about that," Stacy said. "But that means she could be almost anywhere by now. There's hundreds of acres of forest here. It would take weeks to search them all."

"Hundreds? Try thousands. But hopefully, once the fire is out, she'll find her way back home."

Stacy's facial expression seemed to echo Lehigh's thoughts: *If she got out at all.*

***

They returned to the roadblock. Dale Hansen still manned the post, turning back vehicles.

"I'm so excited to meet you, ma'am." Hansen pumped Stacy's hand. "I don't often get to meet famous people."

Stacy blushed. "Famous? Me? I hardly think so."

"I saw you on the TV news this morning. That's fantastic, the big donation you got. Someone out there's a real pet-lover, huh?"

Stacy shot Lehigh a sidelong glance and nodded. "Apparently so, Mr. Hansen."

"Dale, please."

She bowed, a slight nod of her head. "Dale. Speaking of pet-lovers, might Lehigh and I get a chance to take a look inside the house tonight? We're very concerned about the whereabouts of his dog."

Hansen furrowed his brow. "They've extinguished the house fire, but the trees are still burning. We expect that to burn out by morning. I suppose you could get in after that."

"Have firefighters entered the house?" Lehigh asked.

Hansen nodded. "What's left of it. I'm no insurance adjuster, but to me it sounded like a total loss. What the fire didn't get, the water damage probably did."

Lehigh emitted a heavy sigh. "Insurance…I haven't even thought about calling them yet. But tell me. The firefighters that entered my house. Did they report any sign of Lucky?"

Hansen grimaced. "No, Mr. Carter. Sorry."

Stacy grabbed Lehigh's arm, smiling. "Maybe she did escape then!"

"Let's hope so," Lehigh said with a sigh. "Maybe we all got a little lucky."

***

The next real information Lehigh obtained about the fire came by way of the front page story in the Clarkesville News the next morning.

FIRE DESTROYS HOME, 40 ACRES

A fire in a west Clarkesville home spread to a prime stand of commercial forest, destroying the house and as much as forty acres of trees, according to Mt. Hood County Fire Chief Henry McBride.

The cause of the fire is not yet known, but investigators on the scene hinted that arson was a possible cause. "It's unusual to see a fire spread so quickly from a home so carefully segregated from timber," McBride said. "The trail of the fire is also suspicious."

Some logging industry experts downplayed the arson suggestion, blaming instead the "poor" way the burned segment was managed. "This shows the failure of so-called 'holistic forestry management' approaches," said one timber company official, who spoke on condition of anonymity. "The failure to remove extensive fuel build-up on the forest floor through salvage logging puts our whole area at risk."

"What a load of crap!" Lehigh tossed the paper to the motel room's drab gray carpet, then kicked it airborne against the wall. "There wasn't any 'excess fuel' anywhere in my holdings. Not a twig!"

It only then occurred to him that the paper ran the story without contacting him. His anger doubled, cooling only when he realized that he hadn't told anyone except Stacy where he'd gone. Few people knew his cell phone number, and he obviously couldn't answer at home.

He retrieved the paper, sat on the lumpy double bed, and scanned the article for more tidbits. The reporter referred to him only as a "local forester." Big timber companies complained about how Lehigh's so-called "alternative management" style put forests at risk and how giving them a freer hand at forest management would make the community safer. The article quoted Senator McBride as demanding a "full investigation."

"What a crock of baloney!" Lehigh railed to Stacy on the phone a few minutes later. "First of all, I do have a free hand in managing my land. It's private property, after all. Second, what's so 'alternative' about me? Just because I don't spray everything that sways in a stiff breeze and I don't clear-cut. That don't make me a tree-hugging enviro-nut!"

"I don't think 'alternative' is such a bad word," Stacy said.

"If you're a customer or potential customer, it's the kiss of death," he said. "I'd be surprised if I don't lose half of my business over this. Who owns that stupid newspaper, anyway?"

"The same people that own everything else around here," Stacy said. "Cal-Tex Lumber."

Lehigh halted his pacing. Icicles crept down his spine. "That," he said, "explains a lot."

***

"Do you have any concrete evidence that might link Mr. van Paten, Mr. Thornburgh, or Mr. Brockton to the fire?" the young deputy asked in a bored, officious voice. He'd been interviewing Lehigh for almost an hour in the sheriff's satellite location on Brady Mountain Road, a modest brick outpost boasting only the barest necessities of an office—which, apparently, did not include heat.

"I've told you everything I know." Lehigh blew on his hands and rubbed them together. "All I can tell you is, they're the only ones who might have it in for me."

"No unhappy clients, competitors…?"

Lehigh shook his head. "None that have ever said anything to me, anyway. We're a pretty small community, all in all. Everyone knows everybody."

"You haven't given me much to go on," the deputy said.

"Threatening to kill me and running me off the road aren't much to go on?" Lehigh shook his head in wonder. "What-all do you need? A taped confession?"

"Did you get the license plate of that BMW that day?" the deputy asked, still in his dry, bored voice. He drummed his pen on the soft black surface of the gray gunmetal desk.

"I can get it," Lehigh said.

The cop shook his head. "I'm afraid that's not going to work." He sighed. "Mr. Carter, we'll ask them some questions, but–"

"Won't that just tip them off and allow them to cover their tracks?"

"What would you have me do?" the deputy asked.

Lehigh shrugged, defeated. "I don't know. Thanks, officer."

***

Police cordoned off the burned area with yellow tape reading, "Police Investigation Scene—Do Not Enter." Lehigh spent much of the next day roaming the forest outside the perimeter of the taped-off area, well away from the house, checking the status of his adjacent stands and keeping an eye peeled, to no avail, for signs of Lucky. One thing cheered him: his diligent efforts to keep his lands clear of dead underbrush had paid off, limiting the fire's spread and intensity. His commercial losses would amount to far less than he had feared. But the fire reduced his house to charred rubble.

At sunset he drove into town, and stopped by the clinic on the way to the motel, but Stacy had already left for the day. "She mentioned going to dinner with Donna at the Mexican place," Annie-Marie said. "By the way, Mr. Carter, have you found any sign of Lucky?"

"No, Annie-Marie. Thank you for asking."

"That poor dog. I do hope she's all right. She must be starving."

"I know how she feels," Lehigh said. "I haven't eaten since breakfast."

He found Stacy and Donna sipping their second round of drinks from salt-rimmed glasses at Margarita Mary's on the main drag in town. Mariachi music blared amidst flashing colorful lights strung around the otherwise dim room. "Hope I'm not interrupting a private party," he said, sliding in next to Stacy on the booth's bench seat. Donna made a sour face, but offered no objection.

"Paul called me again today." Stacy forced some of her enchilada onto Lehigh's fork. "He was furious, saying you'd sic'd the cops on him."

"*He's* mad? My house is burned down, plus forty acres of prime forest, and he's ticked that the police have a few questions to ask of the only man with a grudge against me?" He forked another huge mouthful of enchilada. Salty melted cheese, beef and salsa coated his tongue.

"Hey, don't kill the messenger!" She pulled her plate back in front of her.

He swallowed. "Sorry."

"If he didn't have anything to do with it, he shouldn't be worried about a couple of questions," Donna said into her drink. "I say, it's about time someone called him on his creepy nonsense."

Lehigh made a fist. "If I get my hands on him, I'll–"

"Listen, Lehigh," Stacy said. "I know I've said that Paul has a temper, but I don't think he'd stoop to burning your house down." She waved off Donna's huff of disagreement. "Not by his own hand, anyway. He has too much to lose."

"He did threaten–"

Stacy pinched his leg and glanced sideways at Donna.

He cleared his throat. "Yeah, I suppose. Whatever."

An uncomfortable silence fell between them. Lehigh wished Donna would leave, and by the way she glared at him and clattered her fork against her plate, he figured she felt the same about him. Stacy remained silent, offering neither of them any relief.

After ten minutes of awkward small talk, Lehigh could take no more. Wiping his face with his napkin, he stood and donned his hat and coat. "Sorry to barge in on your girl time," he said. "Stace, I guess we'll talk later." Donna stared at her lap.

"Where are you going?" Stacy asked.

"I guess to the motel. Where else?"

Stacy turned to face her friend. "Will you excuse us for a moment?"

"Haven't I been doing that all night?" Donna slid out of the booth.

"Please don't get up," Lehigh said. "Stacy, why don't you and I mosey outside a sec?"

"Of course. I'm sorry, Donna." Stacy jumped to her feet and shrugged into her jacket.

Donna slid back into the booth. "I'll order us another round of margaritas." Hints of a smile crept back onto her face.

Outside, standing under the green and yellow blinking neon sign advertising half-priced happy hour drinks, Lehigh held up his hands. "I'm sorry I interrupted your evening. I didn't think–"

"No, I should apologize," Stacy said. "To both of you. I shouldn't try to control everything. Donna's going to learn everything eventually, anyhow. It's just that everything's so tense, and so…I don't know."

"If Paul really wants to get rid of me–"

"I know you think he set this fire, but I just can't picture him doing it." A chill breeze scattered loose napkins and candy wrappers across the parking lot. Stacy shivered. "Not personally, anyway. Those goons from Cal-Tex, sure, but Paul—he's awful, and mean, but not a mobster, or an arsonist. Or…a killer."

Lehigh gazed at the horizon. "Tell that to Lucky. If we ever see her again, that is."

"We will, Lehigh. I know we will."

He shrugged. "I hope so. If not…" He turned back to her. "Tell Paul to watch out."

She stepped back from him. "Think about what you're saying here. If he is involved in this arson, particularly if it has anything to do with that money—that could implicate my father, too. He'd be ruined politically. He could go to prison."

"You're father isn't responsible for what Paul does. Although I'm sure your father wouldn't mind if I disappeared off the face of the earth."

"Don't say that! My father's political ambition may move him to do things we wouldn't do, but even he wouldn't stoop to…" She fought for words. "Taking you out." She made a face as if she wanted to spit out something bitter, and tears welled in her eyes.

"But Paul, on the other hand…?"

She blinked away the tears and leaned the top of her head into his chest. "I don't know. Paul can get pretty nasty. But even he has limits."

He rested his hands on her shoulders. "I just hope his limits end at burning my house down."

"I still don't think–"

"But if he did." He stroked her back with his thumbs. "Even if he just paid to have it done, let's hope he stops there. Because if he tries anything further—well, I have to defend myself."

Stacy lifted her face so she could see him. "I don't think it'll come to that. I have to hope that he wasn't involved in setting the fire." She leaned back into him. "Maybe those Cal-Tex thugs, or maybe no one. Maybe it really was an accident."

"Maybe. I hope so. But what if it wasn't? What if Paul really was involved?"

She took a step back and held his hands in a firm grip. "If he's involved, I promise you, I'll hold the press conference–"

"Bah! A press conference! So–"

"To tell the world what a scum he is. And I'll turn him into the cops myself, no matter what that means for Daddy. Okay?" Her eyes shone, twin orbs of blue flame searing his face with steely determination.

Lehigh surrendered a wry smile and pulled her close again. "Okay. Deal." He held her for a long moment.

Finally she broke the embrace. "I should get back inside. Donna's waiting."

Lehigh nodded. "Tell her I'm sorry I ruined your girls' night out."

Stacy smiled. "I will, and I'm sure she'll let you buy her a few margaritas some time to make it up to her."

"Okay." He sighed. "Well, I guess it's off to the motel."

She scowled. "I hate that you have to live like that." She paused a moment, then pretended to pick a bit of lint from his shoulder. "Would you consider another option?"

"What other option? Rent an apartment? I suppose I should, but I wouldn't know where to look."

"No, silly. I have plenty of room. Stay with me."

"Stacy!" Lehigh grinned. "Are you suggesting we shack up?"

"What I'm suggesting," Stacy said, "is that you stop wasting your money on a flea-bag motel, and take a friend up on her offer of hospitality."

"When you put it like that," he said, "there's no way I can refuse."

**

Lehigh spent much of the next morning with an insurance adjuster by the name of Brian Kelly, a portly man with a thin crown of dark hair encircling his shiny dome. They met in Kelly's cramped, dingy office about a mile from Stacy's clinic. The sharp, acrid smell of industrial cleaner blended with rather than eliminated a subtle mustiness and the faint but persistent aroma of stale tobacco. The combination had Lehigh breathing through his mouth and wishing for an early escape.

"What I've learned from the police," the adjuster said, "is that there is cause to suspect arson."

"I knew it!" Lehigh slapped the arm of his chair. "If I get my hands on the goons who did this, I'll–"

Kelly cleared this throat, a little louder than anyone ever needed to. "Have the police interviewed you or briefed you about this?"

"Not much," Lehigh said. "But I'm not so easily reached. My home phone's gone, of course, and my cell number's unlisted. Even so, Buck Summers has never kept my best interests very close to his heart."

The adjuster slid a card across his cluttered desk. "Here's the number to call to get in touch with the lead detective on the investigation. I suggest you do it soon."

Lehigh glanced at the card and slipped it into his shirt pocket. "I will. Is there anything you can tell me now?"

"Unfortunately not. But you can help me help you. We'll need you to list your personal property and the values of it all on this form. Oh, and the details of when you bought each item, for depreciation purposes."

"Is everything gone?"

The adjuster squinted at Lehigh for a second or two and tapped his pen on a yellow legal pad. "You say you haven't been back to your house?"

Lehigh shook his head. "Cops said stay away until they call me, and last I looked the whole thing was still taped off. Crime scene investigation, and all that."

"Mr. Carter, I think it's time we took a ride."

Kelly drove the two of them to the fire scene in his late-model Taurus and explained the paperwork Lehigh would have to do on the way. "Unfortunately, I suspect a lot of your files were destroyed in the fire," Kelly said, "seeing as it appeared to have started in your office."

"My office? How could that be? Was it an electrical fire?"

Kelly gave Lehigh a sidelong look and shook his head. "Mr. Carter, I don't mean to insult you, but in an arson case the fires don't start on their own. Somebody set this fire."

Lehigh grimaced. "I see. So, what'd they do? Pour gasoline all over everything and light a match?"

Kelly's head bobbed. "From what I saw on my site visit, yes."

"Wait. You've been there? Has everyone been there except me?"

"They seemed most interested in burning your office," Kelly went on, "but it looked to me like the arsonist spread gas pretty much everywhere, based on the path of the fire." One hand flipped off the wheel for a moment to illustrate the splashing of fuel, then resumed its death-like grip.

"The path of the fire? You can tell how the fire spread?"

Kelly nodded. "I've seen enough of these over the years.

These guys weren't very creative. They splashed gas from the office right down your hallway to the living room and bedroom. They splashed the kitchen pretty thoroughly, too."

Lehigh stared at him. In spite of his anger, hope dawned. "Wait. That means they had to have gotten inside to set this fire, right?"

"Of course. So?"

"If they got in, then maybe—just maybe—Lucky got out."

"That's a strong possibility, Mr. Carter. And perhaps," Kelly said, turning into Lehigh's long gravel driveway, "we'll know very shortly."

CHAPTER 15

The Man Who Would Be Governor tapped a manicured fingernail on his dark wooden desk. He regarded the young man before him with a distrust he'd never felt toward him before. That simply would not do. Not in such a close, trusted aide. Certainly not in the man in whom he entrusted his campaign treasury.

No. That would not do a-tall.

"Have I done something personally to offend you?" Paul asked. "Has Stacy complained? Because I–"

"Let's leave my daughter out of this for now, shall we?" the Senator said. "If we can. I have a feeling she may somehow be a motivator for some of this trouble, however."

"Trouble, sir?" Paul wrinkled his brow and sat forward in his chair, knitting his fingers into a sweaty zipper.

"This money that one of my contributors says he gave to you." McBride waved the single sheet of numbers in the air toward the younger man's face. "I don't see it accounted for. Anywhere!" His sudden sharpness of tone startled Paul back into his chair. Calmer, he said, "Perhaps you'd care to explain."

"Which contributor?"

"Dammit, you know which contributor!" Senator McBride slammed the paper onto his desk. The loud smack of his palm onto the heavy wood made Paul jump again.

"Sir, there are so many contrib–"

"How many give fifty thousand dollars in cash that suddenly goes missing?" McBride glared at his visitor. "Hand-delivered, I might add. To you." He kept his steely gray eyes locked on Paul's twitching face while he waited for an answer.

"Sir, that money was stolen."

"Stolen? By whom?"

"Lehigh Carter. The man that your daughter is now living with."

"The man who WHAT?" McBride bellowed. He picked up the phone, then slammed it down again. "Wait—hold that thought. First tell me how you let this idiot Carter get his hands on my campaign money. Surely you're smart enough to guard my funds from a damned lumberjack."

Paul hung his head. "Senator, it appears that the Cal-Tex men accidentally gave it to him."

"Gave it?"

"Yes, sir. They mistook him for me. Apparently he played along and even made promises on your behalf."

"This is lunacy!"

"Yes, sir."

"How could they possibly–"

"I don't know, sir."

McBride squinted at the man with whom he'd entrusted the small fortune he needed to realize his life's ambition. The man he'd hand-picked to be his son-in-law, to provide for and protect his only daughter for the rest of her life. He shook his head in disgust. "How can you be sure it's him?"

"The two men saw them embrace, and assumed it was me. They also described his face and pickup truck—both match Carter's. And there's the kicker."

"What's the kicker?"

Paul cleared his throat. "You know that press conference you helped your daughter with a week ago? Announcing the anonymous receipt of fifty thousand dollars?"

Blazing heat enveloped the face of The Man Who Would Be Governor.

***

Senator McBride slowed his pure-white Chrysler New Yorker into Stacy's driveway so as not to kick up mud onto the car's clean whitewalls. He drove only American vehicles, ever, and he kept them pristine, inside and out. He had an image to maintain, after all—to the point that he would forego his precious cigars while driving.

He half-hoped to see Carter's truck parked in the driveway. The other half of him prayed it would not be, and the prayerful side won. Perhaps Paul was mistaken about him living there, then. Even the most brilliant of aides make mistakes sometimes.

He parked behind Stacy's car, resting in its usual spot near the house, as expected. He hated wasting his time knocking on doors of empty homes, so he never went anywhere without calling first. That call, of course, could explain Carter's absence.

He sauntered to the front door, giving his daughter ample opportunity to greet him at the door. But it remained closed even after he reached the front steps. With a huff, he rang the bell, waited five seconds, and rang the bell again. His ire built even in the few moments he lingered before the wide wooden door swung open.

"Hi Daddy!" Stacy smiled and reached out for their customary hug and kiss on the cheek. His mood softened. He could never stay mad at his little girl.

"Will you stay for dinner?" She closed the door behind him.

"I'm sorry, no," he said with a rueful smile. He draped his coat over a chair. "As much as I love your home cooked meals, I'm afraid the campaign beckons."

"Another rubber chicken tonight at the Roadside Inn?" she asked with a grin.

"I swear, if I have to eat at that place again, I'm going to grow feathers and start clucking." He took a seat on the sofa. "But I would accept a glass of Oregon Pinot if it were offered."

"Coming right up." She escaped through the open doorway into the kitchen. "Make yourself at home."

She returned in moments with his wine and sat across from him in an old wooden rocker, her favorite chair since high school. McBride had insisted she take it with her when she and Steven married ten years before. "So, what compels you to take a break from campaigning?" she asked. "I feel honored."

"Well, it is campaign business, of a sort." He cleared his

throat. "Paul informed me that your, ah, friend, Mr. Lehigh Carter, may have taken something that belongs to me. Or, should I say, to my supporters. An intended campaign donation."

Stacy's face flushed. She halted her slow rocking and planted both feet on the floor. "You know about the cash?"

His face warmed. "So it's true then."

"No!" Stacy buried her head in her hands. McBride sipped his wine. Finally she raised her head to face him again. "What I mean is, Lehigh didn't steal the money. Those two bozos from Cal-Tex–"

"You know who they are?" His hands shook. He set down the drink.

"Of course. They introduced themselves. Lehigh didn't have to steal the money. They mistook him for Paul and gave it to him."

"He took it, knowing their intention?"

A long, slow nod. "Yes, he did. But what was he supposed to do? Tell them 'I'm sorry, I'm not the person you're trying to bribe with an illegal campaign contribution?'"

He jerked forward in the chair. "Bribe! How dare you insinuate–"

She crossed her arms. "Come on. I'm not naive."

"You are far more naive than you think. In any case, what makes you think this contribution was illegal?"

She glared at him and sat upright in her chair. "Daddy, really. It was a secret meeting in the woods, and a large sum of money—cash, even. If it was all above board and legit, why wouldn't they just write a check to your super-PAC?"

McBride opened his mouth, but no words came out. He raised his hand in a gesture of explanation—but still, silence.

Stacy peered at him. "This money," she said. "Is there a record of it anywhere? Don't all contributions have to be reported?"

McBride coughed. "I'm not, er, fully familiar with the details of the transaction–"

"Cut the crap, Daddy. You do know, or you wouldn't be

here, accusing Lehigh of anything. Which raises another point: why are you talking to me about this rather than him? It's not like you to hide behind another person when you have an issue to discuss with someone."

McBride collapsed back into the sofa. "Actually, I half-expected to find him here. I was told he'd moved in with you."

"Moved in? Who told you that?" She gripped both arms of her chair.

He turned away from her hostile stare. "I have my sources."

"Paul."

"I know a lot of people."

"Dammit, Daddy, answer me. Was it Paul?" She leaned forward, bringing her face close to his.

He shrugged one shoulder and refused to meet her eyes. "What does it matter? What matters to me is, is it true? Is he living with you?"

She stood and turned away from him. "I offered to let him stay with me while he's sorting things out. You may have heard that his house burned down."

"I did hear that. That was a tragic accident and I'm sorry to hear it. But–"

She whirled to face him. "It was no accident. It was arson. Someone burned his house down—and may have killed his dog in the process. Bastards!"

"Stacy, your language this evening is pure sewage. Now, honey, listen. I know you're trying to do the Christian thing in offering him a roof over his head in his time of need, but you must recognize how this appears to people."

"What are you talking about?" she shouted. "The man's house just burned down. He has no place to live. If you're concerned about people talking, why don't you start by keeping your own mouth shut about it? And Paul's?"

"Don't talk to me in that tone of voice!" His face warmed again and he started to rise.

"Don't talk to me like a child!" Hands on hips, she towered over him, her face inches from his. Her glare forced him back onto the couch.

"Stacy, what I'm talking about here is appearances. How is this going to look if my daughter is shacking up with some hayseed logger while engaged to another man?"

"Hayseed? What? And I am not engaged to another man!"

McBride's cheeks puffed. "Have you forgotten our agreement?"

"Agreement? Daddy, tell me this 'appearances' issue isn't about your damned campaign." She straightened and stepped away from him, arms crossed, facing her large picture window.

He tried a softer tone. "It's not about the campaign. That's a concern, of course. But your mother and I both feel—"

"Oh, so Mother is all concerned too, is she? Funny, the phone's been awfully silent—a pretty rare event when Mother wants to discuss something with me. I don't ever recall her being shy with expressing her point of view when it comes to me."

He sighed. "Okay, I took it upon myself to bring this up with you. I haven't told your mother what I know. But you know how she'd feel about this."

"No. Please tell me, in her own words, if you don't mind."

"Don't get sarcastic with me."

Again she whirled back to face him, arms crossed. "If it's all the same with you, I'd rather not even discuss this with you. It's none of your business."

He stood and took a step toward her. "But it is my business. What you're doing affects me. Yes, it might affect my campaign, too, if word gets around. And in a small town like this—"

"To hell with the campaign! If you're so concerned about getting elected—and I know you are—you should concern yourself more with the people you associate with and worry less about my relationships. Those Cal-Tex thugs and their bribes—"

"There was no bribe!"

"For God's sake. Do I have to say it again? Lehigh was there. He told me what they said. They wanted to buy your approval of a looser logging policy. They were very specific."

He shrugged and sipped his wine. "They hardly need to do that. My position on that issue is clear. Opening up logging lands to a greater harvest and allowing the private sector a freer hand to manage our forests more effectively–"

"Spare me the campaign speech, will you?"

He sighed. "Okay. But honey, listen. This Carter fellow—he can't live with you. Not during the campaign. If my opponents get ahold of that, I'll be humiliated."

Her smile crackled saccharine. "Then I suppose it's in both of our interests to keep this matter private, isn't it?"

**

In twenty-two years of politics—ten in the state senate, eight in the lower house, and four years before that as County Commissioner—George McBride had grown unused to accepting a firm "no" to anything. People always compromise, according to his experience, if given an alternative to stalemate. As such, he always got his way, at least in part.

But leaving his daughter's house, he had nothing to show for it—not even a bargaining chip.

He'd raised her to be a strong, intelligent woman, one who could think for and fend for herself, unafraid to confront the more well-possessed and more powerful. But he'd also raised her to be loyal, and a team player. To put family first. To honor her mother and father. Somewhere along the line, something had happened to change all of that. Something recent. Very recent.

Right around the time Lehigh Carter came along, to be precise.

He started his New Yorker, still fuming. She'd remained stubborn about letting that idiot Carter live with her—an abomination, that, for so many reasons, and yet another departure from her moral, Christian upbringing. Worse, she'd managed to turn the tables on him with regard to the money. He pounded the wheel and reversed the car in preparation for his three-point U-turn. Damn! He even helped her with the press conference. He had gone on record, lauding the anonymous cash donor. To top it off, she threatened to go public with the details of the whole seedy transaction if he went after Carter. He doubted she'd make good on that threat, but even if she didn't,

Carter might. He'd have to play that carefully. Another hard-learned lesson from politics: never back a man into a corner. Always give him a face-saving way out.

He exited her driveway onto the quiet two-lane road, knowing he had no bargaining chips on this one—with her. But with Lehigh Carter, perhaps he had a few.

Lost in thought, he barely noticed the man driving a Ford F150 in the opposite direction, staring hard at him as he drove by.

***

Lehigh recognized McBride's car from a distance as soon as it pulled out of Stacy's driveway. Given the Senator's well-known preference for having people come to him—and his ability to make that happen—his appearance at Stacy's at this particular moment meant one of two things: either the Senator needed something from her, or he had something to hide.

Or both.

Or—

Lehigh's chest tightened. He slowed his car as the Senator drove past.

Or, he was checking up on his daughter—and whoever else might be around.

Which meant it was a good thing he happened to be out for this particular visit. But next time, he might not be so lucky.

Distracted, he almost didn't notice the black Plymouth sedan that pulled away from the side of the road in front of Stacy's house, trailing Senator McBride's car by only twenty or thirty yards. He spotted it just as the car's nose crossed the center crest of the unmarked pavement, continuing across the lane into his, accelerating–

He swerved, missing the oncoming car by inches. The offending vehicle burned rubber passing McBride's lumbering cruiser and disappeared out of sight. Lehigh's truck choked on the side of the road, struggling to keep running at low speed in fourth gear.

But Lehigh's mind was not on the near-accident he'd just

escaped, nor on the Senator's paranoid meddling, nor on being late for dinner with Stacy.

His mind was on the barrel of the enormous gun that had been pointed directly at him from behind the disappearing car's windshield.

PART 4

Into Hiding

CHAPTER 16

At the entrance to Stacy's driveway, Lehigh made a snap decision. Rather than turn in, he zoomed by her property to the next corner, hung a right, and sped through town into the darkening hills.

Toward Pappy's house.

He made it there in under twenty minutes, driveway to driveway. He pulled halfway up the drive toward the house, then stopped, turned the engine off, and sat with both hands resting on the wheel. He hadn't visited Pappy's on a day other than Sunday in over six years. Not since that day Maw had gotten hold of the gun and blown out all four of his tires, the headlights, half the front grille, and both windshields. He'd hidden in the old barn loft for two hours while Pappy talked her into relinquishing the rifle. Since then, he visited them only during her church services, and even then he often drove by the church first to make sure she was there.

Midweek visits risked seeing her—or, more to the point, her seeing him. But he had no other option, nowhere else to turn. If Pappy couldn't help him–

"Git, boy!"

Maw stood on the porch some forty feet away, waving a broomstick like a hockey player high-sticking on open ice. She wore a simple calf-length country print dress over a dark blue long-sleeved undershirt and dirt-brown tennis shoes. Her face, flushed red against her halo of white hair, contorted into twisted lines more tangled than a roll of barbed wire. She shook the broom at him as if to sweep him away.

"Git, I say. Get along or I'll…I'll…" Her head swiveled side to side as if searching for something to throw at him.

He lowered a window. "I'll stay out here," he said. "Could you send Pappy—"

"You'll stay out, and get further out," she yelled. Brown spittle ran down her wrinkled chin. A wad of chewing tobacco flew out of her mouth to the ground.

"I just want to ask Pappy—"

"The answer's no, whatever it is." She scrambled down the steps, found her chaw and stuffed it back into her mouth. She raised the broom over her head as if preparing to chop wood. "Now, get, or I'll crack your head open."

"Maw, please. Just send out Pappy."

She strode toward him, eyes blood-red and wide, and closed within striking distance of the truck. She stopped, planted her feet wide, drew back the broom, and—

"Irene!" Pappy's gravelly voice interrupted the vicious blow sure to come a moment later. Maw spun around to face him.

"I'm taking care of this," she said.

"Let me talk to the boy," Pappy said.

"He knows better than to come here." Maw turned back to Lehigh and delivered a half-hearted blow to his headlights with the straw end of the broom. Lehigh flicked them off. Let her think she did some damage.

"There ain't no use talking," she said. "He don't listen anyhow." She huffed and strode back to the porch in her trademark wide-footed duck-waddle. Still mad, but no longer violent.

Pappy passed her going the other direction on the steps, muttered something to her and patted her rear. She swatted his with the broom and laughed, then glared again at Lehigh.

Pappy ambled to the truck, leaning hard on his cane. He stopped at Lehigh's door and rested his free arm across the open window. "The hell?" he asked.

Lehigh drew a deep breath, then exhaled a slow, noisy burst of nervous air. "You heard about the house?"

Pappy nodded. "Who done it? You?"

"Pappy. Come on." He shook his head and drummed on the

steering wheel. "Looks like I pissed off the wrong folk."

Pappy turned to glance at Maw, standing on the front porch, aiming the broom handle at Lehigh like a rifle. He turned back to Lehigh and grinned. "That's a bad habit you got."

"Yah." He cleared his throat. "Look, I got nowhere to go."

The old man chewed on something that looked like an old scrap of leather sliding across his tongue. "Yep. You sure don't." Chewed some more.

"I was hoping–"

"Like I said, boy. You sure don't." He stared hard at Lehigh. "Lookit, son. That house was all that gave your Maw any hope at all for you. Some sense that you'd turn out a halfway decent human being. Maybe give her a couple grandkids someday, assuming you find a woman idiot enough to marry you." He dropped his gaze to his feet. "Now, well…she'd just as soon feed you to the coyotes."

Lehigh gazed into his rear-view mirror. "And I suppose you ain't got no say in the matter."

"Don't take that tone with me, boy." Pappy's glare sliced Lehigh's resolve in half, then in half again. "You know how hard I work just to keep her half-sane. It's all I can do to keep her from getting naked and chasing the chickens around with a shovel. The only link to the real world she's got is this place." He swept an arm across the wooded lot. "What keeps her going is, everything stays the same. You being here don't help things."

Lehigh nodded. "Okay. Well. I guess I see where I stand." He started the truck. "See you Sunday?"

Pappy held his gaze for several seconds, unmoving, unflinching. "Let's take a few weeks off of that and see where we stand," he said in a raspy voice.

"Pappy? You too?" Lehigh blinked.

Pappy lowered his eyes. "You keep me posted on what the police say about the fire. The arson, they call it. You let me know if they prove you ain't done it." He rapped the truck with his cane. "Then we'll talk."

He turned away and walked back to the house. He went up the stairs, took Maw by the arm, and led her inside, never looking back at his son.

***

Lehigh took back roads to downtown Clarkesville rather than the highway. Too many emotions swirled in his mind to risk any high-speed driving. On the way, he improvised a new plan.

He made two quick stops—at WinCo for groceries, and at an overpriced but reliable outfitter's store. Within the hour he'd reached the highway westbound, gaining altitude and losing sunlight with every passing minute.

He reached his property at dusk and parked just outside the yellow tape that marked the burnt area around his house. The remaining canopy of Douglas firs and Lodgepole pines turned dusk into darkness, so he grabbed his flashlight before getting out of the truck. He unlocked the door to his metal outbuilding, undamaged by the fire that had consumed his house several days before, and loaded the gear he needed into the bed of his pickup. Re-locking the shed door, he made another impulsive decision.

He stepped into the charred remains of his house, shining his flashlight ahead of him so he could pick his path through the clutter. He followed the burned path on his floor leading from the kitchen through the living room into his office. He focused the bright center of the beam on the dark "V" charring the wall to the now open roof. Even the fire-resistant drywall had burned. According to the insurance adjuster, that meant the arsonist had soaked the wall with combustible fuel. The police were analyzing samples of burned and unburned materials to determine the exact fuel used with certainty, but Kelly had guessed gasoline or kerosene. "Both are cheap and effective," he explained. "Because of that, they're very popular among arsonists."

He flashed the light around the office. His file cabinets lay on their side, their former contents now a pile of ashes strewn across the floor. His desktop sat empty. The phone lay off-hook in a heap of charred papers and desk implements in the corner. His computer lay in a jumble of wires, metal, and broken glass—

destroyed by the fire, or the fighting of it.

He flicked the flashlight about the room, still taking inventory, then flicked it back and forth around the desk. He bent low and searched again. Then again, slowly.

Still, what he sought remained hidden.

Or, missing.

He knelt, flashing the light just above floor level, under and around the desk, then toward the computer junk piled in the corner. He stepped around the desk to get a different angle on the mess. Still no sight of the rectangular metal machine.

He straightened, scratching behind his ear, then shook his head. "I don't get it," he said aloud. "I'd understand someone stealing a computer. But why the heck would they rob me of my old manual typewriter?"

***

He set up camp alongside the brook that bisected his holdings, about a half-mile downhill of his house's charred remains. A stiff westerly breeze, typical of the Cascade foothills, created a challenge for setting up his tent, but long experience allowed him to overcome nature's obstacles. A gas-powered space heater helped him shake off the chill. He'd considered building a fire, but recent events recommended otherwise. Besides, he didn't want to attract attention. Tonight, solitude was his friend.

As it always had been. Before strange people came into his life, attacking him, burning down his home, stealing his property. Before Paul, before Stacy, before Lucky. Before all of that, when escaping to the thickets of the forest allowed him to eliminate all the noise in his life. Some people—Maw, for example—went to church for spiritual guidance and peace, but Lehigh visited his own cathedral in the woods. Towering pines and redwoods formed the canopy, massive Sitka spruces the pillars and walls, and lush ferns, wild ginger, and flowering berries decorated the altar of the earth. He had a house—or, used to—but the forest was his home.

Still, he felt bad about having ditched Stacy's hospitality, and worse about leaving without warning. He should have called her, but he knew she'd try very hard to talk him out of it. She probably would have succeeded, too, in spite of his being convinced that he was doing the right thing.

Which was…what, exactly? He struggled with that, and would have had a hard time explaining it to her. But he belonged on the land—his land. His home, if not his own bed. Whatever these arsonists were after, it was going to happen here, on his home turf. Not hiding in the city, feeling unsettled and alien.

He felt safer in the woods. His whole life had been about forests and trees. They provided a comfort zone, both physical and psychological. They provided his livelihood, for one thing, but also a way of life: fuel for his fireplace, privacy, cool shade, peaceful quiet, homes for critters (some of which became food), and soon, building materials for a new home.

And the quiet. Most of all, the quiet.

He'd already decided to rebuild on the same spot, for practical reasons and sentimental ones. In his mind he even had a rough floor plan, a new and improved version of the 1950's ranch that had burned. It'd be a little bigger, more modern, with more space.

Space for a dog. Maybe even a dog door, so she could come and go as she pleased.

Space for Stacy, too, if she'd have him. After tonight's rash decision, he couldn't be sure. Nor did he have any idea if she'd be willing to live on his land, out in the country, away from all of her friends and community. But if she'd have him, he'd have her. That he knew. If nothing else came of all this, he knew at least that.

He pulled his cell phone out of his coat pocket and turned it on. "Low battery," the phone warned him with a beep. Damn. Hopefully the charge would hold long enough to call her. The phone beeped a second time, indicating messages waiting. He dialed voicemail as the phone beeped its low-power warning again. He had no way to recharge it—he'd left the recharger in the office, now a charred, waterlogged mess.

"Lehigh?" came the first message. "Stacy here. Where are

you? I thought you were coming–"

With another beep, the phone powered down, its battery spent.

***

After several hours of restless sleep, Lehigh rolled out of his sleeping bag and pulled his jeans over his thick cotton long johns. His breath misted in the dark air. He built a small cooking fire just outside the tent and brewed a pot of strong coffee that he gulped down while tearing through a plateful of bacon and eggs.

The food, coffee, and fire warmed and revived him, the perfect complement to the fresh air and quiet of camping. With his cell phone effectively dead and no one knowing where to find him, he had achieved the solitude he hadn't even realized he'd craved throughout the hustle and bustle of the days since the fire. He felt a twinge of regret about leaving Stacy's place without warning. She'd be upset, but once he explained, surely she'd understand.

He also had gained clarity on what he needed to do about his situation. The first thing, he'd already achieved—getting out of sight of whoever was after him. More to the point, he'd gotten out of Stacy's perimeter, which seemed to be the problem. While he had no proof, his gut told him that Paul was behind the burning of his house and forest. He'd not only threatened Lehigh and tried to scare him that day on the highway, but he'd been humiliated by the money transfer screw-up.

What's more, the other potential culprits—rival foresters or angry customers—were unlikely villains in this case. For one, he had no angry customers and no business rivals jealous enough to go to such extremes. Second, from an economic viewpoint, the burned area did not represent a particularly valuable stretch of trees. Nor could the land be developed under current zoning restrictions—if he'd even agree to sell it, which he wouldn't. He didn't want neighbors. He wanted privacy.

He'd also gained clarity about a second thing. Finding Lucky had to become a priority. He missed the dog's gentle company and worried for her safety. This late in the fall, just before hibernation season, an injured animal in the forest became fodder for bear, wolves, and other predators much larger and more vicious than a domesticated mutt. After taking the trouble to adopt and care for her these past few weeks—and, with that, overcoming his life-long fear of dogs—he couldn't let all of that go to waste.

He checked the bowl of kibble he'd left out the night before, some distance from the tent. Empty, but that didn't tell him much. Squirrels or raccoons probably ate it. Still, setting out her favorite food remained his best shot at luring her in. Besides, dog food wouldn't do him any good if she wasn't around to eat it. He refilled the bowl, then returned to put out the fire and pack up his gear.

He finished loading his truck well past daybreak. Today he'd get back to work. As much as he needed them, his forest—and his missing dog—needed him, too. He drove toward the next stand of trees, one eye peeled for a stray yellow hound.

**

"Ow!"

Stacy yanked her hand back from the Jack Russell Terrier's head and shoved her stinging finger into her mouth. Freed of his restraints, the tiny dog lurched to its right, nearly sliding off the stainless exam table, and away from Dr. Lewis's invasive anal probe.

"Control your dog, please, Mrs. Whitehead!" Dr. Lewis said to the white-haired, cowering figure seated to the right of the table. "Are you all right, Stacy?"

"I'm fine," Stacy mumbled around the digit still lodged between her lips. "He didn't break skin. It just stings a little."

"I don't understand." Mrs. Whitehead, on the verge of tears, scampered over to scoop up the quivering animal. "Toby's never snapped at anyone before."

"If I had a dollar for every time I've heard that," Dr. Lewis said, "I could pay off my both my mortgages." She accepted the animal from its owner and set him back on the table.

"I'm so sorry," Mrs. Whitehead said. "Toby, what's gotten into you? Bad boy!"

"I'm fine, really," Stacy said. "It's my fault. I was distracted, and I moved my hand in front of his snout at just the wrong moment." She shook off Mrs. Whitehead's and Dr. Lewis's objections. No doubt the dog sensed her tension.

Her mind wandered to Lehigh for perhaps the fiftieth time in the last sixty seconds, and her face flushed. Where the hell was he? Why hadn't he called? She excused herself from the exam room, found a volunteer to assist in her place, grabbed her purse and headed to the ladies room.

She washed her hands and confirmed that the little dog's nip hadn't left a scratch, then checked her cell phone. No calls—from Lehigh, anyway. Paul had tried a dozen times. With a huff she deleted all of his voicemail messages unheard, stuffed her phone back into her purse, and stepped back into the hallway.

"Ms. McBride!" Anne-Marie's voice rang out. "Come quick. You have to see this!"

Stacy walked as fast as her legs could carry her to the reception area. Anne-Marie's short, chubby finger pointed out the window into the parking lot. "What?" Stacy asked. "What should I be looking for?"

Anne-Marie pointed her finger further to the left. "Over there," she said. "Behind those trash cans. Isn't that Mr. Carter's dog?"

A yellow hound came into view, sniffing at a discarded KFC wrapper on the pavement. Stacy caught her breath. "Yes, I think it is Lucky!" she said. "Thank you, Anne-Marie!" She grabbed a leash from the stash hanging on the hook in the lobby and ran outside. The door slammed behind her, startling the dog. The hound glanced once at her, then trotted in the opposite direction.

"Lucky!" she called. "Stay!"

The dog paused and glanced over its shoulder. After a few moments, the dog sat.

"Good girl," Stacy said. The dog's tail fluttered a moment, as did its soft pink tongue. Stacy coaxed the dog inside and checked the dog's belly for stitches, then its tags. "Lucky, it is you," she said, patting her head. Lucky gulped down two bowls of food in seconds, then waited by the bowl with an expectant look.

"She wants more," Anne-Marie said. "She's so skinny. Poor thing must have been starving."

"Let's get her into an examination room and have Dr. Lewis take a look at her," Stacy said.

"But Ms. McBride, we're all booked up with people waiting."

"They'll wait longer. This is an emergency." Stacy squatted to pet the dog, and Lucky licked her face. "She has a few cuts and bruises, but I don't see any burn marks. She must've escaped before the fire. Thank goodness!"

"Shall I call Mr. Carter and let him know we've found his dog?" Anne-Marie picked up the phone.

"Yes, please. If you don't reach him, I'd like you to try again every half-hour until you do. Call his cell number—his home phone is disconnected." She scribbled his number on a note pad, tore off the page and handed it to Anne-Marie. Then she walked the dog into the examination room just vacated by Toby and Mrs. Whitehead.

"That room hasn't been cleaned," Anne-Marie said in protest.

"I'll clean it," Stacy said. "Just get Dr. Lewis in here."

***

"Lucky has once again lived up to her name," Dr. Lewis said after a quick examination. "A little malnourished and dehydrated, but otherwise healthy. Even her stitches look good. In fact they're ready to come out."

"Good girl!" Stacy cooed to the dog. To Dr. Lewis she said, "I'll put her in a kennel and get her some more food and water. Hopefully we can reach Mr. Carter soon so he can come get her." Her forehead creased, and she petted the dog for several more seconds.

"Stacy," Dr. Lewis asked, "do you mean to tell me that you haven't been able to reach your boyfriend?"

Stacy's chin hit her chest. "What did you just call him?"

"Don't be surprised. Everybody knows," Dr. Lewis said. "You haven't exactly been discreet."

Stacy slumped and hugged the dog, long and tight. "He disappeared yesterday, and I haven't heard from him at all. Frankly, I'm worried. This isn't like him."

Dr. Lewis chuckled. "Actually it sounds just like the Lehigh Carter I've always known. But you know him better, so I'll defer to your judgment. Anyway, I have more patients waiting. Good work, dear." She shuffled out of the room with a friendly pat to Lucky's head.

"Well, Lucky," Stacy said, "I'm glad you found us. Now we need to find Lehigh." She sighed. "You don't think anything's happened to him, do you?"

Lucky's silent reply offered no encouragement.

Dr. Lewis removed Lucky's stitches late in the afternoon, and Anne-Marie led her to a large private cage in the kennels so that night staff could keep an eye on her. Stacy drove away from the clinic a few minutes after seven, exhausted and still worried that she hadn't heard from Lehigh. Since rekindling their relationship, he'd called her at least daily, and had never missed two consecutive days.

Her cell chirped. Caller ID displayed only "Unavailable." Ever hopeful, she answered.

"About time you took a call from me," the familiar voice sneered. "Is there some old McBride tradition that you don't speak to your fiancé for a year before the wedding?"

"Paul," she said, "would you just leave me alone?"

"Why so testy?" he asked. "Is Lehigh ignoring you again? Old habits die hard, you know."

"What do you know about his whereabouts?" Stacy tried to keep the worry out of her voice. She braked hard to avoid running a red light she noticed at the last moment.

"I know he didn't sleep at your house last night. Unless I'm very mistaken about the pattern of Lehigh Carter's life as it pertains to you, he won't be seeing you tonight, either. But don't worry. I'm sure everything will be better when you try again in another twelve years."

"Where is he?" Stacy said. "If you know—"

"I don't know where he is. I just know where he isn't. He's not at your house, and he's not in his own. Very suspicious, wouldn't you say?"

"It's not him I'm suspicious of. If I find out you had a hand in any of this—"

"Oh, go stuff your idle threats, Stacy," Paul said. "I'm not afraid of you, or your father, or your idiot boyfriend. In fact, at this point I hold all the cards in this game."

"What are you talking about?" Stacy's voice rose to just under a shout. "What game? Have you done something to Lehigh?"

Paul's laughter cackled in her ear. "Thus far, my dear, I haven't had to do a thing. He's managing to screw up his own life quite nicely without any help from me."

"He's not the one who burned down his house!"

"Oh no?" The sneer in his voice made her cringe. "Then why does he keep returning to the scene of the crime? I'm sure you and he both know that destroying evidence is a felony."

"Destroying—? He wasn't destroying evidence. He was looking for his dog."

"Is that his story? He must not have looked too hard. I heard the dog turned up safely at your clinic today. Without Carter."

"How did you—"

"Very suspicious, Stacy. Very, very suspicious." With that, the line went dead.

Infuriated, Stacy pulled her car to the side of the road and speed-dialed Paul's number, pushing the buttons so hard on her phone's keypad that her entire finger went white. She reached voicemail, hung up, and dialed again. She repeated this another half-dozen times, each time angrier than the time before, until Paul eventually answered.

"Persistent, aren't you?" he said with a chuckle.

"Don't get all smug with me, mister. In fact we can start this conversation with an apology from you. You know how I hate being hung up on."

"Apologize? Oh, sure. Just as soon as you and Carter return

my stolen money."

"We stole nothing! That money was never yours in the first place. Now start with the apology, mister, or else I'll–"

"You'll what? Hang up on me? Big deal. You called me, remember? Or maybe you plan to steal another fifty grand for a lost kitties fund?"

"I told you, I–"

"I'll tell you what you won't do. You'll never get into a position to screw me over again, Miss Oh-by-the-way, I-met-somebody-else-and-couldn't-be-bothered-to-tell-you. When are you going to apologize for that?"

Stacy took a long, deep breath and counted to ten, then exhaled. "You and I were never a good match, Paul. Anyway it was all just a means to an end for you. I know about Daddy's plans for you. A nice cushy job in the state bureaucracy, way above your abilities. Which department did he promise you? Finance? Forestry? Health?"

"My career is not at issue here, and I don't give a rat's ass what you think of my abilities any more. Two weeks ago that mattered more to me than anything. Now…"

"Now, and forever, the only thing that has ever mattered to you is you." Heat rose again in her voice. "But unlike you, I have people I care about, and–"

"Yes, and I'm not one of them."

Stacy grimaced and tried to keep her voice level. "Where's Lehigh?"

"How would I know?"

"You knew about Lucky coming back."

"Lucky?"

"The dog."

"Oh. Well, word gets around."

"And what 'word' do you have about Lehigh?"

"The only word for him is *Loser.*"

"Paul! What do you know about his whereabouts?"

"If I knew, why would I tell you?"

She put on her pouty voice. "Because I'm asking."

"Pfft. That's not enough anymore."

She gritted her teeth. "Have you done anything to him? You, or your henchmen?"

"Not yet. But if I find him, I'll decide then."

"Don't you dare hurt him!"

Paul laughed. "What are you going to do to stop me?"

"I'm going to hang up and call the police!"

His voice got very grave. "Stacy, do not go to the police. I'm warning you. If you do, I'm going to flat-out publicly accuse you and Loser Lehigh of stealing that money. Consequences be damned."

"You'd go to jail! And Daddy–"

"You'd be surprised at what might happen. Remember who helped get all of the judges elected around here."

Air whistled through her teeth. "Keep away from me, you bastard! And from Lehigh."

Paul snorted. "I recommend the same to you. Because if you get between him and me, I can't predict what might happen."

Once again, the line went dead. This time, she did not call back.

CHAPTER 17

Lehigh woke with the dawn, his new custom since he began sleeping in the tent. He'd repitched camp on the southernmost reaches of his forest holdings, far away from Clarkesville. Far from phones, lights, noise, people…especially a certain angry, unpredictable person of the lawyerly persuasion.

He couldn't hide out forever, and it bothered him to have skipped out on Stacy without notice. He missed her terribly and wished he could let her know he was safe. With his phone dead, his only option would be to head into town to call or leave a note. But if Paul or one of his minions spotted him, they might try to kill him again.

Besides, he still had to find Lucky.

He dressed in warm clothes to fight off the morning chill and stepped out of the tent. A light drizzle coated his hair and skin, and the night's rain left his firewood unusable. Worse, he'd run out of cooking fuel. "Damn," he said aloud. "No coffee this morning."

He checked the food dish he'd left out for Lucky. He found it upside down, several feet from where he'd left it. Squirrels again, no doubt. Lucky would have left the bowl where she found it. More likely, she'd have finished off the food, then smelled his scent and pawed at the tent to wake him. He'd have heard that.

He ate a mix of nuts, raisins, and dried cranberries from his supply pouch and shook off his caffeine withdrawal headache. He packed up his gear in record time and drove back toward the road through a wide natural path through the trees. He'd done some thinning here a few years back and cleared the underbrush, creating an open, old-growth feel to this particular stand. The tall Douglas firs added to that effect. Sometimes he hated having to harvest the grand old trees, but if he didn't, he'd starve. Besides, selling a little bit of the older growth kept him in business and thus protected the rest from the likes of Cal-Tex and their bulldozing ways.

He drove out the logging road and paused at the highway to listen for oncoming vehicles. Hearing none, he pulled onto the pavement, heading toward old man Patterson's general store in Twin Falls, a small town where few people knew him. He could buy supplies, and maybe find a pay phone—if one even existed anymore.

Lost in thought, he nearly collided head-on with an oncoming vehicle hugging the double-yellow center line around a blind curve. He swerved and braked, skidding to a stop in the loose dirt and gravel on the shoulder. Focused on avoiding the crash, he didn't get much of a look at the other vehicle, which disappeared behind him as if nothing had happened.

"What a jerk," he muttered. "Well, at least he didn't point a gun at me." He rested a moment, then edged his car back toward the pavement—

And just missed being sideswiped by another vehicle zooming around the curve behind him!

As with the near collision of a few moments before, the car sped out of view in an instant, as if the driver had never seen him. "Am I invisible today?" Lehigh said.

He kept his speed well below the limit. His hands shook but maintained a firm grip on the steering wheel. Hot sweat dampened the rim of his baseball cap. He took a few deep breaths and eased his truck back onto the highway, passing the spot where moments before the second vehicle had disappeared ahead of him at high speed.

Rounding a corner a few moments later, he spotted the vehicle, idling on the shoulder of the highway.

He slowed further and pulled in behind the car, a black Plymouth sedan with dark tinted windows. As his truck drew near, the Plymouth's engine roared and the car sped off, spitting gravel into Lehigh's front grill.

"What the hell?" He sat a moment, engine running, then shrugged. "Must've just been waiting to make sure I hadn't crashed." He pulled back onto the highway, still jittery, but managed to reach highway speed this time. The highway straightened, providing a forward view of several hundred yards. No black Plymouth in sight. "Well, he sure was in a hurry," he said.

About a mile later, he turned right at an old logging road that bisected another of his holdings and drove on to Twin Falls. There were a few other trucks in the general store's small lot, none that he recognized. A distracted teenage boy stood behind the cash register—also a stranger. Good. He made quick business of gathering his supplies: matches, fuel, a few replacement tent stakes, a small coil of rope, some groceries, and soap. He poured himself a cup of fresh weak coffee from the metal pots perched suggestively next to the donut rack while another customer checked out. He waited for the customer to leave, then approached the counter, head down, and grunted a semi-audible "hello" to the young cashier.

The kid rang up his goods. "Twenty-nine d-dollars and f-fifty-seven cents," he said.

Lehigh opened his wallet and sighed. Not enough cash. "You take credit cards?" he asked.

The boy shook his head. "We g-got an ATM in the b-back if you want."

"I'll be right back." Lehigh took a fifty dollar cash advance on his Visa and returned to the counter. He slipped the kid a twenty and two fives, and put the rest of the cash into his wallet.

"Here's your ch-change, s-sir." The kid handed him the coins. Lehigh thanked him and hurried out of the store. Approaching his truck, he froze in his tracks.

Two spots away from his truck sat a black Plymouth sedan.

Lehigh set his mouth in a line and strode straight to the Plymouth's driver's side. He rapped on the window with a key. The window powered down. A vaguely familiar man in a fedora and black sunglasses stared back at him.

"Do I know you?" Lehigh asked. The man shook his head. "Are you following me?" Again a shake of the head and no facial expression.

"Do you talk?" he asked.

The man turned away and the window rose back to its closed position.

Lehigh blew out a big breath between his lips, shook his head, and returned to his truck. He drove away, keeping his eye on the unmoving Plymouth, but no one exited or entered the car as he watched.

Half a mile away, it struck him: he'd forgotten to call Stacy. "Dammit!" He pounded the wheel. "Well, I ain't going back there. It'll just have to wait until tomorrow."

***

Inside Patterson's General Store, Thornburgh rapped the large, smooth onyx ring on his left hand on the service counter. "Hey, kid," he said, "What did that guy in the ball cap just buy?"

"I-I don't know, I-"

Thornburgh slammed his pudgy hand on the counter. "Don't blow smoke at me, kid. What'd he get? Ammo? Fuel? Come on, spill it."

"J-just some c-camping s-stuff," the kid replied. "C-coffee, tent stakes, m-matches—"

"Matches?" Thornburgh's lip curled into a mean smile. "Good, very good." He picked up a slip of paper off the floor. "Did he use the ATM?"

The kid nodded. "We don't t-take c-credit cards."

"You do take cash though, don't you?" Thornburgh slid two fifties onto the counter.

The kid looked at the money, then back at Thornburgh. "I d-don't understand."

Thornburgh leaned over the counter and stared into the kid's watery eyes. "I was never here this morning. Right?" He stuffed the bills into the kid's shirt pocket and the two of them nodded in unison. "Good boy. Now, what's your name?"

***

Stacy's home phone split the cold morning air like a fire alarm as she sat in front of her make-up mirror, applying eyeliner. Startled, she smudged an errant line across her eyelid. "Who could be calling me at six-thirty in the morning?"

"Stacy?" Anne-Marie's worried voice sounded tinny in her ear. "I'm sorry to wake you, but it's an emergency."

"I was awake." Stacy tried to keep the annoyance out of her voice, but she doubted her success. She reached for her coffee. "What's the emergency?"

"I'm not a hunnert per cent sure," Anne-Marie said, "but I think someone broke into the clinic last night."

"What?" Stacy slammed her coffee cup onto the dresser. Brown liquid spilled onto the existing circular stains in the bureau's fine mahogany finish. "Is anything damaged or missing?"

"The front door's broke." Anne-Marie's voice quivered. "The petty cash box is gone, and some medicines, I think. But the worst thing is—oh, Ms. McBride, I'm so sorry."

"What?" Stacy said again, almost a shout. "What else is wrong, Anne-Marie? Tell me, tell me!"

"Well…some of the cages were opened, and a few of the animals escaped."

"Oh, no!" Stacy's head ached. "Which ones?" She could already imagine the nightmare of telling the pet owners the news.

"Yes'm. Mrs. Hathaway's Labradoodle, the Dursten's six-year-old Siamese, those two little chihuahuas we just took in yesterday, and…and…I'm so sorry, Ms. McBride."

Stacy counted to five before asking again. She gripped her make-up table with white knuckles to steady herself. "And?"

"Miss…Mr. Carter's dog, ma'am. Lucky has escaped."

"Call the Sheriff," Stacy said. "Tell them everything you've told me. I'll be there as fast as I can. Don't touch anything."

"Yes'm. Uh, but, ma'am, there are a couple of animals still loose here in the clinic…"

Stacy sighed. "Of course, re-cage the animals first—and shut the door. But otherwise, leave everything as you see it."

"Yes'm. Ma'am, it's a mess."

"In more ways than one, Anne-Marie."

Stacy placed the receiver back in its cradle and popped two aspirin into her mouth, washing it down with a gulp of coffee. She winced at her reflection in the mirror, then stood. "Screw it," she said. "That's more than enough make-up for today." She poured the rest of her coffee down her wide-open throat and slammed the cup on the dresser. So much for breakfast. Throwing a hairbrush into her purse, she flew out her front door, letting it slam unlocked behind her.

Two diagonally-parked blue-and-white police cruisers occupied the clinic's three best parking spaces when she arrived. She sighed and parked alongside Anne-Marie's car. A uniformed deputy greeted her at the door.

"Morning, Miss McBride," he said. She knew him well. Jared Barkley had been a standout three-letter varsity athlete until a series of injuries sidelined him at the end of baseball season in his senior year of high school. Tall, sturdy, and clean-cut, he had remained in good shape in the nearly twenty years since graduation. Only a touch of gray lightened the black buzz-cut he still favored. He held the door open for her. "Looks like you've had a little excitement."

"Never a dull moment in Clarkesville." She chuckled. She'd written something very similar to that in his yearbook. He gave no sign of remembering the quip. She stepped inside the lobby and he hung up her coat for her.

"We've got a few questions, if you have a moment," Barkley said.

"I've got a few myself. How bad is the damage?" She led him back to her office.

Barkley shrugged. "Not so bad. Insurance will likely cover most of it. Ms. McBride, have you had any trouble recently with any of your customers?"

"No, Jared. Things have been pretty quiet on that front."

"Ms. McBride–"

"Stacy, please. After all the years I've known you." She offered him a seat, which he accepted.

"Stacy, that money donated a while back. That was cash, wasn't it?"

She nodded. "Fifty thousand. But that went straight to the bank that same morning. I'd never keep that kind of money around here."

"I figured," he said, "but the person who broke in may not have. Your cash box was stolen. Do you know how much was in there?"

She pulled a ledger out of her top desk drawer. "We balance it daily. Last night it had sixty-four dollars and twelve cents." She closed the book. "We accept payment mostly in checks and credit cards these days. We never keep more than a hundred bucks on hand, if we can help it."

"Wise policy." He jotted something on his notepad, then paused. "I understand some animals are missing, including a stray?"

"A stray? Oh, you must mean Lucky. She's actually Lehigh Carter's dog."

"We'll be checking with each of the owners as soon as possible. Do you have a number for Mr. Carter? I heard about his house fire, so I don't suppose I can reach him there."

She scribbled on a scrap of paper. "Here's his cell number. But I'll warn you, he hasn't been answering it lately. I haven't been able to reach him for several days."

Barkley's eyebrow arched high on his forehead. "He's gone missing?"

She shrugged. "Let's just say he's been hard to reach."

Barkley studied her a moment, then stood and took the number from her. "If Mr. Carter does call—please, be in touch right away."

Her eyes grew wide. "You're not saying he's a suspect? Lehigh couldn't have–"

"All I'm saying, Ms. McBride—Stacy—is that I need to speak to him as soon as possible." He tipped his hat, nodded once, and strode through her office door.

***

"Paul, why do you keep calling me?" Stacy blew an exasperated breath into her desk phone. She'd gotten very little work done all morning due to the commotion over the break-in, the scramble to recover escaped pets, and the avalanche of cancellations and pet evacuations that streamed in once the news broke.

"I have some information I thought you might appreciate," Paul replied. "It's about your good friend Lehigh Carter. Or don't you want to know his whereabouts anymore?"

Stacy's heart stopped for a moment. When she regained her composure, her words came in a torrent.

"Of course I want to know! Where is he? Have you seen him? Is he all right? Was his dog with him? Did you talk to him? Where–"

"Slow down!" Paul laughed. Traffic noises sounded in the background. "One question at a time. I don't know the answer to all of them, but this much I can tell you. Your friend Carter was seen in the vicinity of your clinic around 5:30 this morning, in his pickup truck."

"By the clinic? Are you sure? What was he doing? Did you see–"

"Hold on, hold on," Paul said. "I didn't see him, but an, ah, associate of mine did. He was dressed in a red flannel shirt, a blue baseball cap, and jeans. He looked like he hadn't shaved in a couple of days. As far as what he was doing, I can't say. But didn't you have some trouble at the clinic this morning? Something about a break-in?"

Stacy sighed for the hundredth time of the morning and leaned forward, her open palm supporting her aching head, elbows propped on the desk. "Yes, we did. But surely you don't think Lehigh had anything to do with it."

"Me? Oh, no, I don't think he has the balls to try anything so bold. But the Sheriff—hold on, I need to set the phone down a sec."

"The Sheriff!" Stacy straightened in her chair. "What did you tell the Sheriff? Paul? Hello, are you there?" Paul chuckled on the other end of the line, but then all sound was muffled.

After a few seconds, Paul's voice returned. "Sorry, I needed to downshift. Too many morons on the road these days! Anyway, it seems the police are looking for him."

"What did you say to them?" Her voice reached a fever pitch.

"Only what I just told you."

"You make it sound—I don't know, sinister. What are you up to?"

"Oh, nothing. Just trying to be helpful." He laughed again.

"Paul van Paten, I swear, if the police suspect Lehigh because of you, I'll–I'll–"

"Now, sugar, calm down. I assure you, I'm only looking out for you. I sure hope nothing I said would raise the suspicion of the law against your friend." With a cackling laugh, Paul closed the connection.

"Pig!" Stacy slammed down the phone. Then, remembering where she was, she buried her head in her hands amidst the pile of papers crowding her messy desk.

***

Minutes later, a knock came at Stacy's door. She lifted her aching head out of her hands and shook her shoulders all around. "Yes?"

"Ms. McBride," Anne-Marie's worried voice stole through the door. "There's something wrong with some of the dogs. I think you should come see."

Stacy bolted through the door and sped by Anne-Marie toward the kennels. "Which dogs?" she asked.

"Two of the ones that were let loose in the break-in. Mrs. Huckaby's Bijon-Frisé and that Border-Aussie mix from Cooper Auto."

"Damn!" Stacy said. "I was afraid of that." She burst through the swinging doors into the kennels. Anne-Marie trailed behind. Dr. Lewis tended to the Bijon-Frisé on a stainless steel table in the center of the room. Lying on its side with a black tongue hanging out of its panting mouth and eyes peering through thin brown slits, the dog did not look at all well.

"What's the verdict, Doctor?" Stacy asked.

Dr. Lewis turned, her face a mirror of Stacy's worry. "Poison. Probably rat poison. I have volunteers searching the facility. Agnes might get through it," she said, pointing to the sheepdog in a nearby kennel, "but I'm afraid that Teddy here is not faring so well."

Stacy fought down a wave of nausea along with the anger ready to burst from her veins. "Who would do such a vile thing?"

"Ms. McBride," came a new voice from the doorway. Amy, a young volunteer whose auburn ponytail curved over the shoulder of her blue scrubs, waited for Stacy's attention.

"What now?" Stacy snapped. "Oh, I'm sorry, Amy. What is it?"

"Jared Barkley from the sheriff's office just called. He wants to know if you've seen or heard from Mr. Carter."

"Tell him no, but I'll be in touch as soon as I do."

Amy nodded. "He said to tell you one more thing." She hesitated, red-faced and trembling.

"Yes? What did he say?"

Amy swallowed a few times and wrung her hands. "He said to tell you that they've put out an all-points bulletin for Mr. Carter. Sheriff's orders. Ma'am, they mean to arrest him. They think he's done all this."

"That's insane," Stacy said. "Lehigh would never do such a thing."

"Yes'm. Would you like me to ring him back for you? I told him about the sick dogs."

"No, thank you. I'll call him myself."

"Yes'm." Amy cleared her throat. "Dr. Lewis? I found something."

Dr. Lewis turned away from the ailing canine to face Amy. "What is it, dear?"

Amy held out an empty carton of rat poison. "It was in the trash, along with some hamburger packaging from Safeway. One of those five-pound tubes, the cheap kind."

"No actual poison itself?" Dr. Lewis asked. Stacy slumped into a chair.

"No'm. I hope it's okay that I told Sergeant Barkley about this, too. He's going to send somebody over for it."

"That's fine," Stacy said, her voice wary. "Let me know when they arrive." She dropped her head all the way back and stared at the ceiling. "My God," she said. "What else could possibly go wrong today?"

CHAPTER 18

Lehigh pitched camp mid-morning near a stream cutting through a deep ravine on the east side of his property, the side closer to town and not far from the spot on the highway where he'd first spotted Lucky. If the dog headed that way once, she might do it again.

He needed a bath. After six days in the woods, he could no longer stand his own odor. He walked downstream along the bank to where the stream collected into a calm pool and dipped his hand into the water. Damn! Too cold. Frigid, even. Okay, Plan B—a warm sponge-off. Dicey—he'd have to build a fire and risk discovery. He filled a pair of canteens and returned to camp.

Despite his trepidations, he built a relatively smokeless fire, heated a small pot of water, and sponged off without incident. He made coffee, cooked some oatmeal and fried up a slab of bacon—his best meal in a week.

After eating, he doused the fire and, pushing his luck a little, opted not to break camp. His goal for the day was to find Lucky, and he needed to give the dog a chance to find him, too. That meant staying still. Bears were always a risk, but they tended not to wander this close to town, so he felt safe leaving a little kibble and leftover bacon out as bait.

His search of the immediate vicinity proved fruitless, and he expanded his exploration with slow, ever-widening circles. He didn't dare return to the road in daylight. He'd finally connected the face of the man at the store with the payola mishap. With thugs like Thornburgh wandering around, he couldn't afford to present any sort of open target. As a result he had to search on foot. He called and whistled for Lucky every few minutes, but that just scared away a few deer and countless squirrels, birds, and rabbits. His energy faded and his pace slowed. Still he trudged on, munching only on a small bag of trail mix and a few swigs of water from a canteen. His hunger grew, but no doubt it paled by comparison to what Lucky must have been suffering. His campsite's stockpile still boasted several cans of tuna fish, some baked beans, beef jerky and dried fruits. Not elegant dining, but a feast compared to an injured dog's late-autumn scrounging.

By the time the afternoon sun broke through the thick blanket of clouds, the rumbling in his stomach echoed louder than his footsteps. Sunset neared and his legs ached from constant walking over the uneven forest floor. Disappointed and exhausted, he returned to camp at dusk—and found it in a shambles.

His tent lay flat on the ground. The bowl of bait had been knocked over, and his clothes and other belongings lay scattered asunder. "Damned raccoons!" He gathered his belongings.

He picked up the aluminum bowl that had held the kibble. As he straightened, his eye caught a glint of chrome a few feet away. Still bent over, he took a couple of steps closer. He picked up a small metal object and stared at it.

"You're alive!" he whispered. He closed his fist around Lucky's ID tag. "You found me!" He closed his eyes in silent thanks, then opened them, searching the horizon.

"Lucky!" he shouted. "Where are you?"

But the silent forest gave no answer.

He searched the site for more clues of Lucky's whereabouts. About fifty feet from the tent, he discovered small tufts of yellow fur, and amidst the fur, an unbuckled dog collar. He recognized it as hers immediately. Picking it up, red liquid darkened his fingertips. Dried blood also speckled the occasional fur tuft on the ground.

"What did you get into, Lucky?" he said. "Did you pull those stitches out again? Or did you wrassle a raccoon...or some other critter?"

He sat on his haunches, searching the ground for more clues. A small tan and white object caught his eye. Leaning over, he reached it easily and held it in his fingers. "Well, Lucky," he said, "unless you've developed some awfully bad habits, I'd say you had human company." He dropped the half-smoked cigarette back to the ground, next to a scrap of cellophane and a spent match—trash that should have blown away in the early morning's steady wind. The litterbug's visit had been recent.

As recent as the dog's, anyway. Maybe—probably—simultaneous.

"I don't like this," he mumbled. An ache formed in his gut. "I don't like this at all."

He cleaned up the campsite, removing every trace, including the cigarette. He set the collar on his truck's dashboard and drove toward town.

He'd driven less than a mile when red and blue lights flashed in his rear-view mirror. He pulled over and rolled down his window, waiting.

"Please step outside of the vehicle, sir." Sheriff Buck Summers stood a few feet away from his pickup, about even with the front of the bed, with his right hand on his hip—close to his unsnapped holster.

"Okay," Lehigh called out. "I'm coming." He unlatched the door.

"Slowly!" Summers called back.

Lehigh paused with the door ajar a few inches, then eased it open with his left arm. He swung both feet into the Sheriff's view, then slid to the ground, arms wide. After waiting a moment, he took two slow steps away from the truck.

"Are you Lehigh Carter?" Summers asked.

"God's sakes, Buck, you've known me for twenty years."

"Just following protocol," he said. "Mr. Carter, you're under arrest."

***

He used his one phone call to reach Stacy. She answered her cell on the first ring.

"Hey there, darlin'," he said as if he were inviting her over for ice cream.

"Lehigh!" she exclaimed. "Oh, my God. I'm so glad to hear your voice. I've been so worried about you!"

"I've missed you too." For a moment he found it hard to speak. "I'm in a bit of a bind at the moment, though."

"What kind of a bind? Are you okay?"

"I'm fine," he said in a weary voice. "But, um…well, honey, I don't know how else to say this. I'm gonna need you to bail me out of jail."

Stacy drove like a NASCAR champion across town to the county lockup where Lehigh was being held on charges of arson, breaking and entering, vandalism, and cruelty to animals. "It's a wonder they didn't throw in jaywalking and terrorism," she snapped to Donna. Her friend had insisted on joining her, ostensibly for moral support, but more likely to keep Stacy from killing someone.

"Don't give them any ideas," Donna said. "Cops love to trump up the charges so they have a bargaining chip in court. They do that all the time on TV. Whoa! Easy, girl."

"The whole thing's ridiculous." Stacy's tires squealed around a corner. Donna held her stomach, her face white. Stacy gunned the engine again. "Lehigh had no motive to do any of this. Why would he burn his own house down? Why poison dogs? The whole thing stinks of a setup!" She blared her horn at an idiot driver going only five over the speed limit. "Get out of my way!" She banged on the steering wheel.

"Easy, girl," Donna said. "Let's get there in one piece. Now who would've set him up? Paul?"

"Paul, or his cronies. Who else?" Stacy smacked the horn again and hit the brake so she wouldn't rear-end the moron forcing her to tail-gate. Donna bounced off her shoulder strap into her seat, then braced herself against the door. Not that it would help much.

Stacy's cell phone rang. She answered it over Donna's protest.

"You rotten son of a bitch!" she shouted into the phone. "If

I find out you had anything to do with this—"

"Easy, easy," Paul said. "While I share the Sheriff's suspicions of your mountain man-friend, I'm not the one with any pull around here. You can look a lot closer to home for that."

"Are you saying my father accused him?" Stacy's voice hit screech level, and Donna winced, still braced in her seat. Somehow, Stacy's driving got even worse while talking on her cell phone. "Why would Daddy do a thing like that?"

"Oh, I don't know," Paul said in an oily voice. "Maybe he's just concerned about his daughter's well-being and safety. I mean, if the guy's crazy enough to poison dogs and burn his own property—"

"Lehigh did not poison or burn anything!" Stacy yelled. "You mean, vengeful bastard. You put Daddy up to this, didn't you? You fed him lies, knowing the cops would jump if he snapped his fingers. Oh, I hate you!" She ended the call and thumped her phone down on the seat, then whipped the steering wheel hard right to avoid colliding with an oncoming car. "If that thing rings, and it's Paul, throw it out the window."

"With pleasure," Donna said. "Now, slow down!"

Stacy's phone rang again about a mile away from county lockup. Donna glanced at the caller ID screen. "It's your dad," she said with a sigh. "Do you want to take it?"

Stacy grabbed the phone from her. "Daddy!" she exclaimed. "Have you heard? They've arrested Lehigh."

"Well, that is good news." The Senator's voice boomed loud in Stacy's ear. "You, and this entire community, are much safer with that violent criminal behind bars."

Stacy took a hard right turn much too fast. "Violent criminal? Are you crazy?"

Donna rolled her eyes. "Seems to run in the family," she muttered.

"Well, things do look mighty suspicious for him, you have to admit," McBride said. "First his house burns down, and his dog goes missing—and we all know his history with dogs."

"He loves that dog!" Stacy slammed on her brakes again.

Donna went white and closed her eyes, mumbling a prayer Stacy half-remembered from childhood.

"Hmph," the Senator said. "Then why did he try to poison it? You have to admit, he did disappear at a rather inopportune time."

"He was being stalked, Daddy. Paul is somehow behind all this. So if you really want to find some suspicious, violent characters, you need look no further than your campaign treasurer."

"That's ridiculous," McBride said. "Why, Paul is a perfect gentle–"

"Stacy! Stop!" Donna yelled. "Red light!"

Once again Stacy's brakes squealed. Her car lurched to a halt some four feet across the white line marking the intersection.

"Daddy," she breathed hard into the phone, "you are blind when it comes to Paul. I can't believe I was ever involved with him myself." Donna nodded emphatically.

"You're the blind one," McBride said. "Carter's a menace. I'm happy he's off the streets."

"Don't celebrate too much. He'll be out of that jail cell in ten minutes, I promise you."

"Or five," Donna said, holding her stomach.

"What?" McBride said. "Stacy, you don't plan on posting his bail?"

"I do." She zoomed around a Volkswagen in a no-passing zone.

"That's lunacy!"

"The only lunacy is that he was accused in the first place. I can't believe you'd do this to me."

"It's for your own safety, and the safety of this community. You'll thank me for this someday."

"My safety? Don't you mean, the safety of your stupid campaign?" She hung up the phone and tossed it to Donna. "Add Daddy to the list of people to toss this thing for."

"Happily." Donna turned off the phone. "Now calm down. The Sheriff's office is just a couple of blocks away. I don't recommend that you go in there mad."

Stacy ignored Donna's advice and stormed into the building ready to tear someone's head off. "I'm here to bail Lehigh Carter out of jail," she said to the deputy behind the reception desk. She didn't shout, but her voice dripped with venom.

Deputy Dwayne Latner limped a few steps from his seat behind the counter to a computer screen and clicked on the keyboard for a few moments. "How do you spell Lehigh?" he asked.

"L-E-H-I-G-H. For heaven's sake, how many Carters did you arrest today?" Stacy thumped her purse onto the counter and gripped it with whitening fingers.

"Ah, yes. Well, I have good news. Mr. Carter won't require bail—yet. You see, he hasn't yet been officially charged, much less arraigned. The bad news..." Latner paused to take a long look over his horn-rimmed glasses. "He's still being questioned, so it'll be a while."

"How long?" Stacy asked.

Dwayne shrugged. "Depends on the questions, and the answers. I'll let them know you're here. You are...?"

"Haven't we met? Like, a dozen times or more?" Stacy fumed, watching the deputy's expressionless face scan the screen. "I'm Stacy McBride. Daughter of Senator George McBride, the next governor of Oregon."

"I don't care if you're the daughter of Frankenstein," Latner said. "It won't change a thing. They'll be done when they're done. Have a seat, Miss McBride. I'll let you know when something changes."

Donna tugged at her arm. "Come on, Stacy. There's an espresso shop across the street. Let me buy you an egg nog latte."

Stacy shook her arm free. "I'm not leaving until Lehigh does."

"That could be a while," the deputy said. "You might as well get the coffee. In fact," he said, reaching for his wallet, "would you mind bringing me back a mocha?"

Stacy stared at him, mouth hanging open. "That's bold."

Latner shrugged and put his wallet away. "Sorry. Just thought

I'd ask. They make a great mocha over there."

Stacy left her cell number with the deputy and allowed Donna to drag her across the street. Mo's Mochas boasted a crowded, slender service counter and a row of chipped Formica-topped tables, each just large enough to hold a cup or two of coffee and a donut. A half-dozen patrons formed a line that extended out the front door.

"Good thing we have lots of time," Stacy said.

"Oh, chin up." Donna gave her a quick side-hug. "Things could be a lot worse. At least he's not going to jail...yet."

"No, but I know a few people who should be," Stacy said. "Starting with Paul van Paten."

Donna giggled. A few patrons in line turned to stare for a moment. "Shh," Donna said. "You never know who his friends are."

"Oh yes I do," Stacy said. "They all have lots of money."

***

The blond man with the crew cut made an abrupt decision to surrender his coveted place in line for Clarkesville's best mocha and bolted for the door, nearly colliding with the two whispering women who had mentioned his boss's name. Moving away from the door, he speed-dialed his cell phone.

"Bad news about Carter," he said. "I don't think the cops are going to keep him."

***

The police released Lehigh about an hour later after questioning him repeatedly about his recent whereabouts. Buck Summers, Jared Barkley and a frumpy, graying detective named Wadsworth took turns giving him the third degree, but Lehigh's story remained consistent. "Don't leave town," Wadsworth said after Latner returned his belongings. "I'm sure we'll want to talk again soon."

"Do you have a place to stay?" asked Barkley.

"He'll be staying with me," Stacy piped in before Lehigh could reply. "I'll keep him close." Lehigh caught the glint in her eye and smiled for the first time all day.

"It's sure good to see you," he said once they left the building. "I have so much to tell you. I don't even know where to begin."

"Start with 'I'm sorry for ditching you and disappearing for several days,' and we'll go from there." She wrapped her arms around his chest and hugged him, her chin draped over his shoulder from behind. "You crazy fool. You had me worried sick."

Lehigh gestured behind him toward the Sheriff's office. "For good reason, I guess."

"I'm sure you two have a lot to discuss...in private," Donna said from the back seat. "So, why don't you get me home so you can get started?"

Lehigh fed them the basics of his outdoor life of the previous several days, becoming most animated when he revealed evidence of Lucky at his campsite. "I just wish I'd seen her," he said.

"Lehigh, Lucky's okay," Stacy said, excited. "Or at least she was. She showed up at the clinic the other day. But then–"

"Someone broke in, right?" Lehigh said. "And Lucky ran away. The cops thought I'd done it. Stacy, she only runs away from serious danger—like the house fire. I suspect she ran from the clinic for the same reason."

"Smart dog," Donna said. "Some of the others got poisoned."

"The cops questioned me about that, too." Lehigh turned to face Donna. "I reckon Lucky recognized the men and ran. Which means, they may be the same guys that burned my house down."

"But why attack the clinic?" Stacy asked.

"To set me up. These guys are dead set on getting rid of me—and I don't think they're done. Which is why I took off last week, Stacy." Lehigh turned back toward her, the corners of his mouth and eyes sagging. "I couldn't keep putting you in danger. And I won't now. Which is why I can't accept your offer of a place to stay."

"Baloney. You're staying with me. We promised the detectives."

"I can't, Stacy."

"I insist."

"Insist all you want. I'm going to a motel."

"In what vehicle? Not mine."

He stared at her. "I'd assumed you'd bring me to get my truck out of impoundment."

She shook her head. "Only if you promise to stay with me."

"That's dirty pool."

Donna's cackling diverted Lehigh's attention. "Welcome to planet McBride," she said. "They have their own rules."

After a moment, Lehigh grinned. "All right," he said. "I guess you've got me over a barrel."

Stacy flashed him a wicked smile. "Not yet," she said in a low voice, "but I like the way you think."

Donna roared with laughter. Lehigh's face warmed and he pretended to take a sudden interest in roadside vegetation.

Stacy dropped Donna off at her place, then backtracked toward her own house. Lehigh's brow furrowed a few minutes into the return trip.

"What's the matter?" Stacy squeezed his hand.

"That black Plymouth in back of us. Wasn't it following us on the way to Donna's, too?"

Stacy glanced in the rear-view mirror and shrugged. "Might've been. I haven't been paying close attention. Are you sure you're not just hyper-suspicious right now?"

Lehigh's face broke into a wry smile. "Maybe. I just want to be careful. Hey, we should turn right up here."

"To see if they follow us?"

"Well, more important, to see if, by pure luck, my truck is still on the side of the highway where they arrested me."

Stacy made the turn, and Lehigh swiveled to watch the car behind them. It slowed at the intersection, but continued past. Lehigh let out a sigh of relief. "I guess I'm just being paranoid."

Some minutes later, Lehigh held her arm. "There—up ahead. That's my truck." Stacy pulled in behind it. Banners plastered on the front and rear windshields read: "TOW—DO NOT DRIVE."

Lehigh groaned. "This is ridiculous."

Stacy grabbed her cell phone, looked through her call history, and pressed the "Send" button.

"Who are you calling?" Lehigh asked.

She spoke into the phone. "May I speak to Deputy Jared Barkley?"

Lehigh waited while Stacy navigated the police bureaucracy, finding answers to the question of whether they could drive the truck. He admired her creative tenacity, always polite, sometimes flirty, insistent but not pushy. Finally she hung up.

"They're sending a deputy right away," she said. "We're lucky. Somebody forgot to tell the towing company to haul your truck to impound. You probably won't have to pay any fees."

"Probably?" he said. "If they didn't tow it, that seems pretty cut and dried."

"You'd think," she said. "But if life with George McBride taught me anything, it's that government policies often make very little sense."

"If your father's willing to fix that," Lehigh said, "maybe I'll vote for him after all."

"Wow," Stacy said. "I'm going to check the temperature outside. I think Hell just froze over."

Lehigh pulled her close. They sat quietly for several minutes in her car. A car whizzed by. Lehigh sat upright. "There's that Plymouth again!" he said.

"The one that was following us?"

He nodded. Once the black Plymouth disappeared from sight, he got out of Stacy's car and strode to his pickup. A moment later he pounded the hood, then turned to Stacy, who had followed him.

"I'm not so sure that leaving my car here was an accident." He pointed to the passenger side door. Glass covered the seat of the truck, and the window was missing. Another damned window repair. He'd spent a fortune at Cascade Glass in the past month.

He squinted in the direction the Plymouth had gone, then spat. "No wonder they knew how to find us so fast."

Deputy Barkley arrived soon after and released the truck to Lehigh's possession. Lehigh filed a report about the broken window, but the deputy gave him little hope of finding the culprit. "Could've been anyone," Barkley said. "All's we really know is that they didn't want to steal it. Otherwise we'd be searching chop shops in Portland by now."

Lehigh drove it straight to the repair shop and waved off Stacy's suggestion of filing an insurance claim. "It's gonna be way under my deductible," he said. He took inventory and discovered that the thieves had stolen some random camping gear from the back of the pickup.

He shook his head in wonder. A five dollar dog dish, Lucky's collar, a length of rope, and a twenty-dollar lantern were gone, but the thieves left a five hundred dollar tent undisturbed. "Obviously," the mechanic said, "they didn't know what they were doing."

"I'm not so sure," he said to the mechanic's puzzled stare.

He spent the afternoon catching up on things he'd pushed aside while hiding out in the woods—mail, recharging his cell phone, checking messages, and dealing with the fire insurance claim. By the time Stacy got home at six o'clock, he was exhausted. "I've had easier days chopping wood and clearing brush," he said over a quick dinner in front of the TV. "I don't know how people in offices do it."

"I wouldn't mind going to bed a little early," Stacy said with a mischievous smile. She rubbed his shoulders with her free hand, balancing a glass of red wine in the other. "I can promise you a more comfy bed than you've slept in lately."

He pulled her close for a long, passionate kiss. "I'm not quite ready to sleep just yet."

"Who's talking about sleep?" She giggled and tugged at his belt. "I only suggested an early bedtime."

He let out a low growl, sprang to his feet, and lifted her into his arms. She screeched naughty laughter as he buried his face into her chest and hauled her into her bedroom, kicking the door shut behind them.

***

Lehigh woke from a blissful slumber some hours later, listening to the rain drip off clogged gutters in sync with Stacy's deep, regular breathing. After a few moments he heard a thump and the sound of a car door closing and remembered that they'd left the TV on. "I'm gonna go turn everything off," he whispered in her ear. She made no response. He smiled. Such a sound sleeper. He could get used to that.

He pulled on a robe before heading into the main room. Stacy often left her blinds open, and no sense flashing the neighbors, even if they were too far away to see anything. He turned off the TV mid-commercial, locked the front door, then flicked the outside light switch to "off."

Then on. Off and on again, a couple more times. The amount of outside light flooding in the window remained unchanged.

"Bulb must be burned out," he mumbled. No matter. He grabbed a replacement from the coat closet. He opened the door, bulb in hand, and stopped in his tracks, staring in shock at the lump of golden fur lying prostrate on the darkened front steps.

CHAPTER 19

Lehigh knelt down and touched the dog's golden fur. The body felt cold and rigid. He scanned the ID tag. Sure enough, it read "Lucky."

"Somebody's got a sick sense of humor." Lehigh shook his head in disgust.

"Who does?" Stacy's voice preceded her to the doorway. She shivered barefoot in a flimsy pink robe. "Why are you squatting there with the door open? It's freezing!"

Lehigh leaned to one side so she could see around him. Her jaw dropped and her eyes swelled with tears. "Lucky?"

"Not unless she's had a sex change operation recently." He pointed to the dog's groin, clearly evincing male body parts. He removed the dog's name tag and held it up so she could see it. "What we have here is an imposter."

Stacy moaned and leaned against the wall, head in hands. He shut the door and pulled her close. They hugged for a minute, maybe two, swaying in a slow silent rhythm. "Why is this happening?" she asked after a while. "Who hates us so much?"

"I got a theory or two about that," he said, "but you ain't gonna like it."

She sniffled, then held her head back so she could see his eyes. Her lips worked a moment or two before she spoke. Finally the word came. "Paul?"

"Who else?" He squeezed her by the hips and held her eyes in his gaze. "Look, I seriously doubt the police would find a single fingerprint—Paul's or anyone else's—on that collar. But this was done at his bidding, if not by his own hand. Just like the break-in at the clinic, and the fire at my house. I'm certain of it."

"But what proof do we have?"

"None. That's the problem."

A loud knock sounded on the door. They exchanged quizzical looks. "Who would come a-knockin' in the middle of the night?" he asked.

The knock sounded again. "Ms. McBride? It's Officer Barkley. If you're up, could you open up, please?"

Stacy stepped to the door and flung it open. Two uniformed deputies framed the doorway. Barkley dropped his gaze to her feet, but his partner gawked at her.

"Jared?" she asked. "What's the matter?"

"Sorry to disturb you, ma'am," Barkley said. "We got a complaint about some animal cruelty—ah, Mr. Carter." He nodded at Lehigh over her shoulder. "Sir, the complaint actually involves you."

"Does it involve the dog at your feet?" Lehigh asked.

Barkley shot him a puzzled stare, glanced to the ground, and returned his gaze to Lehigh. "Sir? I don't understand."

Lehigh and Stacy checked the doorstep again. The dog's body was gone.

"Well, that's weird," Lehigh said.

"What's weird?" Barkley raised an eyebrow. "And what do you know about the dog?"

"Why don't you come in, Officers?" Stacy said.

"Thank you, Ms. McBride." The two deputies followed Stacy into the living room. Lehigh stepped aside so that the two men could pass, then closed the door behind them. After stammering a moment, Barkley pulled a sheet of paper from his jacket pocket. "I should advise you both that I have a warrant to search the premises." He held the paper out to Stacy.

She unfolded the page and scanned it quickly. "I don't get it," she said. "Was there a complaint filed against me for some reason?"

Barkley nodded. "We got an anonymous tip. A witness saw or heard something that led them to believe an animal—well, to be exact, a dog—was being mistreated on these premises."

"What? When?" Stacy and Lehigh said in unison.

"Earlier this evening. Do you mind if I look around while I ask questions?"

Stacy frowned. "Actually," she said, "if you don't mind, I'd love to get dressed first. I don't feel quite comfortable chatting here in my nightie."

"Of course," Barkley said. "But I'll need to check that room before you go in there."

"Jared? What the–" Stacy glared at him. "Fine," she said. "How about the bathroom? Can I use that, or do you want to make sure I haven't flushed a Chihuahua down the toilet first?"

Lehigh choked back a laugh, and even Barkley grinned. "I think we're looking for a larger dog than that," the other deputy said.

The house search took under fifteen minutes. Lehigh made coffee while Stacy changed into jeans, a sweatshirt, and tennis shoes, then he did the same. "Coffee?" he offered all around when the pot stopped sputtering.

"I'd love some, thanks," Barkley said. "Black, two sugars." Lehigh handed him a steaming mug a moment later. Barkley sipped it and nodded with approval. "You make it strong, like my Ma used to."

"Careful. There might be dog poison in it," Stacy said.

Barkley hesitated mid-sip, then chuckled. "Lucky I'm not a dog, I guess."

"Where else do you need to look?" Lehigh sat next to Stacy on her sofa and caressed her leg with his free hand.

"Outdoors." Barkley's gaze lingered on the spot where Lehigh's hand squeezed Stacy's knee. "Can you put a light on, please?" He pulled his flashlight from his belt. "If not, I'll make do."

"I'll get it." Lehigh gave Stacy's leg one more squeeze. "But I think it's a waste of time."

Lehigh showed Barkley to the back door and flicked on the light. "It's kind of dim, but..." His voice trailed off as he stared out the window.

"Something wrong?" Barkley took a big swallow of coffee, set his nearly-empty mug on the counter, and opened the back door.

In a hole next to a pile of fresh dirt, a yellow dog lay as still as a mountain pond.

"That dog was on the front steps a few minutes before you arrived," Lehigh explained some ten minutes later. They had rejoined Stacy in the living room with refilled coffee cups and a fresh sense of worry.

"Who moved it out back, then?" Barkley's partner asked.

"Whoever dropped it on the steps, I reckon," Lehigh said. "They probably ran when they saw your car pull up. Otherwise the dog would've been buried by now."

"Unless their intention was to leave it in plain view for the police to see," Stacy said. "Didn't you say you were responding to an anonymous tip? I bet the same folks who killed and moved the dog called it in—but got their timing wrong. This whole thing is nothing but a frame-up."

"I'm inclined to agree," Barkley said, "since it isn't your dog. Still, I wish I'd checked the bathroom before you used it." To Stacy's puzzled stare, he explained, "To see if there was dirt from the yard present—in the sink, or on the towels. Not that I don't believe you, but it's something I wish I could say I checked first. Sheriff Summers will chew me out for that."

"What's next?" Lehigh asked.

"We'll bring the dog in for an autopsy, and we'll need to dust the shovels out there for prints. You, too," he indicated to Lehigh and Stacy.

"That's ridiculous!" Stacy said. "Are you charging me with a crime?"

"They're her tools," Lehigh said. "Her prints will be all over them."

"Of course," Barkley said. "But once we eliminate yours, we can work with any others that show up to identify the culprit. That goes for the dog's collar, too."

"Makes sense," Lehigh said. "But you didn't answer Stacy's question. Are we suspects?"

"I'm not arresting you," Barkley said. "My superiors may disagree, but it's my call. In fact, my inclination is to try to keep the details of this quiet. Whoever is doing this is getting desperate to mess with you two, and he's going to make a mistake soon."

"A mistake?" Lehigh asked.

"Such as revealing knowledge of this incident he shouldn't know. Or the anonymous complainer might call back, wondering why nothing's been done, and maybe we can learn more. You two should keep mum, too, by the way."

"Agreed," Lehigh said, and Stacy nodded. "If that's possible."

***

"We have good news and bad news," Brian Kelly told Lehigh in a meeting at the insurance office a few days later. "The good news is that you should be able to rebuild and refurnish your home with very little money out of pocket, particularly if you do a lot of the work yourself."

"And the bad news?" Lehigh steeled himself for the worst.

Kelly grimaced. "So long as you're still officially under investigation for the arson charges, we can't award you a dime."

"But that could take months—maybe years!" Lehigh's skin warmed from the top of his forehead to his shirt collar, and he clenched his fists in his lap.

"I'm sorry," Kelly said. "You understand our position."

"You should understand mine!" Lehigh stomped around the cramped office, searching for something to maul. "I have no home, my business records are destroyed, and now I'm a suspect in a burglary and the death of a damned dog. My own dog is missing, my business is a shambles..." He leaned over Kelly's desk, his neck muscles taut. "I pay my premiums on time. I'm entitled to that insurance money, and you sumbitches–"

"Please, calm down." Kelly indicated the chair and waited for Lehigh to sit. In a soothing, monotonic voice, he said, "I understand why you'd be upset. But when you look at it logically, you'll understand. The law clearly spells out the procedure here."

"Damned right I'm upset," Lehigh said, but Kelly's even demeanor had helped calm him. "I'm powerless. I have no recourse."

"Well, you have some," Kelly said. "Your grand jury trial is next week, isn't that right?"

Lehigh stared at him. "What are you talking about?"

"Your arson case. Haven't you received a subpoena?"

Lehigh shook his head. "Remember, my house burned down. I haven't received any mail in weeks."

"This should have been served to you in person, by a county deputy."

"Where? I've been living in a tent until a few nights ago. I'd have expected the cops would've told me that when they had me locked in their little room, asking me all those questions."

"Mr. Carter, have you even spoken to a lawyer?"

Lehigh shook his head again. "I don't even know one."

Kelly pulled a business card from his Rolodex and handed it to Lehigh. "I'm not supposed to do this, but I like you, Mr. Carter. So, here. Call this guy. He's the best."

Lehigh glanced at the card, did a double-take, and burst out laughing.

"What's so funny?" Kelly asked.

Lehigh slid the card back across the adjuster's desk and stood. "I do know this guy," he said. "I don't think I'd get a very fair trial if he were my lawyer."

"Why not? He's very good."

Lehigh smirked and put on his ball cap. "Because," he said, "I don't believe I'd be well-represented by the man who still calls my girlfriend his fiancée. In fact, I believe this man—Mr. Paul van Paten—is trying to kill me."

***

"Paul knows everybody at the sheriff's office," Stacy said to Lehigh later that evening. Her paring knife whacked through carrots with loud slaps onto a wooden cutting board. "He practically owns the place. I'm certain he had a hand in this."

"They said they tried serving me the subpoena at my house, which is stupid, since they're accusing me of burning it down." Lehigh's spittle sprayed the countertop next to her. He wiped it off with a shirt sleeve. "Then they tried here, so they say. Did anyone ever come here looking for me while I was out?"

"Never." She shoved a carrot slice into his mouth. "At least, not while I was here. I tell you, if I do find out that Paul is behind this, I will get him disbarred."

"That sumbitch, he better hope I never find him alone in the forest someday." Lehigh smacked a fist into his open palm. "I've had about enough of him."

"How did it go with the lawyer? Daddy says he's one of the best." She mixed the veggies into a salad in a large wooden bowl between them.

"Hah! That's what the insurance guy said about Paul."

"He is good at what he does." She took him by the hand and led him into the living room.

"He's good at being a pain in the butt."

Stacy pushed him onto the couch, then covered his body with hers and squeezed him hard. "I'm sorry. I've brought you nothing but trouble since…well, you know."

Lehigh chuckled and held her even tighter. "So ironic, isn't it?"

"What's ironic?"

"I find a dog we name 'Lucky', and ever since I've had nothing but bad luck."

She swatted the air in front of his nose. "Nothing but bad luck?"

"Okay. Not entirely. But if I ever do find that dog again, I'm changing her name to Trouble."

Her smile crumpled. "We'll find her, Lehigh. Now, tell me about the meeting with your lawyer."

Lehigh sighed. "He doesn't seem to think they have much on the arson charge, but I'm the so-called 'natural suspect.'"

"That's ridiculous. Why would you burn down your own house?"

"Insurance fraud, he says."

"What else have they got?"

"In terms of breaking and entering at the clinic and all that, he did some checking and apparently the cops have a witness saying I was at the scene that morning."

"You were miles away."

"I was alone. No alibi. He says I may be in trouble on that one."

"It's your testimony against theirs, then. They can't convict you on that."

Lehigh shrugged. "It's a grand jury, Stace. I don't get to testify, apparently. Only the prosecution. They don't convict anyone, they just indict, which is a fancy name for charging me formally with a crime."

"Listen to you, learning all these fancy legal terms!" She cuddled close again. At length she asked, "Will they put you in jail?"

"No way," he said with bravado. After a pause, he added, "At least, I don't think so."

***

"The State calls James Thornburgh."

Lehigh shifted to watch Thornburgh enter the courtroom, a drafty, wood-paneled chamber several times wider than it was deep. In contrast to the heavier man's swagger, Lehigh itched and sweated uncomfortably in his ill-fitting suit. The two men made brief eye contact before the clerk swore in the witness.

The prosecutor, a round, balding man no taller than Lehigh's armpits, stood at his table a few feet to Lehigh's right. "Mr. Thornburgh," the prosecutor asked, "are you familiar with the accused, Mr. Lehigh Carter?"

"Yes, sir, although our meeting was quite accidental." His smug smile matched his earlier swagger.

"Please explain, Mr. Thornburgh."

"I had arranged a private meeting with Mr. Paul van Paten at a dinner party at the home of Senator George McBride. We were going to discuss a possible contribution to the Senator's potential gubernatorial campaign."

"What happened?"

"I didn't know Mr. van Paten yet. I was told he was engaged to the Senator's daughter. I saw a man kissing her by a pickup truck, and presumed it was him."

"But it wasn't?"

"No, sir. It turned out to be Lehigh Carter. But I didn't know that."

"So you met with Mr. Carter instead?"

"Yes, sir. We greeted him as Mr. van Paten and he did not correct us. We conversed a bit and he even made promises on the Senator's behalf."

Lehigh grimaced. Thornburgh's version of the story painted a pretty bleak picture.

"How did you learn of Mr. Carter's true identity?" the prosecutor asked.

"Mr. van Paten called later, asking why we hadn't shown up. We met him in person later that evening."

"What about the money?" Lehigh whispered to his attorney, seated to his right. "Aren't they going to talk about that?"

His attorney, a white-haired, block-jawed barrel of a man named Constantine Richards, shook his head, close-lipped. He held up a finger to shush his client. Lehigh obeyed.

"Now," the prosecutor said, "tell me what you saw on the morning of October twenty-sixth."

"I was up early, getting coffee at Starbucks before heading out for a drive to Portland for an eight a.m. meeting. It was about five-thirty a.m. On my way out, I happened to look across the street toward the veterinary clinic."

"Clarkesville Animal Hospital, to be precise?"

"Yes, sir."

"Go on."

"I saw a man sitting in a Ford pickup, just like the one Mr. Carter drives. Just like the one I saw Mr. Carter standing next to, that day at Senator McBride's. He was parked right by the clinic's front door."

"Did the man remain in the truck?"

"No, sir. He got out and opened his tool box in the back of his truck. He pulled out a small crowbar and something else. I couldn't quite tell what it was, but it looked kind of like a screwdriver."

"I did not!" Lehigh whispered. "I wasn't even there!"

Again, Richards held a finger to his lips. Lehigh huffed, but kept quiet.

"Did you recognize the man?" asked the prosecutor.

"Yes, sir. It was Lehigh Carter, that man sitting right over there." He pointed at Lehigh.

"Did you see what happened next?"

"No, sir. I had to get going, or I'd have been late to my meeting in Portland."

The prosecutor smiled and nodded once. "Thank you, Mr. Thornburgh. That will be all."

Thornburgh's crony Brockton testified next, miraculously also "just happening" to be out and about early that morning. He claimed to have seen Lehigh driving away from the clinic a few minutes after six a.m. with a yellow hound next to him on the front seat. "He seemed to be in a real hurry," Brockton said, wide-eyed and innocent.

Brian Kelly confirmed that Lehigh stood to collect "several hundred thousand dollars" on a successful fire claim. "Two hundred, net," Lehigh muttered to Richards, only to be shushed again.

Forensics officers stated that the fire was definitely an act of arson. Traces of gasoline had been found in several places in and around the house. Only Lehigh's fingerprints could be identified at the scene, including on a discarded gas can and some unburned matches. "From my own tool shed," Lehigh whispered, once again drawing a stern glance of reproach from his lawyer.

The sales clerk from a gas station in Twin Falls testified that Lehigh had bought gas from his station in the suspicious can not long before the fire. Lab analysis showed that the station's gas chemically matched the fuel used to start Lehigh's house fire.

"This is crazy!" Lehigh whispered to his lawyer. "All this proves is that they stole gas from my shed to burn my house down."

"Sh!" Richards replied without looking at him. "We'll get our chance to rebut at the trial. For now, just listen."

"Easy for you to say," Lehigh whispered back. "You're not the one going to jail for no reason."

The grand jury didn't deliberate long. They returned an indictment on the arson, break-in, poisoning, and theft charges in under an hour. The prosecutor pleaded for Lehigh to be held without bail, but Lehigh's attorney surprised him with his counter-argument.

"If it please the court, I offer the following affidavit signed this morning by Ms. Stacy Lynn McBride of Clarkesville," Richards said. "She has offered to keep Mr. Carter in her custody until his trial. As the daughter of George McBride, who is in fact President Pro Tempore of the Oregon Senate and himself a former Mt. Hood County judge, she makes a strong argument that in her care, Mr. Carter would not be a 'flight risk'."

Lehigh gawked at his attorney. Stacy never mentioned meeting with Richards, much less signing an affidavit. The lawyers wrangled over Lehigh's potential for becoming a fugitive from justice. Ultimately, the judge sided with Lehigh.

"Given the status and reputation of not only Ms. McBride, but of the entire McBride family," Judge Kimball said, "I concur with defense counsel that, in her watchful care, Mr. Carter would not be a flight risk. Mr. Carter, you are released into Ms. McBride's custody. You are ordered not to leave the state until your trial." With a few more instructions to the attorneys, the courtroom adjourned.

***

Richards paced the floor of Stacy's modest living room, frowning. His client was not being helpful. No alibi, and no countervailing evidence. Just a lot of wild theories about being framed. How often had he heard such nonsense?

He sighed, stopped pacing, and pushed his frameless glasses up over the bridge of his considerable Roman nose. Facing his client, he repeated the question he'd asked a dozen times already. "Think again, Mr. Carter. Did anyone see you or talk to you that morning, or the night before, the clinic break-in?"

Lehigh squeezed two fingers together between his eyebrows.

"I just can't remember. All the days sort of run together."

"It was the last Tuesday of October. You were arrested later that day. Come, Mr. Carter. It was just over a week ago."

"Well…let me think. That would have been the day I went to Patterson's General Store out in Twin Falls. That was pretty early in the morning. I may have a receipt somewhere."

"Find it! I'll want to speak to the sales clerk. What time was that?"

"Early. It was just light out. Say, six-thirty or seven."

Richards grimaced. "Six-thirty would be much better. How long of a drive is that from the clinic?"

Lehigh shrugged. "Half-hour, forty-five minutes."

"No good, then," the attorney replied. "Did you see anyone else you knew?"

Lehigh snapped his fingers. "Yes!" he said. "That guy who testified—Thornburgh. He was at the general store, in the parking lot. I couldn't place his face at the time, but I'm sure it was him."

"Very good. Well, perhaps. If you're right, then he perjured himself today. We'll see how nervous he gets about serving jail time just to help his cronies in their little scheme."

"Wouldn't that implicate him in the break-in and arson, though?"

"Maybe, maybe not. We can always see if the D.A.'s office is willing to strike a deal. Assuming Thornburgh is. If not, perhaps Mr. Brockton."

"I can't see it happening," Lehigh said. "They're Paul's boys. After they screwed up that money drop—well, they're humiliated. They probably hate my guts, too."

"Perhaps not enough to go to prison over it," Richards said.

"Can't we get them for the illegal cash contribution to McBride's campaign?" Lehigh asked.

"I'll definitely bring it up when I depose them," Richards said. "The risk is that you could be charged with receipt of stolen funds—or with outright stealing."

"But they gave it to me!" Lehigh said.

Richards sank into the chair next to Lehigh. "You knew they

intended to give it to Paul van Paten. If you had turned it over to the police, you'd be free and clear. But your clever little ploy of setting up the 'Lucky Dog' fund implicates you."

Lehigh sighed. "So what we've got here is a game of chicken."

"If you like."

"I'm already in trouble. I reckon I've got more reason to deal."

Richards smiled. "Good to hear. I'll definitely let them understand the risk they're taking."

Lehigh thought a moment. "So much for the break-in. But I'm more worried about that damned arson charge."

"Understandably. But you shouldn't be. Their case is weak—completely circumstantial. Unless they're holding something back."

"You'll want to have a jaw session with Paul about that. Or I will."

"Don't do that!" Richards shook a long finger at him. "I don't want you doing any investigating on your own. You could end up providing—or creating—evidence against yourself."

Lehigh scowled. "I feel useless. Until this case is over, I can't even collect on insurance and get my house rebuilt."

"That is unfortunately true. Perhaps your business affairs need tending." He opened his briefcase, perched next to his chair, and fussed with some papers inside.

"Yeah, but my records—the ones that survived, anyway—are in the house, now a crime scene and off-limits to me. Assuming they didn't burn to a crisp."

"I'll petition the court to obtain possession of all of your files, and copies of any they may have taken into evidence. That they are required to do."

Lehigh managed his first smile of the day. "Thanks. That'd help a ton."

"If there is anything else you need, don't hesitate to ask. Remember, I am your advocate. I work for you."

Lehigh winced. Yeah, at $300 an hour. "I'll keep that in mind." He imagined Lucky foraging for scarce food in the cold, nearly barren forest. "I reckon I can find other things to do."

"Excellent. But remember: keep Ms. McBride and myself informed of your whereabouts. The last thing you want right now is a violation of court orders to stay put. That would just play into the prosecution's hands."

"I will, Mr. Richards." He shook his attorney's hand, coping as best he could with the choking feeling that came over him at that very moment.

***

Lehigh kept his promise with perfect diligence for the next several days. As agreed, he left notes or called whenever he left the house, when he arrived at his intended destination, and when he deviated from or changed his plans in any way.

By the weekend, though, the situation chafed his nerves. He felt like he was already in prison—an innocent man serving time for someone else's crime. "Why don't they just go ahead and lock me up?" he complained to Stacy. "I can't stop and take a leak without calling Big Brother to tell him which direction my pecker's pointing."

"It's just for a few months," she said. "Don't you dare take any chances or you'll find yourself in county lockup."

But the following week, he omitted the minor deviations from his planned itineraries. A stop at the grocery store for bread and milk, a detour around a construction zone, a quick drop into a neighborhood tavern for lunch and a beer—surely, they didn't need him to report these details.

He never went anywhere significant, anyway. He stayed inside county lines, mostly just killing time, keeping an eye out for Lucky and asking people if they'd seen the dog. Most hadn't. A few thought they had, but their suggestions turned out to be dead ends or false leads.

One morning in early December, leaving Dot's Diner after a hearty breakfast, a yellow hound trotted across the road a few hundred yards off. Lehigh called out to the dog, but it didn't respond. Probably too far away to hear him. He raced to his truck, keeping an eye on the dog. It disappeared into the brush on the side of the road, carrying a piece of trash in its mouth. He couldn't be sure it was Lucky, but it warranted a look-see.

He drove to where he'd last spotted the dog. Slowing the truck to a stop, he rolled down the window and called out: "Lucky! Lucky? Come here, girl!"

Something rustled the tall brush some ten yards in front of his truck and moved away from him. He drove along the shoulder, following the dog's apparent path, calling out every so often. But the dog didn't emerge.

After a good mile or so, the noise disappeared into a forested glade. "She's headed toward my property," Lehigh said. "It's her. It's Lucky!"

He parked the truck on the shoulder and hurried out, not bothering to lock it. He kept nothing in there worth stealing anyway, except his phone. And he'd only be a minute.

He plunged into the dense thicket, calling out Lucky's name. Again something rustled ahead of him in the distance. But he couldn't see the dog, nor his truck parked on the road behind him.

***

The black Plymouth pulled off to the side of the road and parked behind the familiar Ford F150 pickup truck. The driver, a muscular man with a blond crew-cut, speed-dialed his boss.

"Found him," he said. "And from what I can see, he's alone."

"Give me your coordinates," his boss said. "I'll send in the rest of the team."

"We'll need dogs," the blond man said.

The boss laughed. "I know someone with a great team of search dogs. A good friend of mine, who just happens to be looking for the same man. He also has guns…and wears a uniform with a badge on it." He laughed again, and cut the connection.

CHAPTER 20

Stacy waited through the obligatory four rings, then Lehigh's voicemail greeting, fuming. "You're supposed to keep your phone with you," she said over his recording.

At the beep, she calmed her voice. "Hey, honey, it's me." Deep breath. Do not nag. "I wondered whether you'd want to join me for a late-morning coffee. Call me A.S.A.P., okay?"

She set the phone on her desk and spent twenty minutes preparing a six-month checkup appointment reminder for a single client, a task that normally took about thirty seconds. "Call me, dammit," she said. But her phone remained silent.

She dialed again, but this time she hung up midway through the greeting. Stuffing her phone into her purse, she whisked down the hall and past Anne-Marie at reception. "I'm going home for an early lunch," she said.

"Say hello to Mr. Carter for me," Anne-Marie said.

"Will do," Stacy said, more hopeful than confident. This morning he'd told her he'd be "out running errands" today, which meant at least a pass by his property, looking for Lucky. With the unexpected but welcome break from Oregon's relentless winter rains, he could be gone most of the day.

She could hardly blame him. Once the rains returned, they'd both be cooped up inside for months. For an outside guy like Lehigh, largely idled work-wise by recent events, sitting around indoors all day could be maddening.

A sheriff's patrol car pulled into traffic behind her a few minutes from home, and followed her into her driveway. She parked, hopped out of her car, and greeted Sheriff Summers through the open driver's side window of the patrol car.

"Something I can help you with, Buck?"

"Evening, Ms. McBride." His overlarge dark Polaroids, unnecessary in the gray light, made a pointed sweep of her gravel drive. "Mr. Carter's vehicle is absent. Do you know his whereabouts?"

"Lehigh's out running errands in town," Stacy said. "Is there something in partic–"

"Where, exactly, is he?"

"In town, as I said. He–"

"Exactly, ma'am. Where exactly is he?"

Stacy snorted. "At one store or another. Honestly, Buck, I can't be expected to monitor his every move."

"As a matter of fact," Summers said, "that's exactly what we expect, and what you signed up to do, under the conditions of his court order. When-abouts do you expect him back?"

"Around four or five o'clock." Pure guesswork, but she spoke with confidence. "He had a lot to do."

"With all due respect, he could be clear to Canada by five o'clock," Summers said. "So I'm afraid that's not good enough. Can you phone him, please, and establish his whereabouts?"

"Sure," Stacy said. "But can we wait just a minute? I really need to use the restroom. I'll just pop inside and–"

"I'll join you indoors, if you don't mind." The Sheriff opened his car door and his foot hit gravel before she could respond.

He followed her to the front door. Stacy fumbled with her keys, nerves making the simple task of finding and inserting the proper key into the lock an agonizing chore. "Please have a seat," she said once inside. She waited until he sat on the sofa, hat in hand, before she disappeared behind the bathroom door.

Sitting on the toilet, she dialed Lehigh again, with the same frustrating results. She saw no point in leaving another message, so she put the phone back into her purse, hurriedly washed and dried her hands, and returned to the living room.

To her surprise, Summers wasn't there. She found him in the dining room, staring down at a folded piece of paper on the table.

"Can I help you with something?" Irritation crept into her

voice.

"Have you seen this note?" He handed her the paper. She unfolded it and read its typed words: "Stacie: I won't be back. Sorry—I can't go to jail. Love, Lehigh."

"If I'm not mistaken," Summers said, "this note constitutes evidence of Lehigh Carter jumping bail."

Stacy's skin flashed heat from the top of her head to her boots. "This is a forgery!"

He squinted at her. "What makes you so sure?"

"Everything about it! First, the misspelling of my name. Second, the fact that it's typed. He hand-writes everything unless it's a business matter. Besides, there's no typewriter in this house."

Summers pointed behind her. "There appears to be one right there."

Her eyes followed the direction of his finger. Sure enough, an ancient 43-key Olivetti rested on a small table in the corner.

"That's Lehigh's typewriter," she whispered. "How did it get here?"

"I'm sure the judge will want to know that himself." He reached out his hand and nodded once at the note. "I'll be needing that, if you don't mind."

She handed the page to him, numb. Summers pulled a small notepad from his pocket, tore off a sheet of paper and inserted it into the roller. After laying his handkerchief across the center of the keyboard, he typed for a few seconds, then lifted the entire machine under his arm. "They'll need this downtown," he said.

"Wait a second," Stacy said. "Do you have a warrant for that?"

He stared at her for a moment, blinked, then set the typewriter back down with a heavy sigh. He pulled a cell phone from his belt and dialed. "It'll just take a moment."

Stacy eased herself into a chair in the living room and, after a quick search of her purse, dialed the number of Constantine Richards. His secretary patched her through moments later.

"I think Lehigh's in trouble," she said. "Come quickly."

***

Richards didn't make it to Stacy's before the warrant came through, so Buck made off with the typewriter and note by the time he arrived. Richards listened to her story with dignified calm, which helped settle Stacy down.

"There was no evidence of forced entry?" Richards sat on her sofa, sipping tea.

Seated across from him in her living room, Stacy knitted her hands in her lap. "None. The house was locked, top to bottom. I checked while we waited for the warrant. Is that tea warm enough? I could–"

"It's lovely, thank you. Are you sure the house was locked when you both left this morning?"

"Positive. We left together, and I always check both the front and back doors. I'm kind of paranoid like that."

"That leaves two possibilities," Richards said. "Either Mr. Carter did bring it here, or the intruder had a key."

"How would they have gotten a key?" Stacy asked. "Oh my God! That means they can get in here at any time! I should change my locks."

"Assuming it wasn't Mr. Carter. But if he did bring it, and typed that note–"

"He didn't! I know him. He wouldn't run." She edged forward on her chair.

"I must remind you of his disappearance just a short while ago."

"That was before the indictment," Stacy said. "Lehigh knows he's not going to jail. He told me last night how sure he was that the jury wouldn't convict him, once they heard all of the evidence."

"It would seem unlikely to me as well that he would flee," Richards said. "However, since we haven't heard from him, and cannot reach him, we must consider that possibility."

"Mr. Richards," Stacy asked, her voice rising, "don't you believe he's innocent?"

"What I believe is irrelevant." He set down his teacup.

"Irrelevant? Mr. Richards, how can you defend him if–if–"

"It's my job, Ms. McBride. It's one I do very well, irrespective of my beliefs."

She wanted to ask him how many criminals he'd set free, but the ringing of his cell phone interrupted them.

"Richards," he said into the phone. "Who? I see. What did he say?" After a long pause, Richards nodded. "Aha. Very well. Thank you for letting me know."

He hung up. "The police have put out an all-points-bulletin and are organizing a search for Mr. Carter. They believe he is attempting to flee the state."

Stacy leaped to her feet. "That's ridiculous!"

"Let's hope so. If he's found anywhere outside of the county, I'm afraid it will be impossible to keep him out of state custody until his trial."

Stacy gripped his arm. "Mr. Richards, I'm going to go find him—before the police do."

Richards pleaded with her to stay out of it, but Stacy could not be dissuaded. She drove first to Dot's, the greasy-spoon diner at which he often had breakfast.

"He's a popular guy today," the gray-haired counter matron said. Dot chuckled and wiped the counter with an almost-clean rag. "You're the third person that's asked for him since he left. The other two were cops. Well, two pair of cops, one after t' other. Is Lehigh in trouble with John Law?"

"He might be, but it's not his fault." Stacy ignored the older woman's eye roll. "Did he say where he was going?"

"Looking for a dog, I think. He was asking people if they'd seen 'er. Don't know why. Damn butt-sniffers is nothing but messes and trouble if you ask me."

Stacy suppressed the urge to return the eye roll. "Did he say which direction he'd be going?"

"Nope."

More counter-wiping. The rag left greasy streaks on the gray-speckled Formica. Stacy vowed never to eat there. She turned to leave, then stopped. "You said two groups of cops asked for him?"

"Yup. Least, one group was. T'other, I presumed so. Same

look about 'em: short hair, dark suits, very official-sounding guys."

"One of them big, blond-haired, and kind of dumb-looking?"

Dot cocked an eyebrow and examined her dirty rag. "Blond, sure. Big, kinda. I don't know about dumb-looking. I don't like to judge, 'specially when it comes to cops."

"The other one—short guy, curly-haired, kind of pudgy?"

Dot stole a glance at her own waist, then a sour one at Stacy's. "No pudgier than anyone else 'round here. But yeah. Curly hair, what he had left of it."

"Thank you." Stacy pushed open the front door.

"Coffee for the road?" Dot pointed one finger at a half-empty pot. "Made it fresh an hour ago."

Stacy glanced again at the greasy rag. "No, thanks," she said. "Another time, maybe." When pigs fly.

She drove in concentric circles from the coffee shop until the town's tiny grid gave way to lonely highways and peach orchards. At length she opted for the highway that headed west, toward Lehigh's property, figuring he'd search for Lucky there.

She spotted his truck about a mile down the road. She pulled in behind it and got out. The truck's dome light illuminated the empty cab. The driver's side door hung open an inch. Nothing visible inside: no keys, no cell phone, not even a map.

A set of tire tracks curved into the mud behind the truck, then back onto the highway. Footprints the size and shape of a man's dress shoe dotted the mud between the empty tracks and the truck. A path of trampled grass led from the front of the pickup into the dense brush. A second trampled path wove around it until both disappeared into the trees.

One set of tracks was probably his—and one, clearly, was not.

CHAPTER 21

Lehigh struggled against the thin nylon ropes cutting into his wrists and ankles. Every movement tore his skin, already rubbed raw by two hours of pulling and wiggling. Instead of loosening, however, the bonds only tightened. The gag stuffed into and tied around his mouth made it difficult to breathe, much less shout for help. He'd woken with a blindfold wrapped tight around his head, tight enough to create uncomfortable pressure on the sore spot on the back of his skull.

He hadn't seen the face of the man who hit him, but he had a pretty good idea who put him up to it. Even if he didn't personally tie the knots, Paul van Paten's virtual fingerprints were all over the gags and restraining ropes. He'd caught a brief glance at a vaguely familiar lump-shaped man some three or four feet to his left a moment after something hard thumped his skull from behind. The throbbing pain in his head fogged his memory. Brockman? Stockton? Something like that. One of Paul's henchmen. The dumb one.

Smart enough to stalk and trap Lehigh, though.

Footsteps crunched in the leaves and brush over the sounds of the wind in the trees, although he felt no breeze on his exposed skin. The noise seemed to come from behind him, and overhead. Knowing his property as well as he did, he could tell exactly where they'd left him: in a deep gully, once a streambed, now dry and hidden from view of a casual passer-by. He could even picture the two trees growing up the side of the ravine to which they'd tied the ropes that spread his arms and legs to the point of aching: one a sinewy birch, the other a sturdy lodgepole pine.

The footsteps drew nearer.

After several moments he heard a muffled voice, then laughter. Three voices, all men. He stopped tugging on the ropes and listened. Three sets of footsteps—three separate walking rhythms. Then, in the distance, another sound: barking. Lots of it. Several dogs, excited, hunting prey.

He knew who the prey was, too: him. Before long, they'd find him. Then they'd start biting, snarling, tearing at his skin…

He shook himself, forcing the image from his mind. The barking grew louder. The dogs would arrive soon. German shepherds, no doubt, like Uncle Ted's: relentless, vicious, horrible.

The voices rose and fell again, and the footsteps grew close. The men—at least some of them—descended the side of the gully. Judging by their unsteady thrashing, these were not woodsmen, not used to climbing up and down steep, soggy trails and hillsides. One of them slipped and cursed. Another laughed. The third shushed them both. "Don't attract attention," he said. "We have things to do before our friends arrive."

That voice. Lehigh recognized its sneering quality immediately: Paul van Paten.

"Well, it looks like our little stray dog is still here," Paul said. The other two men laughed, their voices, like Paul's, coming from in front of Lehigh now. He remembered their names: Thornburgh, the curly-haired dumpy one, and Brockton, the taller blond guy. Lehigh bit hard on the gag in his mouth. The barking grew a little louder, a little closer.

"S'matter, little dog? You didn't want to run away?" Paul said. "Poor puppy. He's all tied up."

"Poor doggie," Thornburgh said.

Brockton laughed. "Maybe we left his leash too tight."

"Well." Paul stepped closer, a few feet in front of Lehigh. "Maybe we should loosen it a bit."

"Ooh, I don't know," Thornburgh said. "Then he might run away. The cops might not like that."

"Oh, running away would be bad," Paul said.

"Very bad," Brockton said.

"Our canine friends might get all excited," Thornburgh said. "You never know what an excited dog will do."

The barking grew louder. He could distinguish one dog's bark from another's now, and could count them. But no need. There were several…more than enough.

"I wonder what would happen to him if he were to get loose," Brockton said, and giggled.

"Doesn't seem fair that he's all tied up, with all those dogs coming for him," Thornburgh said. "If I were him, I'd want to get loose and maybe run away."

"We couldn't allow that to happen," van Paten said. "Get away, that is." Brockton and Thornburgh laughed again.

Now other men's voices shouted over the dogs. They seemed to be coming from every direction. Closing in. Angry. Snarling. Hunting. Biting.

Leaves crunched at his feet. A man grunted, very close. A hand slid up the side of his head and lifted the blindfold. He blinked open his eyes, and the three men came into view. The crew-cutted Brockton retreated from him with the blindfold in his hand, while Thornburgh and van Paten stood back, hands at waist level.

Hands holding guns—pointed at Lehigh.

"Well, hello there. Welcome to the party," Paul said with a sneer. He took a step forward. "I see you've noticed the, ah, predicament you're in. That's good. I wouldn't want you to misunderstand the terms of this negotiation."

Lehigh cocked an eyebrow. Paul raised his voice to project over the noise of the dogs.

"Yes, negotiation. What are you negotiating for, you might ask?"

"Yeah, what's he negotiating for?" Brockton laughed again.

"More like, what does he have to negotiate with?" Thornburgh spat. "I wouldn't call it a position of strength."

"Very observant." Paul nudged the barrel of his pistol against Lehigh's temple. With his other hand he loosened the gag, letting it drop to the earth. Lehigh worked his jaw and lips, still sore from having been bound for who-knows-how-many hours. Two, plus however long he'd been unconscious.

"You might think we're here to give you a chance to save your life," Paul said. "You could, say, make a promise to admit your guilt to the cops when they get here, in exchange for having us call off the dogs. Is that what you're thinking, Carter?"

"I ain't thinking anything, Paul."

"I figured as much," Paul said. "You never struck me as much of a thinker." Brockton burst out laughing. Thornburgh chuckled.

Lehigh met Paul's eyes with an icy glare. "I ain't admitting to arson, or dog-killing, or any of the other crap you've done. If you're expecting that, well, I reckon you'd better just shoot me right now, cuz it ain't gonna happen."

"I thought you might start out with that negotiating position," Paul said. "We'll see how long you stick to that." He nodded once to Thornburgh and Brockton and took a step back as the two men approached. Still pointing their pistols at his ribs, they untied his legs. Paul aimed his pistol at the bridge of Lehigh's nose. "Now they're going to untie your arms," he said. "You'd better hold still, or…" He paused, waiting for Lehigh.

The barking turned to howling, a cacophony. Lehigh judged the dogs weren't more than a few hundred yards away in any direction, and closing fast. How would his three captors escape? He stared at van Paten, unblinking.

"Boss?" Thornburgh's voice sounded behind Lehigh's ear.

"Go ahead," Paul said. "He's not going anywhere. Yet." The two ropes fell free. Lehigh rubbed his wrists where the ropes had cut into his skin. Thornburgh and Brockton stepped sideways around him, back in front alongside Paul, a few feet out of arm's reach.

"You know what to do now, Carter." Paul aimed his pistol at Lehigh's head.

"'Fraid I don't," Lehigh said. How close were those dogs?

Paul waved his gun toward Lehigh's right side, then pointed it back at his head. "Now we negotiate," Paul said. "It's a fairly simple negotiation, really. You confess to your crimes and go to jail…or you run, in which case, you die. What'll it be, Carter?"

Lehigh clenched both fists. "How 'bout I kick all three of your asses?"

"That'd be kind of difficult, since you'd be full of bullets long before you threw a single punch. Not to mention the dogs tearing your throat off. Now come on, Carter. I'm losing patience with you." He aimed the pistol with both hands at Lehigh's chest and scowled. "I changed my mind. You don't get a choice. Run, dammit."

Lehigh spat. "I ain't going to run and let you shoot me in the back. If you want to kill me, you'll have to do it face-to-face."

Paul's scowl deepened. "I thought you might take that point of view," he shouted over the noise of the dogs. Barking caromed down the walls of the canyon, filling the forest with a deafening roar. Paul moved his gun into his left hand, then unbuttoned his jacket without looking and withdrew another small pistol from an inside pocket.

Lehigh recognized his own pistol in van Paten's right hand. "How did you–"

Paul jerked his right hand sideways. The howling and barking muffled the gun's report. Brockton cried out in pain, gripping his foot with both hands. Blood gushed out over his fingers and stained his slacks. "What the hell did you do that for?" Brockton screamed.

"We are now acting in self-defense," Paul said. "Carter just shot you." He emptied the pistol's chamber and magazine into his palm, pocketed the bullets, and held the unloaded gun out to Lehigh. "Take it."

"I ain't that stupid."

"I said *take it!*"

Lehigh stared at him, unmoving. Thornburgh kept his gun aimed at Lehigh, but edged closer to the screaming Brockton, his focus dancing between Paul, Lehigh, and his injured friend.

"Listen, dumbass," Paul said. "I'd be happy to kill you in self-defense, or just gun you down, like you did to your dog. Or let the hounds eat you. Your choice."

Thornburgh reached the howling Brockton and lifted his friend's pants leg, exposing a deep gash and a stream of blood. "Help me!" Brockton yelled. Thornburgh looked to Paul, then Lehigh, then back to Brockton.

"Leave him be," Paul said. "He'll be fine. Keep your gun trained on Carter."

"How'd you know about the dead dog?" Lehigh asked. "We didn't tell anyone about that."

"I know everything that goes on in this county." Paul held up his gun and took careful aim. "Now run, you yellow bastard."

"Boss," Thornburgh said, "I think Brock's hurt kinda bad."

Paul gritted his teeth. "Wait a damned minute, will you? He'll be—"

"It hurts like hell!" Brockton screamed. "I'm bleeding to death here, and you carry on like some Hollywood western bad guy—"

"Would you shut the hell up?" Paul turned toward the two men.

That gave Lehigh the opening he needed. He dove for Paul's legs, tackling him football-style into the muddy leaves. The two rolled downhill into the ravine. Paul pounded him with his fists, but with no leverage, he couldn't muster much strength. A gun fired, but Lehigh felt no pain, and no letup on Paul's part. They slid the last few feet. Lehigh's back tore into the mud and brush with Paul riding him like a sled, crushing the wind out of him. Lehigh struggled to free his arms from under Paul's weight, but couldn't. Paul's head crashed into Lehigh's, two, three times. Lehigh felt, and heard, cracking in his nose. Blood ran down his face. Paul straddled him, knees on his elbows, fists flailing, smashing his face, again, again, pummeling him, each blow intensifying the sharp pain and dizziness and the crazy noise all around.

The beating stopped. Paul stood over him, panting, pointing the gigantic barrel of a pistol into the center of Lehigh's aching, bleeding face. "I said die, you son of a bitch," he said through gasping breaths. His finger squeezed the trigger.

Click. Click. *Click*!

"Wrong gun, dumbass!" Lehigh smashed his fist into Paul's exposed groin.

Paul doubled over. Lehigh sat up and butted his head into Paul's nose, then swung both fists in roundhouse blows to his unprotected face and gut. Paul crumpled to the ground, still gripping the pistol. Lehigh stood, dizzy, and aimed a kick at Paul's knee. Missed. Paul jumped to his feet and swung the gun in one motion, connecting with Lehigh's left temple.

Lehigh sank to the earth, pain exploding across and inside his skull. Eyes squeezed shut, his consciousness ebbed. He wondered if the pain would stop, if Paul had already shot him, if this was how dying felt, and if that confounded barking and shouting would ever stop.

The sounds of barking, snarling, men shouting, and pounding feet—human and otherwise—closed in around him. It rang in his ear, echoed in his head...the familiar bark of Uncle Ted's German shepherd stormed his memory, along with the slashing claws, the sharp gnashing teeth tearing at his arm, the tight grip that would never let go.

"Get off me, you mangy mutt!" Paul screamed.

Why Paul would say that?

Paul screamed again, this time in obvious pain. Lehigh rolled to his side, expecting sharp teeth to puncture his throat any moment. He waved his arms over his face, and found no resistance. The snarling, barking dog, from the sound of it, was at least a few feet away now.

Lehigh opened his eyes. Paul lay on his back, his hands covering his bloody face, staving off the attack of a very familiar-looking yellow Lab-hound mix.

"Lucky!" he exclaimed. "What the hell?"

Lucky turned her head only long enough to acknowledge Lehigh's presence, then clawed and snapped at van Paten's face again. Lehigh found Paul's gun and fired it once into the air. Startled, the dog halted her attack.

"Lucky!" Lehigh shouted. "Back off." He pointed the gun at van Paten. Lucky stepped off him, approaching Lehigh, tail wagging.

"Good girl," he said. "Sit." The dog obeyed.

Thornburgh and Brockton shouted, surrounded by snarling police dogs some thirty yards uphill. Uniformed policemen reached the top of the ravine moments later, rifles raised. "Drop your weapons!" one of them shouted. Lehigh obeyed and raised his hands over his head.

"That you, Carter?" another one shouted. Barkley.

"I'm here." Lehigh's face ached in several places. He tasted blood in his mouth, and his nose felt like fire. "Van Paten's down here with me, too."

"Paul van Paten?" Barkley asked. "Are you serious?"

"Long story," Lehigh said.

Uniformed canine handlers reached Thornburgh and Brockton. Barkley ran past them to Lehigh and Paul. "Looks like you two had a few words," Barkley said.

"More'n that," Lehigh said. "Well, I suppose you're going to arrest me now."

Barkley shrugged. "I think we've got some talking to do." He gestured to Paul. "All of us."

Paul collapsed onto his side and groaned.

CHAPTER 22

The interview lasted over three hours, two of which Lehigh spent alone in the spare whitewashed room, waiting for Detective Wadsworth to return from his frequent trips to wherever cops go while their captors stew. During the infrequent bouts of two-on-one questioning they made him sit in the world's most uncomfortable chair, a junior-high school reject with a flat wooden seat and back bolted to a metal-pipe frame about eight inches too short for comfort. This gave the police the ability to glare down at their suspect, who in turn had to squint into the harsh glare of a bare bulb hanging from the ceiling behind their heads. A long wooden folding table divided the space between Lehigh and his interrogators, a bit too high for him to comfortably rest on his elbows.

The police rehashed the same points over and over again: when had he left the café? How did he find himself tied up in the woods? Had he left the state? Did he type the note? Who, when, where, how? He repeated his answers with resigned calm, never varying his words or his tone. Where they were heading with all this, he had only the vaguest idea.

Between interviews, Lehigh wandered the room, taking in its insignificant details: the scuff marks on the fading paint, cracks in the mortar between the stacked cement blocks comprising the walls, the missing screw from the plate covering the light switch. He guessed that his missing interrogators were either gathering or comparing details from the other detainees in the case—Paul van Paten, Thornburgh, Brockton, and Stacy—or, almost as often, drinking coffee and chatting about nothing, delaying while their captors sweated alone, hoping their stories matched.

On that count, Lehigh liked his odds: three were more likely than two to make a mistake or sell each other out. On the latter point, Lehigh had nothing at all to fear.

The longest gap between his interviews turned out to be his last. Wadsworth pushed open the heavy metal door without warning. His gray suit and soup-stained tie looked like he'd slept in them, and gained twenty pounds while sleeping. He smelled like pipe tobacco. By contrast, Jared Barkley's county-issue uniform remained as crisp as the moment he'd retrieved it from the dry cleaners. Neither man had smiled even once the entire day, and they kept their streak alive with this entrance.

"Take a seat," Wadsworth said. "I've got a few more questions."

"I'll stand. Is my lawyer here yet?"

"I said sit." Wadsworth spat on the gray concrete floor. On top of the tobacco aroma, he reeked of stale coffee and Chinese food. In spite of the rank odor, Lehigh's stomach growled. He'd last eaten ten hours ago.

Lehigh sat. The two cops regarded him with a mix of curiosity and contempt for another half-minute. Finally Wadsworth broke the silence.

"How many keys exist for that shed of yours?"

Lehigh shrugged. "Two. One's on my key chain, the other I kept in my desk."

"Still have the one on your key chain?"

"Yep."

Barkley slid a small MasterLock key across the table. "Is this the one?"

Lehigh examined it without touching. "If that came off my key chain, then yes."

Barkley picked it back up. He pulled another from his pocket and held them together, comparing the two. He nodded once to Wadsworth. "They match." To Lehigh he added: "Good thing for you."

"Why? Where'd that one come from?"

Barkley raised an eyebrow at Wadsworth, who shrugged. "Go ahead and tell him."

Barkley tapped the two keys together on the table. "The second key came from the keychain of James Thornburgh. If the prints we lifted from this key match the unidentified ones on the gas cans at your former home, and the ones at the animal clinic—or any of a hundred other items we've taken in evidence from those sites—you'll be a free man, Mr. Carter."

"But if they don't..." Wadworth's voice trailed off.

"If they don't, I suggest you try matching those to his buddy Brockton, or to Paul van Paten." Lehigh bounced forward onto the front legs of his chair. "Although I'm not sure they'd be dumb-ass enough to leave fingerprints behind."

Barkley snorted. "If Thornburgh was dumb enough..."

"Thornburgh's a mouth-breather who picks the wings off of flies," Lehigh said. "Van Paten's a lawyer with personal access to George McBride and the D.A.'s office. For God's sake, please tell me you recognize the difference."

Wadsworth gritted his teeth. "Watch yourself, Carter."

"Why? Is van Paten a friend of yours, too?"

"Enough!" The detective slapped an open palm on the table.

Lehigh settled his chair back on all fours and held up both hands in surrender. "Sorry. I reckon I ought to let you fellas handle the police work. I'm happy to wait a spell longer if need be. Although I wouldn't mind seeing a menu from that Chinese place you got your take-out from tonight."

Wadsworth's jaw dropped. "How'd you know—"

Barkley waved him off. "Never mind. Carter, I don't need to wait for prints. Your story checks out. As far as I'm concerned, you're free to go."

"Assuming, that is," Wadsworth added, glaring at Barkley, "that you'll continue to cooperate in our ongoing investigation."

"You have my word." Lehigh rose to his feet. "Now, about that take-out place?"

***

Stacy greeted him in the lobby once he reclaimed his personal possessions from the clerk. Her bright smile belied her stooped shoulders, unkempt hair, and smudged makeup. She squeezed him tight after giving him a long kiss. "I'm sorry about how I look. I wanted to go freshen up, but I didn't want to chance missing you."

"You're beautiful," he whispered into her ear. She loosened her embrace, but he held her a few moments longer. "Let's get out of here."

"I thought you'd never ask." She pulled him by the hand out the door into the parking lot.

"Hey," Lehigh said. "Isn't that your Dad's New Yorker? What's he doing here?"

Her smile faded. "It's complicated," she said. "I called him when they said they wanted to question me, figuring he could pull a few strings. Oh, please don't be mad!" Her expression twisted in pain.

Lehigh clenched his jaw and fists. "We don't need his help," he said through gritted teeth. "It's because of him we're in this big-ass mess in the first place."

"Is that what you told them?" she asked in a tight voice. "If so, it was very effective."

"What do you mean?"

She glared at him. "Didn't you know? Now he's in there, being questioned."

He stopped, and she took another step, leaving a gap between them. He wiped his mouth, raised one eyebrow, then answered. "I mentioned his name only in reference to Paul and the whole money thing, and only in response to a direct question."

Her face looked stricken. "Oh, my God, Lehigh. This whole thing could unravel on him. His campaign—"

"It should unravel on him." Lehigh took a step away from her, neck muscles taut. "Look, I'm not saying he burned my house down. But I think Paul did, or maybe those two monkeys he keeps on a chain did it—anyway, somebody connected to him. And he's one of your father's key advisers. How can that not reflect on him?"

"So, Daddy's guilty by association? Is that what you're saying?"

Lehigh sighed, calming a little. "No. But I am saying that it's reasonable to wonder about what type of company he'd keep as governor. Isn't that what politics is all about? Who your allies and trusted advisers are?"

She met his eyes, tight-lipped. After a long pause she turned away. "I suppose. But if all this gets out of hand and into the papers and TV–"

"I can't see how it wouldn't."

She faced him again. "His career will be over. All of his dreams. What he worked his whole life for—gone."

He reached out with both hands, massaging her upper arms. "Maybe now he'll have a little more time to give his wife and family. Maybe now he'll see you as real people, instead of campaign props. I can't see that as being a terrible thing."

She fought back tears, then gave up and wiped one away. "No, I can't say it would be so bad, either. God, if I never have to shake another clammy politician's hand as long as I live—or feel their slimy hands grabbing my ass–"

"What?" Lehigh's eyes and mouth opened wider.

"Haven't I talked about this? Those creeps can't keep their zippers up, even with their own wives in the room. When I complain to Daddy, he always tells me it's 'all part of politics.' Of course, it wasn't his ass being grabbed or him getting propositioned."

"Those rotten sonsobitches! I'll kick their lying asses, every one of them. Who are they? I want names. I want–"

"Calm down! It doesn't matter. It's over." She leaned into his chest. "This whole thing is over. I just want to go home, have a nice dinner, and forget about it. And—oh! I almost forgot!" She broke free of his embrace and ran back to the front door of the police station.

"Where in the hell are you going?" he yelled after her. "Are you crazy?"

She paused at the door, only long enough to yank it open. "They still have Lucky!" she said.

"Wait for me!" he called. She didn't, but he caught up to her at the front desk.

"We're here to get Lucky," she said to the clerk.

"You're in the wrong place," Deputy Latner replied with a sardonic smile. "Hotel's up the block and to the right."

Stacy covered her mouth in horror, finally realizing what she'd said.

Lehigh grinned. "Ya know," he said, "the man's got a point. Maybe the dog could wait an hour or two."

Reddening, she grabbed his hand and turned to face the deputy again.

"We'll be back," she said, and dragged Lehigh out the door.

***

The next day, Brian Kelly, the insurance adjuster, shared more good news with Lehigh. They huddled around a stack of forms spread across the coffee table in Stacy's living room. After walking them through the terms of the policy, Kelly leaned back and pointed to the bottom line of his Claims Adjustment Worksheet. "So, you see, Mr. Carter," he said, "the total payout to you would be just over two hundred twenty thousand dollars, covering both your personal and business property as well as the total loss of your dwelling structure. I hope that is satisfactory."

"I hope so, too." Lehigh raised his eyebrows. "I guess we'll see, once I get some contractors in here to give me a few rebuilding estimates." He stretched back onto Stacy's sofa, taking the pressure off of his lower spine. Two hours of bending close to read the fine print of Kelly's various forms and spreadsheets left him stiff and torpid. The dank January chill didn't help matters any, either.

"If you'd like, I can refer you to some very reputable builders, but I seriously doubt that you could break ground before spring," Kelly said. "Do you have suitable interim lodging arranged? Our adjustment does include an additional allowance for a modest rental, although around here I can't imagine what you'd find other than a double-wide in a lot somewhere."

Lehigh spread his arms wide, indicating the room around them. "Stacy—er, Ms. McBride—allowed as how I could stay on here a bit," he said. "If that's okay. To give her the rent, I mean."

"It's not just okay. I insist!" Stacy entered from the kitchen, wiping her hands on a dish towel. "Staying, I mean. Not the rent part."

Kelly shrugged. "The money's yours, Mr. Carter, whether you spend it on rent or gamble it all in a casino. You should receive a check in the next month or so. Now, unless you have any other questions…"

Stacy pushed Kelly out the door moments later. "I'm so happy that this crap is almost over," she said once they were alone.

He wrapped his arms around her and pulled her closer on the couch. "I'm sorry about your Dad having to end his campaign. I know I said some mean things about him, but I also know how important it was to him—and what he means to you."

Stacy snorted. "The damned campaign was too important, if you ask me. I don't mean to sound harsh, but I think this could be the best thing ever for Daddy. His ambitions were changing him—corrupting him. I mean, he was never going to be recruited for the angels' choir, but the idea of being governor brought out the worst in him. He was like a man possessed."

"He could always run again. As long as he keeps away from people like Paul van Paten."

"Ugh. Him and me both."

Lehigh tried to suppress a smile and failed. "I'll give you a hand with that."

"Oh, you will, will you?" She grinned and nestled deeper into his arms, touching his lips when he seemed to be about to speak. "I don't want to talk about this anymore. Anyway, I have a present for you."

"For me? Why?"

She kissed him, a quick brush of her lips on his. "Call it a Happy Home Settlement present. Close your eyes and I'll bring it in."

He squinted sideways at her. "Stacy, what are you up to?"

"Shush, Mr. Detective. Wait here." Another quick kiss and

she dashed out the door. "Close your eyes!" she called over her shoulder.

He laughed, shook his head, and turned his back to the door. Moments later, he heard commotion outside, followed by a dog's bark.

"Lucky, hush, girl!" he said. Lucky yawned from her pillowy bed in the opposite corner. "Hey!" Lehigh said. "If you were asleep, then how did you...?"

"Okay, you can look," Stacy called.

He turned. She closed the door behind her. "Okay," he said. "I'm looking. What is—"

Then he saw it.

Him.

The puppy. A ball of black fur, about the length of Lehigh's forearm, tethered to a leash leading to Stacy's hand.

"A...another dog?" he said.

"You're not mad, are you?" She gripped the leash in both hands, waiting.

Lehigh grinned. "No, no. I'm not mad. Lucky, are you mad?"

Lucky, already on her feet, stared at the puppy straining at his leash. Stacy kept jabbering. "I thought it'd be good to have a companion for Lucky, you know, while you're so busy with rebuilding your house, and all? This poor little puppy, he's almost ten weeks old, and he's so darling, but for some reason nobody wanted him. Can you imagine? Probably because there was such a large litter, ten puppies, and all of them oh so cute, don't you think? Don't you think he's cute, Lehigh?"

Lehigh bent, picked the puppy up into his arms, and disconnected the leash from his collar. Stepping closer to Lucky, he held the puppy close to the older dog's snout.

"Lehigh, that might not be such a good—"

"Shh," Lehigh said. The two dogs sniffed at each other, tails wagging. The puppy licked Lucky's nose, prompting a surprised bark.

"She likes him!" Stacy said.

"Of course," Lehigh said. "Everyone likes Lucky. You're not surprised, are you?"

"Well…" Stacy grinned. "Nah. So, now all that's left is to name him."

Lehigh lifted the puppy to eye level, held him there for a moment, then set him back onto the floor. "That's easy," he said. "His name's Diamond."

"Diamond? I love it, of course, but—why?"

"Two reasons. One, he's got a nice diamond-shaped patch of white on his chest. And two…well, I've got a present for you, too."

"A present for me? What does that have to do with—?" She stopped and covered her open mouth with one hand. "You mean…Oh, Lehigh. You didn't!"

"Wait here." He exited to the bedroom, and a moment later, returned with his hand behind his back. He grinned like a school boy and pulled his hand around to reveal a small black box in his hand. He popped the curved lid and dropped to one knee. A half-caret stone perched on a slender golden band in the center of black velvet. "I did," he said. "Now please tell me, sometime this year, 'I do.'"

Stacy reached both hands to his shoulders and guided him back to his feet. Wiping tears from both cheeks with the back of her hand, she laughed. "Lehigh, my dear man," she said. "I do."

ACKNOWLEDGMENTS

The Mountain Man's Dog has been in the works for nearly a decade. Many friends, colleagues, and family members –too many to count or even remember—have contributed ideas, feedback, critique, encouragement, and love. I thank you all.

But special thanks goes out to those whose support really pushed me when I needed it to get this story published. They include:

Angela Carlie, Randal Houle, and Paul McKlendin, all members of the North Bank Writers Group, whose chapter-by-chapter critiques made this story better on a weekly basis;

My Beta Readers, Kelley Tyner McAllister and Dominique Rossi, for their invaluable late-in-the-game feedback;

Patsy Silk, whose keen editing eye caught many errors long after my own eyes glazed over;

Steven Novack, for an amazing cover design;

The Willamette Writers Group, the best bunch of writers around;

Patricia and Donald Corbin, my mother and father, who made me love books, and who always encouraged my love of writing;

All of the many furry critters who have made their way into my life and heart, each of whom show up on these pages, one way or another; and,

Renee, the kindest, most patient, most beautiful person I've ever known, whose smile lights up the darkest night and brightens even the sunniest day…I love you.

ABOUT THE AUTHOR

Gary Corbin is a writer, actor, and playwright in Camas, WA, a suburb of Portland, OR. His creative and journalistic work has been published in *BrainstormNW*, the *Portland Tribune*, The *Oregonian*, and *Global Envision*, among others. His plays have enjoyed critical acclaim and have been produced on many Portland-area stages.

Gary is a member of PDX Playwrights, the Portland Area Theater Alliance, the Willamette Writers Group, 9 Bridges Writers, and the North Bank Writers Workshop, and participates in workshops and conferences in the Portland, Oregon area.

A homebrewer as well as a maker of wine, mead, cider, and soft drinks, Gary is a member of the Oregon Brew Crew and a BJCP National Beer Judge. He loves to ski, cook, and root for his beloved Red Sox, and hopes someday to train his dogs to obey. And when that doesn't work, he escapes to the Oregon coast with his sweetheart.

CONNECT WITH GARY CORBIN

Keep up to date with the latest at
http://www.garycorbinwriting.com.

Follow me on Twitter: http://twitter.com/garycorbin

Follow me on Facebook:
https://www.facebook.com/garycorbinwriting

Follow my Amazon Author Page (and review this book!)
http://smarturl.it/GaryCorbinAuthor

Favorite me at Smashwords:
https://www.smashwords.com/profile/view/GaryCorbin

ALSO BY GARY CORBIN

The Mountain Man's Bride

Lehigh Carter's task: prove that his fiancée, Stacy McBride, is innocent of murdering popular Acting Sheriff Jared Barkley. But evidence that she may have had a secret affair with the victim makes even Lehigh wonder if he should fight for her freedom against the corrupt local machine that accused her.

Cooperating with the only honest cop he knows, Lehigh plays a high-stakes game of legal chicken to infiltrate the conspiracy and discover the truth behind Jared Barkley's murder.

Can Lehigh get to the truth behind Jared Barkley's death--and if so, will he like the answers that he finds?

Check out the sample pages from **The Mountain Man's Bride** *below!*

The Mountain Man's Badge

Mountain Man Lehigh Carter, drafted into serving as acting sheriff of Mt. Hood County after exposing his predecessor's corruption, is compelled to arrest his new father-in-law for the murder of Everett Downey, the most despised man in town.

Soon, Lehigh suspects that those most intent on pinning the murder on his father-in-law, George McBride, have reasons far more sinister than blocking Lehigh's agenda of reform.

Can Lehigh uncover the truth behind the crime without becoming the killer's next victim?

Both books available in hardcover, paperback, and all eBook formats.

Lying in Judgment

A man serves on the jury trying a man for the murder that he committed!

Peter Robertson, 33, discovers his wife is cheating on him. Following her suspected boyfriend one night, he erupts into a rage, beats him and leaves him to die...or so he thought. Soon he discovers that he killed the wrong man—a perfect stranger.

Six months later, impaneled on a jury, he realizes that the murder being tried is the one he committed. As jurors one by one declare their intention to convict, Peter's conscience eats away at him and he careens toward nervous breakdown.

Lying in Judgment is a courtroom thriller about a good man's search for redemption for his tragic, fatal mistake, pitted against society's search for justice.

Lying in Vengeance

Two months after serving on the jury trying a man for the murder that he committed, Peter Robertson's worst nightmare comes to fruition: Christine, his beautiful and charming fellow juror, blackmails him with his dark secret.

Her price: Peter must kill again, this time to stop Kyle, the man who torments Christine and threatens her very existence. Peter refuses, only to discover that his best friend Frankie may have committed the act in his place. Or was he framed?

Peter's relentless search for evidence to clear his lifelong pal forces him to confront his demons and risk his own freedom—and his life—as he battles the ruthless, manipulative, and resourceful woman who always seems one step ahead and knows his every move.

Available in hardcover, paperback, audio, and all eBook formats.

FORTHCOMING FROM GARY CORBIN

A Woman of Valor

Rookie policewoman Valorie Dawes was molested as a young girl. Now she pursues a serial child molester—and struggles to control the anger his misdeeds awake in her.

Can Valorie overcome the trauma she suffered as a child and stop this dangerous criminal from hurting others like her—or will her bottled-up anger lead her to take reckless risks that put the people she loves in greater danger?

ISBN: 978-0-9974967-9-6
Available in June, 2019 in hardcover, paperback, audio, and all eBook formats.

Excerpt from

The Mountain Man's Bride

Gary Corbin

CHAPTER 1

Lehigh squinted into the headlights of the oncoming car through the muddy mist on the windshield of his old pickup and navigated the tight curve of the old mountain road. Some part of his brain became aware of the fact that his fiancée, Stacy Lynn McBride, had just said something important, which he had missed, for the two hundredth time too many. And that was only this week.

"Sorry, hon," he said. He adjusted his baseball cap, which didn't really need adjusting, but it gave him something to do while he thought of something smart to say. Which, unfortunately, didn't happen. As usual. "Say again?"

"I said," she said, huffing and crossing her arms over her chest, "because those stupid stores and their idiotic policies, we're going to have to go back to some of those same shops tomorrow. I can't believe they wouldn't extend their sale prices one day early. Why, if someone came into the clinic with a sick cat or dog and we had a special–"

"Back to Portland? Tomorrow?" Lehigh nearly drove off the road. Damned switchbacks. "Stacy, no. I can't. Not on a Monday. I have too much to do, and—well, I just can't."

"Can't, or won't?" She found something fascinating to stare at out the passenger side window. "And what could be so much more important than our wedding? The union of our lives, expressing the foreverness of our love, the–"

"Okay, okay, I'll go." He sighed. "I was hoping to get some work done. You know, to actually pay for all this wedding stuff? It's busy season in the forestry world, and I–"

"Watch out for the deer!"

Lehigh slammed on his brakes and swerved in time to allow the doe to leap across the single-lane eastbound freeway to wooded safety.

"Maybe we should take this road a bit slower," Stacy said. "Unless you hate shopping so much that you can't wait to get away from it."

Lehigh bit back a snotty reply when a toothy grin split her beautiful face, framed by long black hair tumbling down around her shoulders. She sure knew how to push his buttons—good and bad.

"I don't so much mind the shopping," he said, "other than the driving, parking, expense, long lines, rude city people, the wandering around aisle after aisle of stuff I don't want to buy and can't afford, fakey-fake sales people pretending to be my friend, elevator music…"

"Other than that, it's your favorite contact sport." Her grin widened. She rested her hand on his knee, then slid it along his inner thigh, northbound.

"Second favorite." He clamped his hand over hers to arrest its progress. "But the first I can't do while driving, or that will become a contact sport."

"Prude." Her lips pressed together into a crooked smile, her dark eyes sparkling. She leaned over and kissed his stubbly cheek. "You need a shave." She rested her head on his shoulder. "And a shower, mountain man."

"Hey, I took a bath last week." He wrapped his long arm across her shoulders. Still thin at thirty-seven, Stacy could pass for ten years younger, and often she still got asked for ID in bars. He could wrap one arm all the way around her if she stood in front of him, and her tiny waist had added to her frustration— and his—over shopping for a wedding dress that fit right. The diet she'd started the day after he proposed had succeeded—too well, actually.

But he knew where to find soft flesh. He slid his hand upwards until he felt the stiff underwire, then cupped his hand slightly.

"Now look who's risking full contact driving!" She laughed and pushed his hand off her breast. "And watch your speed. You're going ten miles over…"

Red and blue flashing lights reflected in the pickup's rear view mirror. Lucky, their three year old yellow hound, sat up in the jump seat behind Stacy, growling. Diamond, a four month old Lab-Dalmatian mix in the seat behind Lehigh, followed suit.

"Down, dogs," Lehigh said. Lucky quieted first, and Diamond, as always, followed suit.

"I warned you," Stacy said.

Lehigh braked and steered the truck to the side of the highway. "Damn. Another ten minutes and we'd-a been home." He fished in his wallet for his license.

The sheriff's vehicle pulled in behind his truck. A moment later a tall, athletic figure in a beige uniform emerged from the driver's side.

"Omigod," Stacy said. "It's Jared."

"Barkley?" Lehigh squinted in the rear view mirror. "That may be the first good news I've had all day."

"Shush. It is not. I told you I got Donna's maid of honor's dress and head piece picked out."

"I rest my case." He ducked away from a playful swat at his nose.

Lehigh lowered the window and a moment later Barkley stepped into view.

"Evening, Sheriff. Dogs, be quiet." They stopped growling again in the back seat.

"Still Deputy, Mr. Carter. Evening, Stacy. Is that Lucky and Diamond back there?" A puff of fog followed the words from his mouth.

"Hey, Jared." Stacy's voice dripped with honey. "Mighty shocked to see the Acting Sheriff of all of Mt. Hood County working traffic on a Saturday night."

"Duty calls, ma'am. Might I see your license, insurance and registration, Mr. Carter?"

Lehigh groaned and handed his ID cards through the window. "Registration's in the glove box. Mind getting it for me, please, Stace?"

Stacy smiled past him and leaned closer. More than a hint of cleavage showed where her blouse had, moments before, been buttoned to her collar. "Make sure to thank your Momma for that strawberry cake recipe," she said to the deputy. "You should swing by and try some on your day off. If you ever take one."

Barkley emitted a small cough. "Mighty kind of you to offer, but with Sheriff Summers' situation…well, don't let it go bad waiting on me." He smiled at Stacy's chest, then nodded once to Lehigh and handed him back his IDs. "Careful with your speed coming round these turns at night, Mr. Carter. That black ice'll get you this time of year." He tipped his hat and stepped back toward his car.

"Thank you!" Stacy turned and waved out the back window. "Well, that was mighty nice of him." She squeezed Lehigh's arm.

He wiggled away and rolled up the window. "Awfully nice. Next time maybe you ought just get naked for him. Maybe then he'd let us rob a damned wedding store and we'd be done with all this blasted shopping." He started the engine.

"Lehigh, I'm surprised at you. Here you go acting all jealous when all I did was save you a two hundred dollar ticket."

Lehigh slammed the truck into gear and sped the truck back onto the highway. Gravel spewed from his rear wheels onto the front grill and hood of the deputy's still-parked car. "Yeah? What do I get for four hundred? A strip show and a slice of strawberry pie?"

The drove the rest of the way home in heated silence.

***

Lehigh parked his truck behind her car at the end of her hundred-foot gravel drive. Her modest two-bedroom bungalow needed painting and probably a new roof, projects she'd asked him to finish this year—and the source of too many arguments. "I have an entire house to rebuild," he'd pointed out the last time. "Or don't you remember how your last fiancé and his friends felt about me coming back into your life last fall?"

That cheap shot had earned him a night on the couch. Not wanting another, he kept his thoughts about the relative priority of his and her house repairs to himself from then on.

They sat in the truck for nearly a minute, seat belts still buckled, his hands on the wheel, her arms crossed, both staring straight ahead into the misty darkness of the evergreens that bordered her two-acre property. A few times, one or the other drew a sharp breath as if to speak, but no words came.

Lehigh's arms grew tired. He dropped them to his lap and turned to face her. "Look, I'm sorry. This whole wedding thing—"

"Does it bother you?" She faced him too. "Because I seem to recall it being your idea."

"My idea?" He sat flat against the seat and blew noisy air between his teeth. "I seem to recall a certain someone once cutting me out of her life for not asking."

"That was twelve years ago. What's next? Complaints about how I ignored you in high school?" Her dark hair whipped around her face as she turned away from him.

He sighed. "So much for trying to apologize."

"It just seems that ever since we started making plans to actually get married, you've been a total grump." Her head drooped and she recrossed her arms. At some point she'd rebuttoned her blouse. Dammit. "It's as if you're...I don't know. Changing your mind."

"I'm not." He rubbed his stubbly cheeks and weary eyes. "But I'll admit, this is becoming a much bigger deal than I ever wanted it to be."

"Getting married is a big deal."

"Yeah, but does the wedding have to be? Why can't we just get a couple of friends together, go to a Justice of the Peace..."

"My father would kill you, that's why. And my mother would roast you alive first."

The first etchings of a smile crossed his lips. "Ain't that the truth. I just thought that your dad might always want a lower-key event, now that he's dropped out of the governor's race."

"Was forced out. By us."

"By his own bad choices." Lehigh's jaw clenched. Her dad's role in ruining Lehigh's life six months before remained a serious bone of contention between them. One of many. Only the way Senator George McBride told the story, it was Lehigh who ruined the other man's life.

"Still," she said, "it means a lot to him, and that means a lot to me." She took his hand. "I kind of hoped it meant something to you, too."

"Course it does." He squeezed her hand. She leaned against him, rubbing his thumb with her much-smaller, delicate fingers.

In the back seat, one of the dogs (Lucky, no doubt) stretched and whimpered, followed by the other. Lehigh reached back with an expert hand and popped open the king cab door. The dogs bounded out into the darkness, Diamond always two hops behind Lucky's lazy loping gait. Lehigh shut the door behind them. He reached around Stacy and pulled her close again. "What say we sit here a bit?"

She giggled. "It'd be warmer inside."

He hugged her tighter. "Yeah, but it's cozier in here. Besides...we'll be warm enough in a minute."

She slid her hand inside his shirt, onto the bare skin of his muscular chest. "You got a point there, cowboy." She pulled his hand inside her own miraculously unbuttoned-again blouse. Lehigh leaned forward for her kiss and wondered how in the hell she managed to keep doing that without him ever noticing.

***

Lehigh tugged at the collar of his starched, pressed dress shirt and loosened his bolo tie. The white cotton stuck to his neck, clammy in spite of the late winter chill, and he repressed a resurgent gag reflex for the tenth time of the evening. But the uncomfortable clothes couldn't take all the blame for that. At least half the credit belonged to the stuffy dining room, paneled floor to ceiling in tobacco-darkened walnut imported from the east coast. For all of his local-yokel politics, Senator McBride's patrician past seemed to matter more than supporting the Oregon economy when it came to surrounding himself with luxurious creature comforts.

Stacy sidled up next to him and rested her hand against the small of his back. "You look wonderful," she said in a soft voice. "You should wear fitted shirts more often."

"Not if you want me to survive until our wedding day," he said. "But you look amazing. That dress—"

"Has cut off all circulation below my rib cage," she said. "But I'm glad you like it. It's Daddy's favorite too." She pecked him on the cheek.

"Speaking of your old man—"

"Shh!" She shook her head, a quick vibration back and forth as if to hide the action. "He hates being called 'old.'"

"Okay, then. The Esteemed Senator. Where the heck is he?"

"Mom said he's in his—oh, here they come now." She sipped from a glass of Pinot Grigio in her left hand. Lehigh drained the last of the melted ice from his own glass, now devoid of her father's prized 18-year old Scotch. Best not let the Senator see what his wife had so freely offered a half hour before. Bad enough old George found Lehigh beneath contempt without knowing how much he'd had of his favorite liquor.

Catherine McBride, Stacy's mother, led the Senator into the room. Despite her small stature—probably a full foot shorter than Lehigh's 6'1" frame when she wasn't wearing three-inch heels—her regal bearing and teased hairdo elevated her presence in the room. She wore an ankle-length flowing dress that seemed to thin her matronly, if not stout, shape. She strode into the room with confidence and greeted them for the second time that night with hugs and smiles.

The Senator, by contrast, seemed old and stooped, a half-foot shorter than he'd appeared a few months before when the race to become governor seemed his to lose. His full shock of white hair lay flattened against his scalp, and age spots dotted his ruddy, wrinkled face. He mumbled a quick hello to Lehigh, kissed his daughter on the cheek and shuffled over to his seat at the head of the table.

"Dinner will be served in a few moments." Catherine took Lehigh by the arm. "And not a moment too soon, by the likes of you. Don't you feed my future son-in-law?"

"I wouldn't want to spoil his appetite for your legendary dinners," Stacy said with a grin.

"That'll never happen," Lehigh said. "Who's the chef this week?"

"A new fellow from the culinary school in Portland. His name is Antonio. He's amazing—he has no sous-chef. He does everything himself." Christine winked at him and escorted him to his seat. She sat to Lehigh's right and Stacy sat across from him. The Senator took his position at the head of the table.

Lehigh's stomach growled. Early dinners meant skipping lunch and at that moment he could eat one of the Senator's retired show horses, medium-rare.

Almost on cue, a short, chubby man with tufts of curly hair protruding from either side of a white ruffled chef's hat, dressed in kitchen whites and sporting a food-stained apron, whisked into the room. He set a heaping salad plate in front of each guest with nervous dispatch. He ground two twists of pepper on top of the greens without asking and disappeared, neither he nor the four diners having uttered a word.

Lehigh grabbed a fork and had nearly reached his quarry—baby green spinach leaves topped with thinly sliced red onion, chunks of bright red strawberries, crumbled feta cheese and crushed walnuts all tossed in a vinaigrette redolent of chocolate and orange—when a sharp pain pierced his ankle. Stacy glared at him, hands crossed in prayer. His stomach growled again, but he set down his fork and bowed his head on folded hands.

"Bless us, oh Lord, for these, thy gifts…" Catherine recited the prayer as if making it up for the first time, every word an intense plea for God's attention. Which made the damned thing take twice as long as it should. But he couldn't complain—it was four times as long when his Pappy mumbled through it on Sunday mornings. "Amen," they said in unison at the end, and perhaps Lehigh said it a bit too loud, because Stacy kicked him again.

"I have an announcement to make." The Senator stood, a laborious effort. Lehigh chewed the delicious greens and shoved more in. The guy wanted to talk, fine. Some people came to eat.

"Is it about the case?" Stacy asked.

"Partially." The old man's face darkened and he swallowed with some effort. Lehigh had already polished off half of his salad and would have offered half his kingdom for a crust of bread. Hell, a crouton. The Senator cleared his throat. "The State has offered to drop all charges of impropriety against me, in exchange for…" He licked his lips and stared blankly into space, as if he'd forgotten what he'd intended to say. Stacy's fork hovered near her mouth, dripping vinaigrette from bushy spinach leaves. Lehigh shoveled in another heaping mouthful. Talk, pause, whatever. Dinnertime mattered. Politics, not so much.

The Senator cleared his throat. "In exchange for naming names of other fundraising violators in my party and campaign, and…" His gaze dropped and his eyes moistened. He wiped his nose with a napkin, set it down, took a deep breath. "And resigning my Senate seat."

"Daddy, no!" Stacy's fork clattered to her plate. She raced over to her father and wrapped her arms around his neck. "They can't do that. You love the Senate! And the idea of turning against your colleagues–"

"Is reprehensible. Which is why I am declining the offer." McBride hugged his daughter and patted her back. "My lawyers will tell the prosecutors in the morning. But I wanted you to hear it from me first rather than read it in the papers."

Stacy circled back to her seat. "But what does this mean? Will you have to go to trial? All the publicity, the scandal…"

"The spotlight, the opportunity to state his piece in public." Catherine fumbled with her wine glass and held it out to Lehigh. He refilled it from a bottle resting in a clay chiller behind him. Catherine nodded at him and took an approving sip. "Your father relishes the opportunity to debate, don't you, George?"

"In fact I do," the Senator, now seated, said around a mouthful of salad. He pushed a thin slice of onion around his plate with his fork. "Catherine, we agreed not to rehash this debate in front of the kids."

"We aren't kids, Daddy. Lehigh and I are–"

"Partially responsible for this damned mess!" McBride slammed his fist on the table. A chunk of walnut flew onto Lehigh's empty plate. Lehigh suppressed the urge to scoop it into his mouth.

Stacy pushed her chair back from the table, her face and neck muscles tight, her color drawn. "So that's your take on this?" She stood and pointed a finger at her father. "That it's our fault that you and Paul van Paten took cash bribes from corporate donors, broke into my clinic, poisoned animals, burned down Lehigh's house–"

The Senator's face turned crimson. "Perhaps you think I should rot in prison along with the drug addicts and thieves you used to prance around half-naked for? Oh, you thought I didn't know about your 'scholarships' from Mr. Downey's bar!"

"Enough!" Catherine slapped the table with both hands, rattling glasses, plates and silverware. Standing, her hazel eyes blazed. "There shall be no further discussion of this at my dinner table."

"But Mother–"

"Dammit, Catherine, it's my house–"

"Not one word!" Catherine pointed her fork at Stacy, then George. "If we cannot discuss the matter civilly, we simply shall not discuss it. Nor anything else remotely related to it."

Stacy glowered at the remains of her salad, arms crossed. Her father stared at his silverware. Lehigh shifted in his seat. If they could just get past this, the next course would appear any minute. He could smell bread, imagined a plate full of aged cheeses and salted meats...

"Stacy tells me you're spending a lot of time in Portland lately, Lehigh," Catherine said with a forced smile. She sat and gestured for her husband and daughter to do the same. They did, eyes cast down, mouths in matching tight lines. Catherine sipped from her drink. "Tell me, has that new mayor torn out all the freeways and planted gardens like he promised he would?"

Lehigh cleared his throat. "Judging by the traffic, he must have. I never saw a place that hated food so much. I mean, hated cars." Oops. His face warmed. Stacy stifled a giggle.

"Oh, dear, you must be starving!" Catherine rose from the table. "Antonio!" She started for the kitchen.

The short, chubby man burst through the swinging door, nearly crashing into her. He carried a platter in one hand, a basket of bread in the other. "Antipasti!" he said as if making an announcement. "Formaggi, carne, olivia and of course, focaccia." His pronunciation gave each word a few extra syllables, which only served to deepen Lehigh's hunger.

"Meat, cheese, olives and bread, for the unwashed among us," the Senator said with a glance at Lehigh.

"Daddy, don't be rude." Stacy pushed the tray to Lehigh. "Dig in, my love."

"Ladies first." Lehigh imagined every scrap of the immense piles of food being on his fork at once, heading into his mouth.

"Please, dear," Catherine said. "You're our guest, and you're starving." She patted his shoulder on her way back to her seat. "Start us off…but do leave a bite or two for your anorexic bride to be."

"Will there be anything else, signora?" Antonio said in a sing-song voice. "More vino, eh?" he dashed through the kitchen doors before anyone could answer

Lehigh served himself a modest sampling of each item on the tray and a hunk of bread, then passed the tray to Catherine. "Mmms" and "yums" replaced the tense arguments of a few minutes before. After serving himself last, George cleared his throat. "I still would like to finish my announcement."

Catherine sighed. "If you must, dear. But please avoid the topic of you-know-what."

He glanced at her, shook his head. "Of course, dear. What I would like to announce, dear family, is that I've been offered a job. And I plan to accept."

"A job? That's…that's so…ah…exciting, Daddy." Stacy's stammering drew stares from both of her parents and a bemused smile from Lehigh. "Um…who…?"

"Friends of yours, in a way," the Senator said to Lehigh. "The Oregon Lumber Council."

Lehigh frowned. "I'd hardly call them friends. Quite the opposite, in fact, especially lately."

"I don't understand," Stacy said. "Isn't that the lumber industry's statewide lobby? Why wouldn't you consider them allies?"

"If I were owner of Alabama-Pacific Paper or Cal-Tex Lumber instead of Carter Forest Services, I'd love them to death," Lehigh said.

"That'd be more like self-love," Catherine said with a smirk.

"What does that mean?" Stacy asked.

"Two thirds of their board comes from the five largest lumber companies in the west," Lehigh said. "The CEO of Cal-Tex Lumber is the board chair. I guess I'm not too keen on folks who burn my property for sport."

"Daddy!" Stacy tossed her napkin onto her plate. "How could you work for them? After all Lehigh has been through?"

"Baseless, unproven allegations." McBride harrumphed and turned away from the table. "Rumor, innuendo and coincidence."

"Beg pardon." Lehigh dipped another chunk of bread into a plateful of olive oil. "The fact of my house being burnt to a crisp is anything but unproven rumor."

The Senator held up a hand. "But their guilt—their association with the perpetrators–"

"Is stipulated in depositions accepted by a U.S. Court in the plea bargains of two former employees!" Stacy jumped to her feet and pointed a long, manicured finger in her father's face. "You know damned well they're involved!"

"Unauthorized actions of a misguided few, acting independently–"

"Could we please change the subject?" Catherine place one hand to her temples, a pained expression dominating her once-calm face. "Must every dinner conversation we have devolve into political debate and recriminations?"

Silence reigned around the table, other than the exasperated sighs from Stacy and her father. Antonio broke the gloom, bursting into the room with a second round of antipasti and a promise of amazing pasta to follow. His exit produced another long minute of silence.

Lehigh shrugged and scooped a healthy ration of olives and cheeses onto his plate along with another chunk of warm focaccia. "Well, sir. Regardless of my own differences with the OLC—congratulations on your new position, and best of luck to you. What will your role be with them?"

"Government relations," McBride said.

"Lobbying," Catherine said.

"I thought ethics rules prohibited you from lobbying for two years after leaving the Senate. Or is it five?"

"In the first place, I haven't yet left the Senate," McBride said. "I won't start in the new position until my term expires in January. Second, that rule applies to Congress, not the state legislatures. And in any event, such rules would never pass Constitutional muster. It's a violation of my right to free speech."

"I'm glad your job isn't with the Supreme Court, then," Stacy said under her breath.

"I heard that," her father said with a glare.

Lehigh sighed. The pasta could not arrive too soon.